PLAYBOOK

a love story

TRACY EWENS

PLAYBOOK

a love story

Book design by Maureen Cutajar
www.gopublished.com

ISBN: (print) 978-0-9976838-3-7
ISBN: (e-book) 978-0-9976838-2-0

For Maggie.
Who shares my love of glitter.

Chapter One

Annabelle Jeffries was lost in thought. It was nothing new, except this time she almost bought a zebra head. In fact, if it hadn't been for the little girl with the blue toenail polish in line at Cosmo's Costumes, Anna definitely would have left with the wrong rubber mask. She was trying to memorize the names of her new students, using a word association trick her friend and professor-in-crime Cynda Bass had explained, when the little girl's incessant whining to her frazzled mother about "needing boas for the birthday party or everything would be ruined," returned Anna to reality. The snap back to real life was often jarring, but as she noticed the stripes rather than the donkey she ordered, Anna was grateful for it.

There were no zebras in *A Midsummer Night's Dream*.

Stepping out of line, she returned to the back counter of the shop. After a bit of confusion and sifting through stacks of yellow order slips, the heads were switched and Anna paid for her donkey. She grabbed a quick coffee next door and noticed the little girl, now drowning in hot pink boas, climbing into a minivan. Anna chuckled at the sight as she crossed the street to her car. She wondered if her sisters, one with a new baby born in April and the other with a baby on the way, had any idea what they'd gotten themselves—and their lovely husbands—into. It had been a busy and exciting year for her family, but Anna was settled back into the calm normalcy of her routine. The University of California–Berkeley was renowned for the occasional spectacle or spotlight issues, but it was also a university steeped in tradition and history. That was what drew Anna there as an undergrad and what brought her back to teach years later. She recognized how lucky she was to be exactly where she belonged.

There were only two more weeks in September, which meant four remaining class periods of *Macbeth*, Anna thought, clicking her car open and trying not to spill coffee down the front of her top. She tossed her bags onto the passenger seat while her mind shifted to upcoming lectures and the meeting she had next week with the English department curriculum committee. When Greta, the department secretary who always had chocolate-covered almonds on her desk, had called to set up the meeting, she mentioned it was a "casual discussion." Anna had been teaching Shakespeare at UC Berkeley for three years now. That was long enough to know there was nothing casual about the curriculum committee.

The committee was in charge of keeping an eye on the "dissemination of knowledge as it pertains to the English department goals and standards as set forth by the dean." That was what the members told Anna the first year they reviewed her classroom. They'd left her alone last year and she thought she'd proven herself by now, but Anna seemed to be back under the microscope again after recently applying for full-professor tenure. Although she wasn't sure how all the committees worked, they acted more like they were responsible for the brick-by-brick building of the institution, rather than simply the current overseers of its teachings and traditions. Anna found them stodgy and at times stifling, especially since during her first-year review they had declared her teaching style was "a touch unconventional."

Following that review, Anna had tried to tone things down, but it never worked. It was impossible *not* to get excited about the porter scene in between Act II and Act III of *Macbeth* or all the blood and deceit. That's how Shakespeare wanted it. His words all but demanded the work be brought to life, so in a way, she was honoring him by annoying the establishment. Not that she would ever explain her classroom to the committee like that. She loved her job and wanted to keep it, so she at least *tried* to play the game. But maybe she hadn't been trying hard enough if they wanted to meet again.

Macbeth was the first play of the semester, followed by the comedy, *A Midsummer Night's Dream*, which would start mid-October. When she had been hired, the committee had wanted her to cover three plays a semester along with a general overview and history of William Shakespeare. She explained that an overview and history usually put people to sleep and that it was far better to focus on two plays a semester. They'd looked over their glasses at her, and had Anna not possessed "incredibly accomplished credentials," as the man wearing a turtleneck in July had pointed out, they would never have offered her the position.

She had not intended to become a teacher, let alone a professor. Anna was the quiet one of the four Jeffries sisters. Meticulous about her grades, as was expected in her family, but happiest in her head. She'd loved Shakespeare since she was old enough to understand, but once she began studying, a passion grew that surprised even her. Following graduate school and a wonderful professor at Oxford who took their class to the roof every Thursday and instructed them to "shout Shakespeare until they can hear us in Manchester," Anna knew what she wanted to do and how she wanted to do it.

Teachers didn't need to be stuffy or elevated from their students. Learning could be an experience, a life-changing experience. That was what she wanted to give her students, not some snooze-fest that didn't do Will the slightest justice.

After much heated debate, the committee agreed an in-depth study of two plays was sufficient, and Anna would dedicate at least ten days of class time to an overview and historical perspective. It was a compromise that should have settled things, but each year still felt like a push and pull. Climbing into the warmth of her car, she kept thinking about the "casual discussion." What did they want now?

Anna looked over at her packages and tried to focus on the present, as her sister Sage always advised. That little suggestion was simple on the surface, but extremely difficult in practice. The first three years she taught English 117, Anna rented her props in case someone, or the dean for that matter, decided to pinch her and confirm that her dream of igniting young minds with the brilliance of William Shakespeare was not only laughable, but over. But she was a month into her fourth year, her second year as an associate professor. She had even submitted her paperwork and portfolio to seek full-professor status. Being permanent, settled, had become what she wanted more than anything. Her class had been using props all month and would continue in the coming weeks when the rest of the students would have a chance to read aloud. With the purchase of the donkey head, she was now prepared for her next play and "ahead of the game," to use her father's phrase.

The guy who fixed her order at Cosmo's, the one with the impressive beard, had asked if she was an actress. Anna got that a lot. She'd loved Shakespeare all her life, seen every play, some three and four times, but she had never acted in one. She was more of a watcher, an examiner of life in general, sort of like... paint on a scenery wall. Maybe.

"No. I teach."

"In costume?" he'd asked, placing the credit card slip in front of her for a signature.

"We are starting *A Midsummer Night's Dream* next week. I... try to keep things interesting, and Bottom is one of my favorite characters."

He cringed. Anna was used to that too. "Shakespeare?"

She nodded.

"Aww, no way. I never got that guy."

"Hence the mask. I'm trying to change that reaction one class at a time." Her eyes twinkled, but he still looked unconvinced.

It seemed the students who had time for the beauty of Shakespeare were fewer and fewer. She may not have taught The History of Film or even the new class on the Harry Potter series, although she loved those books, but Annabelle worked hard to ensure her class was progressive and engaging. Her seats were full every year, sometimes with a waiting list. It was an honor. She believed a person was given only so much good fortune and with that in mind, gave teaching everything she had. Being able to do what she loved and live in her own world was exceptional, and she wasn't about to squander it by being mediocre.

"Yeah? Sweet. Seems a shame to cover up that face, though." Impressive Beard winked, and Anna was sure she'd blushed. She could never get used to that... flirting. In her mind she was clever, sexy even, but reality was a harsher critic. Flirting required taking what was in her head and freeing it in a way that wasn't awkward or jumbled. Flirts enjoyed the spotlight. Anna was not a flirt.

"Embrace you," Anna's mother used to advise somewhere in the blur of high school when that was virtually impossible, but she remembered it all these years later. That was something, she supposed.

"Nice beard," Anna said, trying for friendly. He was good-looking, sort of. Anna had not been on a date in almost two years, unless she counted the guy who cleaned the shoes at the bowling alley, which she certainly did not think counted. That had been a setup one night after the tournament was over, and he looked so sad waiting for her at the brown Formica table with a pitcher of beer and two mini pizzas. She loved bowling, and since her league bowled at Plank, she enjoyed the food too. But even craft beer and house-made crust couldn't mask his incredibly detailed love of reptiles. That was not a date.

Steve wasn't a bad guy. In fact, she still waved to him every Wednesday during league night, and it looked like he might be dating the new cashier, the one with the snake tattoo on her ankle. Perfect. Anna had thought when she saw them together. Steve deserved to be happy.

And Anna had hers: teaching and her students.

Besides, she wasn't good at being fun and flirty, and it seemed that was what most men wanted. If her job wasn't off-putting enough, her penchant for romantic movies and reading usually ran any relationship into the ground at around week three. But, maybe this guy was...

"Thanks. I like playing dress-up too," he said, winking yet again.

Yikes! Anna laughed, grabbed her bag, and left without another word.

Two of her sisters had found love in addition to their careers. Anna had to admit having a person by her side sounded lovely, but it wasn't for her. She'd been given extra when she became a professor— got to wake up every morning and drive to a fabulous campus. She wasn't going to push her luck by asking for love. Besides, love the way she imagined it didn't exist.

Anna was content. Maybe she wanted to travel more and go back to Spain one day, but she'd bought a small home four months ago. This was her place, where she belonged. The commitment of the donkey head had sealed the deal.

Starting her car, she tried to hold back from rewriting the scene in the costume shop. She needed to live in reality a little more, at least that's what Cynda and her sisters always said. But Anna couldn't help it. She'd been converting real life to fiction for far too long. In her mind, Mr. Sexy Beard would have steered clear of creeper and instead asked for her number or been good at say... knock-knock jokes. He would have had a quirk, a personality, instead of sinking into the obvious. She sighed. Reality was disappointing. Her family hated it when she said that out loud, but it was the truth. Every time, without fail, what she saw was exactly what she got. Especially when it came to men. Men were never a surprise.

"If music be the food of love, play on," she said to her empty car and turned on Ingrid Michaelson. Ingrid spoke to her soul, especially in September. Anna took a sip of her coffee and put it in her cup holder.

It was a gorgeous day. She thought about rolling down her window but decided against it. She loved the breeze, but any time she rolled the windows down, things went flying and made a mess. Anna was not about making a mess. Her life was neat, tidy, and tucked into a quiet corner north of her favorite big city. Her sisters had new families and babies. Anna had her books, Wednesday-night bowling, weekend movie marathons, or the occasional drink with Cynda and her current crazy boyfriend. This one was a nude painter. He didn't paint nudes, he painted *in* the nude.

See, you even have some comedy, Anna thought as she pulled into her parking spot.

Dane Sivac was trying his best not to laugh and doing a decent job so far. He'd only had to "cough" once.

There wasn't time to grab a coffee before this after-morning-practice meeting, and now two guys in suits launched into the "emotional completeness" of every athlete on the football team. Dane almost lost it. Looking over his shoulder to see if there was going to be any sort of caffeine served at this thing, he wondered why the hell everyone else in the room was nodding and smiling on cue. What was going on? After some sappy slideshow complete with music, story time was finally over, and Dane sprang to his feet and made a beeline for the real world.

"Sivac."

Come on. Dane turned to find Head Coach Hall and a woman in a suit wearing a large, shiny necklace that seemed too big for her.

"Before you run out of here, I thought you'd like to meet Dr. Frasier. She's the psychologist working with Trey."

Dane nodded, shook hands, and made nice because his boss was smiling and Dane had been around long enough to know that a happy head coach meant a happy life. "Right. Good to put a face with the name."

"You too. I heard Trey chose a Shakespeare class when I asked him to step out of his comfort zone to bolster his confidence."

Dane raised his eyebrows, hoping that made him look interested in the game his boss and the shrink were playing with his star receiver. Well, his *almost* star receiver. "I did hear that. I'm not sure how that's going, but I'll ask Trey at practice later tonight."

"He seems to be enjoying the class, but I e-mailed you his four-week grade report. He's failing."

"Seriously?"

She nodded. The concerned-but-distant-shrink nod and smile was something Dane hadn't seen in a while. Not since his mother had the clever idea that he himself needed to "discuss his feelings." Christ, shrinks gave Dane the shakes.

"Wow, well, maybe you can work with his teacher," Dane said, his now-desperate need for coffee making him a little twitchy.

"We were hoping you could get in touch with her," Coach Hall said.

"Me?"

"Yeah, sort of explain to the teacher that Trey's taken on a challenge and see if there's anything you can do to help get his grades up."

Dane wanted to laugh, ask his boss if this was some kind of joke. The guy had a good sense of humor, but at the moment he was looking at Dane as if it was the most natural thing in the world for a football coach to monitor an athlete's studies with his Shakespeare professor. Trey wasn't going to lose his scholarship. He wasn't flunking out. It was the first month of school. So he's having a hard time reading about men in tights, Dane thought but did not say.

"Okay. Wouldn't it make more sense for the doctor to talk with his teacher since it was her recommendation?" He tried for polite.

The shrink took a deep "cleansing breath." Dane recognized that too. His mother and sister were big fans of the cleansing breath, but then the doctor's eyes went wide, almost like she'd been mesmerized by something, and when she addressed Dane, she had a bit of a Barbie tilt to her head. The whole effect made her look crazy, which was ironic for a shrink. Something else Dane would not be sharing.

"Let me try to explain, Coach Sivac. On the surface that seems logical, but I don't want Trey having the stigma of seeing a sports psychologist. Granted, I gave him the assignment, but I think it would be best if you were his liaison going forward. It seems more organic if you understand my meaning. Besides, coaches should display an air of approachability for their players, don't you think?"

Like vegetables, organic? Why the hell did it seem like the more pieces of paper these people collected, the harder it was to understand a word they said? Dane nodded because nodding was the go-to these days. And talking right now would certainly get him in trouble.

"Right." He looked to Coach Hall for some confirmation that this woman was a pain in the ass and found nothing but more nodding. "I'll check in with the teacher. Can Trey drop the class? Or audit?"

"I don't want him to drop it. In our session yesterday, he seemed to express a genuine interest in the subject. Furthermore, I don't want him pulling out now, especially since this class is part of his confidence building blocks. I'm sure you'll agree."

"I... actually have no idea what that means."

She giggled. It wasn't a word Dane used a lot, but the sound coming out of her could only be described as a giggle. Giggle with Barbie neck and crazy eyes. This woman reminded him of a character in Harry Potter. The one who wore the weird suits and looked like she was from the fifties. His nieces would know her name.

"Plus, it's stimulating and I think it's good for him."

"But... he's failing."

She nodded.

So that's why it worked so well. It was hard to argue with a nod.

Dane accepted defeat. He was used to going round and round with the women in his life and knew eventually he would be worn down, so he quit while he was ahead.

"Okay. Well, thanks for this talk and the meeting in general. Good fun. I'll get with the teacher."

"Excellent," the shrink said, clasping her hands together, crazy eyes looking pretty damn happy now.

"Coach." Dane nodded as a sign he was now going to back away slowly.

His boss, the man who just last week brought a giant wall of a lineman to tears, nodded too and put his hand on Dane's shoulder. "Thanks for this," he said as he walked him outside the meeting room.

When they were alone, Dane asked in the most politically correct way he could muster, "What the hell?"

"Look, I know it's different, but the higher-ups are on my ass, and you know everything flows downstream. They're responsible for our budget and ultimately the success of our program. If those suits asked me to put on a tutu and dance around the room, I'm not sure I wouldn't give it a shot. I'm sorry about Crazy Eyes in there, but this is the new 'culture' and we need to play nice."

Dane let out a deep breath. "Right. Well, I guess I'm off to get Trey's schedule."

"Hey, just be glad you're old enough to remember when college ball was just a game. Now we're a 'building block in the lives of these young men.'"

Dane laughed and turned back toward his boss. "When I was in college, do you know what my coach's favorite saying was?"

Coach Hall waited, his eyes giving away that he knew it was going to be a good one.

"He used to say, 'You're all playing like a bunch of fucking bunnies.' How do you think that would go over in there?"

His boss roared and held his out-pouched stomach. "That would be—what was on that handout?—'excessive emotional duress.'"

Dane shook his head. "Cut it out. You're scaring me." He turned to leave.

"You'll follow up with the teacher?"

"Do I have a choice?" he asked, pushing through the door.

"No."

Dane shrugged his acceptance and decided he needed coffee and a few doughnuts before venturing into the English department. Yeah, that was going to be a treat.

Chapter Two

"Now that"—Cynda slapped a folded newspaper down on the table—"that right there makes waking up and coming to work all worth it." She pointed to a promo picture in the center of the paper under the heading *High Hopes for Sivac*. Cynda took a seat and opened her lunch while Annabelle looked closer at the picture. Broad shoulders, dark hair, and eyes the color of—what was that color? It didn't matter. The new coach was good-looking.

"Cyn, aren't you still with Nude Todd?"

"Yes, and don't call him that. It makes him sound strange."

Anna lifted her brows, her fork still in her mouth.

"Well, strange-er. Todd and I are still together, but I can appreciate a fine-looking man even if I can't take a shower with him. Oh, yum, can you imagine lathering all of that up and—"

"All right. Maybe you should write romance or teach Byron." Annabelle laughed and tossed the folded paper back to her friend.

"Nah, the shower scene is about all I've got. Anyway, I bring this to your attention because he's new and probably lonely and could use a friend."

"The article says it's his second season. He was brought in last year when some other guy had a temper tantrum and walked off during a game. Never looked back, I guess. It's your man's second year. I doubt he's lonely."

"How do you know all of this?" Cynda asked, again looking at the article.

"Hollis took a picture of the article and sent it to me this morning with a one-line text."

"I'm afraid to ask."

"'At least he's something to look at while you're losing.' Then the emoji with the devil horns."

Cynda laughed. "Well, she's right. He is pretty, and he's still considered new. I think he needs a friend."

"He certainly does not. I'll give you that he's lovely, but he is not alone."

"Lovely? Honestly, Anna, that is take-me-now-on-my-kitchen-table hot. There's nothing lovely about that man."

Anna shook her head and finished eating her tuna salad. She and Cynda had been friends for almost three years, and Anna was immune to her outbursts... even found them entertaining. They'd first met during a meet-and-greet for new English department professors. Cynda walked straight up to Anna, who was hanging near the door waiting for the right opportunity to leave and go back to her cozy office. Cynda had extended her hand and said, "You are the only person in this room who doesn't look like they belong on *Masterpiece Theatre*. I like your skirt and I think we should be friends."

Anna had been floored by her boldness, but she would quickly learn one thing: that was Cynda. She was the oldest in her family, with two younger brothers, and reminded Anna a lot of Hollis, her own oldest sister. Cynda was strong, brilliant, and simply the most entertaining person Anna had ever met. Considering Anna came from a family of highly entertaining women, that said something. She and Cynda could not be more different, but over the years Anna had grown to love her. Cynda Bass never sat on the sidelines. She was a bold splash of life that rarely existed in Anna's reality.

Cynda taught Middle English Lit and a class on Milton, wore clogs in every color of the rainbow, and was currently drinking green tea out of the mug Anna had brought back from London for her last year. It was a Milton quote and read, "Better to reign in hell than serve in heaven." Cynda was flipping through the rest of the paper and eating a vegetable bowl. Anna opened her bag of carrots and waited for the next comment. She knew Cynda; she was sulking. The conversation wasn't over yet.

"Fine, he's not lovely. What has gotten into you today?" Anna asked, breaking the silence.

"I think you should keep him company."

"Me?" Anna clipped her now-empty Tupperware together. "I am absolutely certain I'm not Mr."—she leaned over to read the caption under his picture—"Sivac's type."

"Why not?"

Cynda was usually astute, but right now Anna was beginning to question that. Her friend was looking at her as if it made total sense that a football coach and an in-bed-usually-by-ten (okay, let's be honest, nine thirty) professor would... keep each other company, whatever that meant. Anna wasn't sure how to clarify what she thought was obvious.

"Because he's not my type."

"Honey, he's everyone's—"

"Okay. Let's not launch into another round of how hot the not-so-new football coach is again, please."

"Excuse me," a deep voice from behind Annabelle interrupted them.

Cynda's jaw all but fell to the table. Anna turned but already knew who was standing in the doorway. Of course the coach himself would be right there. That's how reality worked.

"How can we help you?" Cynda asked, standing up like one of those women on a game show, poised to walk him through the prizes he'd just won. "You're Coach Sivac. Welcome to the English lounge."

Easy, Cyn. Down girl.

"I am," the voice said as Anna zipped her lunch box closed. "Thanks. I was looking for"—he pulled a scrap of paper from his pocket—"Ms. Jeffries. She teaches Shakespeare, poor woman. Do you know where I can find her?"

Cynda pointed to Anna right as she stood to leave.

"Oh, sorry. I didn't realize."

Anna turned and would admit her pulse picked up a bit as her eyes took in a pretty potent full view of him, but that was all she was willing to give him. Well, that and the fact that he was taller than he looked in the picture and his eyes made little crescents when he grinned, which he was doing now in an effort to defuse his insult. Anna had known these types of guys all her life. In fact, she'd helped a few of them at the student study center barely graduate college back when she was an undergrad herself. Of course he didn't like Shakespeare and of course he thought she was some miserable shrew. Typical.

"You teach Shakespeare?" he asked, stepping into the lounge, which suddenly felt smaller with him in it. His teeth were white, almost too white. *Is that a coach thing?*

"I do," was all she offered before turning to Cynda, who had at least regained a modicum of composure and was now rinsing her bowl at the sink. "I'll see you later."

"Don't you want to stick around and—"

"I do not." Anna left the lounge and found she had company as she walked toward her office. She assumed he was heading to his car. After all, her blowoff had been quite clear. Trying to ignore him, Anna focused on the rest of her day. She had under an hour before her next class and wanted to fine-tune the last part of her lecture. Today she would focus on Lady Macbeth's death. While she was unpacking boxes the other night, she had an inspired idea to compare Macbeth to modern-day boy bands. The flash of celebrity followed by their fall, usually when they lost their managers, their puppeteers. Lady Mac most definitely held her husband's strings. The idea for class was almost perfect. Anna had already selected a playlist of songs, but in case a committee spy dropped by to check on her class, she wanted to make sure there was enough of their favorite word—substance.

Her thoughts stopped spinning when she realized the coach was still in stride next to her. Too close, as if he had no sense of personal space.

"Can I help you with something?" Anna asked, stopping as they stepped into the afternoon air.

He smiled again, somehow friendly and mocking at the same time. The man felt like static, or magnets. Anna stepped back.

"Yeah, you can. I have a player in your class, Trey—"

"Duncan. Yes, I know. How can I help you?" She met his eyes, which was no easy feat for her, but she wanted to get back to her work. "Are you preparing to offer me say, box seats if I give him an A?" Anna fluttered her eyelashes in animated glee. It was only fair that she got to tease too.

"Would that work?" he asked, his face giving nothing away. Well, it was clear Coach Sivac enjoyed playing games.

She shook her head and turned to continue walking. He laughed.

"Kidding, I was kidding. But, I do want to talk to you about his grade. We received his four-week grade report yesterday and it looks like he's failing. How is that even possible?"

"There have only been two quizzes and four weeks of class participation. Mr. Duncan got a C on both quizzes, which isn't bad considering some of the terms can be challenging at first, but he has all zeros for class participation."

Anna called him Trey in class. She never used proper names unless someone pissed her off or she was attempting to be assertive.

Mr. Sivac scrunched his face, looking almost in pain. "Can't imagine why," he said under his breath, apparently forgetting once again that she was standing right in front of him... front row to his insults.

"Sorry," he said, but she knew he couldn't have cared less.

Empty minds, empty words, Anna thought.

"How did you know I was here about Trey? Has he said something to you? Maybe about why he took the class?" He closed the space between them again as if he had a secret.

Anna was growing impatient and annoyed. Despite the recent cooler weather, she was flushed and warm. Perhaps it was the way such a seemingly boring blue dress shirt stretched over his chest—it was distracting. She was sure a lot of women, Cynda being one of them, would be turned on right now, but for Anna he was more like roller coasters or 3-D movies: too much. She rationalized that she was fixated on chests in general, having watched *The Last of the Mohicans* for the fifth time last night. The fascination would pass, she thought. This football coach was not Daniel Day Lewis.

Anna stepped back. "Mr. Sivac—" *Why does that name sound familiar?*

"Coach."

"I'm sorry?"

"Coach Sivac. Mr. Sivac was my dad, and my grandfather I guess."

Anna laughed. Even with that chest, those shoulders, the man was ridiculous.

"Right. Well, *Coach* Sivac, I teach Shakespeare. It's an elective, not required, so it attracts a certain type of student. Mr. Duncan is six-foot something and easily two of me in weight. It wasn't a stretch for me to conclude he's a quarterback or maybe a linebacker. Young men of his stature don't make up a huge part of my student demographic."

"Receiver. He's a wide receiver."

"Does it matter?"

"Does it matter if Romeo makes it up that balcony?"

Clever. He was quick and Anna normally would have let it go, but not this time. He was trivializing what she did. She was used to it, but lately, with people poking around in her classroom, it was hard to brush things off.

"I suppose it does," she said, keeping her voice steady.

He had the same look Anna's sisters often flashed when she spoke in what they referred to as her Professor Snooty Pants voice. His eyes hadn't rolled yet, but it was only a matter of time.

"I was wondering if you offer some kind of tutoring or office hours. Our head coach doesn't want him to fall behind. Maybe you could talk with him about why he's not participating?" Somehow he was close to her again, almost face-to-face. *Give me a break.*

"Could you... Do you mind stepping back?"

He looked at the space between them and stepped back. "Sorry, I'm not good with boundaries."

"Clearly." Nothing was working on this guy. He should be gone by now, intimidated by the chill in her tone. It was the only secret weapon she had outside of being invisible, but he was getting closer as if he had some kind of force field. Anna tried to pretend the "physicalness" of him wasn't causing her heart to race. Will would be proud of her because even though "physicalness" wasn't a word, it should be, and it perfectly described Coach Sivac. Despite her best efforts, her heart *was* racing, her hands were a little clammy, and she was standing in the courtyard at UC Berkeley as if she were some blushing student in the prime of innocence instead of a professor on her way to full tenure. At least that's how she felt.

Oh, stop it. He's just a guy. There are millions of them. She heard her youngest sister Meg's voice in her head.

Annabelle was older than Meg by two years, but no one ever believed it. Meg seemed born knowing herself. They had a swimming pool in their backyard growing up and spent summers at the beachside cabins their uncle rented out to vacationers. One year, Anna observed that the way each sister approached the water spoke volumes about their place in the family. Anna used the steps or the ladder. That made her the unassuming one. Hollis usually executed a perfect dive, even off a dock or the side of a pool without a diving board. She was methodical. Sage, the second oldest, was always trying some new flip or twist into the pool, which made for the best pictures. She was the vibrant color of the Jeffries sisters. That left Meg, the undisputed Queen of the Cannonball. Simply standing next to Meg made Anna feel adventurous. Meg was fearless. Although Anna was Meg's go-to for life advice, Meg was the voice in Anna's head any time things got a little... nerve-racking, or male. It had always been that way. They were the odd couple, opposites in so many ways, but sisters were usually that way, weren't they? Pieces of a puzzle only they knew how to put together.

Anna caught herself staring out at the courtyard, the flickering of the leaves in a gentle breeze she now felt cooling her warm cheeks. Coach Sivac was staring at her. It must have been her turn in the volley.

"I believe Student Services offers tutoring. As for Trey's participation, the class can be intimidating at first because students bring all their own preconceived ideas about the work and don't give it a chance. My class is different, but it still takes some time."

He was a "direct looker," to use one of Anna's father's terms. The first time she'd heard it was when Hollis's date picked her up in high school. Their father shook his hand and announced, "He's a direct looker. I like that." That guy turned out to be a creep, but her father had his ideas, strongly held rights and wrongs. Anna never liked direct lookers. She preferred to float in and out of eye contact, but this guy was all about being direct apparently.

He said nothing, so she finished up. "I have office hours on Wednesday and Thursday. Trey is more than welcome to bring questions to me during that time."

"Okay, great, so you'll talk with him? Because I've got... people on my ass, and I need to be able to tell them that I've fixed this."

"I try to keep communication open with all my students. Coach, one question, if I might," she said, trying her best to be snide. "If Trey doesn't like Shakespeare or has no interest in participating, why did he take my class in the first place?"

"Yeah, well, that's interesting. Trey is having some issues with his confidence, so Crazy Eyes... I mean, one of our staff gave him an assignment to do something off the field that was out of his comfort zone. See, being a receiver is all about confidence. It's knowing if you train and track, that the ball will be there at the reach. You know?"

He reminded her of those tinfoil popcorn things they used to pop on movie nights when she was growing up. The ones that always burned her fingers when she tried to open them.

Anna swallowed. "I... no, I don't know anything about football."

"Big shock." He laughed.

Anna did not laugh, but instead turned and left him standing there.

Holy shit! He'd grown up around these brainy types, but damn, Trey's professor was a piece of work. One minute he could have sworn she was checking him out and the next she was dismissing him back to recess. Dane caught up with her again as she walked under the arch of the building. He was raised never to call a woman a bitch, but Ms. Jeffries was pushing him.

"Again, sorry. Look, this is taking way more time than I'm sure either of us expected, so I'll cut to the chase. Trey seems to like your class. He's interested, but for some reason he's not participating. Can you fix that?" Dane asked.

"Probably not." She kept walking in a tightly wound way Dane found annoying. Sort of like chewing on tin foil. Yeah, he'd never done that, but it was probably an accurate comparison.

"Listen, I guess you're kind of a big deal. Students seem to love your class, according to this website his... guidance person said he found you on. I guess they rank the teacher?"

"I hate those."

"Okay, well, apparently they like you. Your class is off the charts and—" He stopped. There was no way in hell he was explaining this next part to Little Miss Cardigan. Dane dropped eye contact and put his hands in his pockets. "Anyway, I'll let you go."

"And what?"

He feigned confusion, but outside of a Christmas pageant in the third grade when he was a kick-ass shepherd, he'd never been a good actor.

"You said my class is off the charts and... what's the 'and?'"

"It's not important. And it's a little embarrassing."

Her face suddenly flushed and if he'd thought it possible, she looked vulnerable, nervous even.

"Why would it be embarrassing?" she asked.

Dane took a deep breath, not sure how to put this tactfully. Realizing she'd probably be pissed no matter how he said it, he figured he might as well come out with it. "I guess you're also rated as, and I quote, easy on the eyes, by your previous students. I'm guessing male, maybe some female. I'm not sure."

"What? You're joking."

"Afraid not. Makes no sense to me either, and this is as far as I want to get into—"

"What's that supposed to mean?"

"Nothing." She was staring him down now. Fantastic. "I just don't think of English teachers as easy on the eyes, let alone ones who teach a language that doesn't exist anymore, but what is it you highbrow types say? To each his own?"

She looked at her watch again in that way that made Dane feel underdressed, undereducated. *Oh, sweetheart, been there, done that.*

"Right. Okay, well, this has been enlightening and insulting, so thank you for both. I will talk with Trey, but ultimately he'll need to participate if he wants a passing grade."

There it was again, hurt or angry, Dane couldn't tell, but her face changed and her mouth formed a thin line. Nice mouth when it was shut, he thought as she walked away. Wait, he wasn't finished with her, he needed confirmation she would handhold Trey so Crazy Eyes would leave him alone.

"I'm sorry if I've insulted you, but there's a lot of pressure this year with the team. I don't have the luxury of fairies and whatever other crap is in your precious plays. I have a job to do, a real one in the real world. You know, in 2016. If Trey needs help, a tutor or whatever, then tell me where to get someone like that."

Anna stopped again right before the entrance to another building and smiled at two students walking by. Wow, her whole face changed when she wasn't pissed, and Dane felt his stomach flip a little. Caffeine on an empty stomach, he rationalized. She stepped into him this time, barely coming up to his chest. She was tiny, buttoned-up in a cream-colored sweater that was now accentuating the red in her cheeks.

"I am well aware that it is 2016, Mr. Sivac. I'm not sure you understand—"

"Oh Christ, enough with the back and forth. I just want to check this off so I can report back to my boss that all is good with Trey. Let me give you my number." He pulled out his phone.

"That won't be necessary."

"It is, though. Somehow this 'whole and happy player' thing has become all important. I don't want to be a pain in your ass, but if you have any problems with him or you think there's anything the coaching staff can do, please let me know. There are a lot of eyes on him this season."

When Anna said nothing, he kept going. "You know what? Since you have all your... stuff, just give me your number and I'll text you my information."

"No."

"No, you won't give me your number?"

"Mr.—Ah, Coach Whatever, I make a habit of giving my number to people I like."

"And you don't like me?"

"No."

Dane suddenly noticed her neck, the line of it, and that led to the urge to check if her hair was as soft as it looked. *Oh, that's fantastic, asshole. You've been a monk for almost a year. Let's wake up for the librarian with a chip on her shoulder. Perfect.*

Dane laughed partly at his thoughts, but mostly at her defiant stance and her insistence that she didn't like him. *She was totally checking us out back there,* his ego chimed in.

"I am not sure why we would exchange numbers. I'm sorry you had to drag yourself away from your party-all-the-time crowd and step into the antiquated English lair. There's no need to extend this communication beyond the present. Since Trey is my student, I will talk to him and work to ensure his success. I do not need his coach to help me with that. I have class in"—she looked at her watch again— "a half an hour, so you can head back to your grass now. We're done here."

"Christ, do they rate personality on those websites?" Dane mumbled under his breath. Maybe he was hoping she heard him so she would whip around again all flustered. She sort of reminded him of the fireflies his dad used to catch in a mason jar during summer break so Dane and his sister could see them up close. Bright, fascinating, and completely untouchable.

He noticed her back stiffen as she walked away. Yeah, she heard him but kept going.

"Right. Great talk. Thank you, Professor."

Nothing. She just kept walking. Dane shook his head, maybe grinning a little, but mostly glad that was over. Check in with the teacher, done. *Can we play some ball now, Crazy Eyes?*

Chapter Three

*A*nna was still "learning her class," as she often referred to the early part of each semester. She had a few students with an expanded knowledge of Shakespeare and his works, but the majority were freshmen looking for an elective credit and of course, a few couples. The lovebirds that sat in the front row this semester fascinated Anna as they somehow managed to hold hands during the entire class period unless they were taking a test. Yes, there were always at least one or two couples every semester. The girls most likely convinced that Shakespeare equaled romance and their otherwise uninterested boyfriends lured to class under the guise of getting laid more than the semester they took, say, Statistics with their girlfriends.

Surely, the thought of sex being a leading factor in even one student enrollment would offend the uptight committee. Anna could almost imagine that lecture on "belittling the subject matter," but Will himself would have been thrilled. After all, dirty jokes and innuendo were often tucked into his clever twists and turns of phrase.

Looking out over her class, Anna realized she had at least three, maybe four, Shakespeare-through-the-movies students. These were the kids who would raise their hands mid-lecture and exclaim, "I think that's wrong. He has a gun in the movie." Anna loved these students. They at least had a concept of Shakespeare's words in the modern world, and she made every effort to bring relevancy to Will's words.

Seated in the corner of her classroom, Anna took a sip of water and noticed Trey. The most difficult students to reach were the ones who took copious notes and believed there were right and wrong answers. Trey, it turned out, was one of those students. He was a structured student, with a planner and highlighters Anna could appreciate, but he was about as uncomfortable as she remembered being in school, which didn't make sense to her. He was handsome, clearly bright, and a football player. In her experience, those guys were the life of the party.

Maybe he truly was out of his comfort zone.

Anna thought about her conversation with Coach Sivac. That students thought she was "easy on the eyes." Where were they in the sea of faces? Anna had never thought about how her students perceived her looks or who she was outside the whimsical confines of the classroom setting. The idea of being rated on a scale in such a calculated way was unnerving, almost as unnerving as the man who had delivered the news. He probably took pleasure in seeing her squirm, or for all she knew he made the whole thing up. Guys like that, like him, were often entertained watching those who couldn't catch a ball or chug a beer feel awkward and ridiculous.

She was suddenly uncomfortable, which never happened within her four walls. This was her sanctuary, so she chased his voice out of her head and refocused on the four students finishing up an animated reading of *Macbeth*, Act IV, Scene I. It was such a resplendent scene. "Open, locks, whoever knocks," Anna mouthed the clever language along with Patrice, who was doing an excellent job as the second witch. This was the scene that would seal Macbeth's fate, she would later explain to the class.

At present, the lights were dim and Anna had borrowed a smoke machine from the drama department. Some of her students had never seen anything like it, short of a movie or a video game. Anna could tell by the wide eyes and frozen movements that they were experiencing something rather than trying to find the right answer. There were no notes to take, no passages to highlight as the room was awash with wonder and the magic of a master playwright. It was brilliant, and the joy of teaching flushed away any other silly self-conscious thoughts.

"But no more spooky visions!—Where are the messengers? Come, bring me to them." George, the tallest student in the class next to Trey Duncan, finished the scene. Anna clapped and brought the lights back up.

George high-fived his girlfriend with a big grin on his face. Where else would he be able to show her his "mad skills," as he put it, playing Macbeth than in this very room? His girlfriend, April, kissed him. *The power of Will.*

"That was perfect, all of you. Well done." Anna checked her watch. She'd removed the clock from the classroom wall to help the students focus. She had fifteen more minutes with them. "Why is this scene so important? It's toward the end of the play. The deeds are done. Why bring the witches back?"

Hands went up, and Anna noticed Trey frantically return to taking notes as if he'd fallen asleep and didn't want to forget a single detail of his dream. Anna wanted to call on him, flush him out and get him to join in the conversation instead of trying to write down every word she said, but when he looked up, she had a feeling he wasn't ready, not yet.

"Yes, Maria." Anna pointed toward the back of the classroom. Maria Cristo was a freshman from Mexico. English was her second language, and yet she managed an incredible understanding of the plays.

"Maybe Shakespeare wanted to bring them back toward the end because they were the ones who started all of this?"

Anna nodded. "Continuing the theme, yes. The witches are a thread throughout the play that point to what?"

Finally looking up from his notes, Trey raised his hand.

"Yes, Trey."

He said nothing, and even though Anna heard snickers and some-one say, "Well, that was enlightening," she held his eyes, afraid if she looked away he would never raise his hand again. "What do you think the witches represent, Trey?"

He looked down at his notes, broke eye contact, and she lost him. "Forget it."

More snickers.

"Excuse me. Mr. Swift and Mr. Granville, that behavior is not at all in the spirit of a collaborative class discussion." Both students sat straight and were silent. Anna looked to Trey and realized for the first time, maybe in her life, that beneath all that muscle and physical intimidation rested an insecure kid like the rest of them. She was angry that she'd lost an opportunity to reach him, so she offered up something completely out of character.

"While you may hide behind your books, gentlemen, I'll ask you to please respect Mr. Duncan if only for the fact that he could flatten both of you on the football field without even trying."

The class laughed and as Anna turned on her Smart Board to write down the two major interpretations of the witches in *Macbeth*, the faintest of smiles spread across Trey's face. She felt good, somehow vindicated for his embarrassment, even if her comments did pander to a machismo she would not condone.

Had she just defended a football player? Yes, she had because re-gardless of his sport, Trey was a hard worker and she could tell he was a thinking young man. She always encouraged thinking. Where would she be now if Professor Vance hadn't shown her a different way of looking at Shakespeare's histories her freshman year at Berkeley? Teaching was all about finding different avenues into a student's head. Now she simply needed to figure out a way to reach Trey. Challenge accepted.

Anna stopped by the grocery store after class and less than an hour later pulled into the carport of her home. It was earlier than she

normally arrived home, but she needed to start getting her new house together. Turning off the car, she first reminded herself that she still had to do something about the bushes lining her walkway. She loved them, but they were making it almost impossible to actually get to her front door. Finding a landscaper needed to be on top of her list for the weekend, she decided, which made that the hundredth such conversation she'd had with herself in the few months since becoming a new homeowner.

Near the front of her house, Anna noticed the UPS truck, or more importantly, the man currently navigating around the out-of-control bushes and bravely making his way to her door. She stepped out of the car and hurried across her small patch of grass.

"Sorry about the bushes."

UPS Man looked up, eyes hidden behind dark shades. He was wearing the standard, but inexplicably sexy, brown uniform. His hair was almost black, legs tan. Anna noticed his forearms were lovely and when he smiled, she felt a little woozy. Lack of food, that's all. She needed to eat the apple she'd put in her bag for a snack, she told herself as she tried for a smile back at him.

"Not a problem. How's the house coming? I noticed the Crate & Barrel boxes stopped, so you must be settling in." More smiling.

Anna laughed, or maybe it was a snort. "I'm getting there, thank you."

"That's good news. Your deliveries are a lot more exciting than the previous owners'."

"Oh really." Anna shaded her eyes from the setting sun and looked up at him.

"Let's just say there were a lot of boxes with those 'As seen on TV' stickers."

"You know, some of that stuff is wonderful. You might see those boxes for me eventually. Maybe I'll get a couple of cats too."

He laughed and seemed to take her in with a glance that almost slid across her skin. That was her imagination, she was sure of it. UPS guys were always charming, weren't they? "You don't look like a cat lady yet. Well, it's nice to finally meet you, Annabelle." He handed her a small box.

He knows my name?

Of course he does, dummy, he's UPS.

"Yes, likewise..." She paused in that way a person does when she's soliciting another person's name in return without coming right out.

"Brad." He extended his hand.

Anna shook it and felt a small burst of warmth. "Nice to meet you, Brad. Happy... delivering," she said and walked back to her car for her groceries.

Brad chuckled and she heard the truck start to back up.

Happy delivering? Anna shook her head, grabbed her bags, and went into her house through the side yard. Sometimes she wished life came with a weekly script and maybe a soundtrack. A proper writer would have given her some clever response for Brad, something like — *"Oh, well don't get too... hot out there, Brad," Anna said in a breathy voice as the condensation of her sweet tea glass melted around her fingers.*

Anna laughed. There she went again rewriting reality. She threw her keys onto the kitchen counter and set the bags down. Yes, if only she had a script.

Instead, she was left with her own words, which was fine. She could always peel Brad's clothes off in her imagination. A lot of women were given near-perfect bodies that they worked into fine-tuned instruments. Anna had her imagination — it was practically a triathlete. She would tuck Brad and his yumminess, as Cynda often said, away for one of those days when real life sucked.

"Keep your arms in tight, Birch, and that back leg is still stuttering. Five-yard bursts, again. Hit." Dane stood in the center of the practice field as he worked drills with his guys. There were seventeen receivers on the final roster, eight of them redshirts. Head Coach Hall took most of the inside receivers, which left Dane with ten guys. His one junior, Lincoln Birch, was the hotshot of the group. Since last year, he'd packed on another ten pounds of muscle, but he was still fast, making him an even better asset during running passes.

Asset was probably a politically incorrect term these days, but he'd spent so many days in meetings lately, Dane found himself craving simplicity. He was now inundated with "whole player" and "emotional fitness." Asset was easy compared to all the feelings floating around.

Dane made an effort not to compare his time as a player with his current players, but sometimes that was difficult. It had been almost twelve years since he'd taken the field on their end. He remembered being worked to within an inch of his life, yelled at, and occasionally belittled. It was part of the game, part of the training for when he was faced with guys on the field who couldn't give a crap about his feelings unless it was the feeling of his face smashing inside his helmet.

Dane had not expected coaching at UC Berkeley to include exploring the "emotional wholeness" of anyone, but he was trying to adjust. He liked his job, and deep down in a place Crazy Eyes would probably love venturing to, he wanted to make his dad proud. Yeah, this "feelings" stuff was getting to him.

Birch was a big deal, and no one knew it more than he did. He'd taken Trey, the star freshman, under his wing, but Dane wasn't sure that was a good idea. With their first game next week, Dane was still assessing the strengths and weaknesses of nine of his players, which would be more pronounced once these guys were under the bright lights and in actual play. There was only so much that could be done in practice.

Birch was the only player Dane spent most of his time nitpicking because the kid was close to perfect. Dane knew if Birch could keep some humility intact for another two days, he would perform beautifully in front of the roaring crowd. He was a typical receiver: confident and cocky, a showman. Trey seemed to be coming up right alongside him, minus the confidence he'd exhibited back in high school. That's why Coach Hall brought in Crazy Eyes and apparently made Dane Trey's babysitter, which was fine because right now, impressing the higher-ups was exactly what Dane needed to do. It would solidify his job and give him as stable a future as any coach could ask for, which wasn't much, but he couldn't keep working for USC. There were too many memories, so when Berkeley offered, he jumped. He wanted this to work.

Dane grabbed his water bottle and turned back to keep an eye on the drill. The setting sun was a relief as the heat began to lessen. He had no idea how those coaches in hotter climates worked their players. He pushed the cap back in on his bottle, blew the whistle, and walked onto the field. "Let's work sideline catches. Campbell, this is where I need you to think about dragging rather than the pattering you usually do, okay?" Brian Campbell, another freshman—again too much confidence—nodded and took position. "Set. Hit."

Dane watched as the new freshman quarterback threw pass after pass to his receivers and with the exception of a few glances down at the line, which was easy to correct, the drill went well. And then Trey dropped the ball. The pass was clean; there was no reason.

Dane asked Trey to go again.

He tracked it, found it, and... the ball hit the ground with a familiar wobbly hop.

Dane blew the whistle and walked over to him. "Problem?"

He let out a breath like he wanted to say something, but changed his mind. "No. I'm good. Not sure what happened there."

Dane patted him on the back and signaled for the guys to go again. Trey missed the pass and ran to the back of the line. Dane let it go this time and kept practice moving.

The kid was in his head. For an instant, Dane thought he recognized the weight between Trey's eyes. Dane couldn't figure out Trey's hesitation, or why he kept letting the ball slip away, especially since he had the kind of natural talent most players dreamed about. Maybe there was something personal happening.

Practice was over, and Dane was relieved because watching Trey struggle was frustrating. Dane met with the other coaches in the locker room to go over the plan for Sunday and the revised TV schedule for the opening game. He listened, but his mind was on Trey. If the kid didn't get his head in the game, the shrink was never going to leave any of them alone. It was like this one player had become the poster child for the "whole player" movement. Crazy Eyes had already sent a follow-up e-mail and copied Coach Hall. She said, with way more words than were necessary, that Trey was making progress.

Yeah? Could have fooled me.

Dane couldn't remember the last time talking through feelings had fixed anything. Trey was an athlete with talent, some of it God-given, and the rest earned through sweat and hard work. Dane had a difficult time believing that a few more sessions on the couch were going to keep the ball in this kid's hands. He needed to talk with his friend Jeb, the assistant strength and conditioning coach, tomorrow. Maybe there were other drills, something practical that could get Trey where he needed to be.

Grabbing his bag, Dane threw two of the towels left on the floor into the large laundry bins. The look on Trey's face had stirred things up, brought crap to the surface that Dane had put to bed a long time ago. How the hell had he gotten involved in all of this? Hopefully the kid pulled out of it because if Dane had to hold hands in some therapy session with Crazy Eyes or navigate another meeting with that professor again... aw, hell, now he was thinking about her too.

"Sivac." His boss came around the corner. "Your turn to do the faculty social thing or whatever it's called. They want a rep from each athletic program. You're that rep. Tomorrow night. Starts at six. Wear a collar on your shirt and no jeans. You should be in and out by seven."

"I don't remember drawing straws. I'm stuck with this because..." When Coach Hall said nothing and grinned, Dane finished the sentence for himself. "Because this is only my second year and I'm incredibly charming?"

There it was again, the roaring laughter of the man who was turning out to be one hell of a coach. Dane could learn a lot from him and truly didn't want to screw things up. If that meant making nice with some suits and turtlenecks, that's what he was going to do. He knew his mother would be at the social, and whether he wanted to think about it or not, so would Professor Annabelle Jeffries. Dane had been to a lot of these dress-up-and-say-the-right-thing shindigs growing up.

"That's right, kid. Go charm the pants off them. Maybe next year we'll have someone else to pick on."

"Yeah, yeah." Dane smirked, shook his head, and left to the sound of more laughter.

Chapter Four

Every department had meet and greets and workshops, as well as opportunities to interact with faculty peers. Although these functions were intended for sharing research and teaching techniques, more often than not, Anna found they were mostly for bragging and gossip. The university as a whole also held the Faculty Connection each semester to promote unity among all departments. For Anna, the university structure was again a reality versus fantasy thing. When she'd first applied, she imagined departments working together, a completely free and collaborative environment. Instead, she found the reality of higher academia a bit like high school. Cliques and competition left little room for more than the grown-up equivalent of social climbing. She had not counted on the politics, but with the help of Hollis and her father, she'd learned to navigate it. Anna skated along, expending a good deal of energy making sure not to ruffle any feathers outside the classroom in an effort to protect her freedom inside the classroom. Cynda was her saving grace at these functions, but the minute she stepped away to get another drink, Professor Robert Troupe pounced.

"Jasmine here is a Fulbright scholar. She spent the past year in Oxford," he said, holding the elbow of a woman in a mint-colored dress.

"Oh, that's exciting. Welcome, Jasmine. I do miss Oxford. What was the emphasis of your work?" Anna asked, doing her best extrovert impersonation.

Mint Dress had a tiny gap between her front teeth. Anna focused on that when the woman gave her a tight, not-friendly-at-all grin and said, "I don't want to share at the moment. I'm working on a book."

"Right. Sure." Anna turned to make a quick visit the ladies' room when the bells of Sather Tower rang out, indicating it was only six o'clock. She once again cursed herself for having been early and wondered how much longer she would need to endure. Then she saw Coach Sivac.

He was over by the bar talking to a tall woman with short dark hair. Anna had no idea who the woman was and told herself she didn't care, but somehow she couldn't take her eyes off them either. She was about to look away when he glanced up and caught her. Anna was acutely aware of her breathing as he excused himself, eyes flicking back toward her again. He was in slacks that were anything but the coach pants of her high school memories and a dark button-up shirt. Holding a glass of wine, not a beer like he was supposed to drink, he walked toward her, and Anna was reminded of those sultry car commercials professional athletes did.

Shouldn't these cold marble walls be a sanctuary for those of us less athletically inclined? she thought. Why would a football coach be at a faculty function? *Because he's an employee of the university too, Anna. Don't be such a snob.* Meg was back in her head. Perfect, just what she needed. Oh God, she was too tired to break out Professor Snooty Pants, so Anna tried something different.

"Why do I know your last name?" she asked before Dane could get out what promised to be something sarcastic, if his easy grin was any indication.

"I'm sure it's because you can't stop thinking about me since our fateful encounter. You probably have a thing for jocks. Deep down," he joked and seemed almost sexy now that it was dark out.

So much for avoiding the sarcasm. Anna took the glass of wine off a passing tray. She needed something to do with her hands... and red wine was her favorite.

"I can assure you that is not the case." She sipped and turned the wineglass by the stem, still trying to place his name. She'd heard it before. Maybe his wife worked here too? She glanced at his left hand. No ring. That didn't mean anything these days. Coach Sivac appeared comfortable in all situations and was clearly enjoying watching her stew. He was like one of those moderators at a spelling bee who, Anna always thought, secretly wanted the speller to mess up.

"My mother is the new dean of the law school. For the record, I had a job here first," he finally said.

"That's right. Wow, she's your mother?"

Dane nodded. "Confirmed. We have pictures."

"Huh."

"Surprised I have a mother, or thought she'd be in a football jersey holding a cherry pie?"

"I... am surprised your mother is the dean of the law school. Mainly, I'll admit, because football and law school don't often go together, at least in my mind. From what I've heard, she's an accomplished woman. But no, I did not imagine your mother baking."

"Football jersey, though."

"Maybe. If I gave any thought to you or your parents, which I have not, yes, I suppose I'd envision those parking lot rallies where they line up all the cars."

"Tailgates."

"Yes, those, and jerseys. Maybe some of those obnoxious foam fingers too."

Dane laughed, and Anna took another large sip of wine. This felt like flirting, and she didn't do that. Well, maybe she practiced in the mirror after she took a shower or finished watching a great movie, but flirting was never a real-world thing.

"I can understand that. Stereotypes are powerful. Your dad probably smokes a pipe." Dane cocked a brow.

Anna shook her head and fought the warm comfort slipping under her surface. He was sharp and stimulating to talk with. "No. My dad doesn't smoke. Loves football, actually," Anna said under her breath.

"What was that?" he asked.

"Nothing."

"Your dad loves football, really?"

"See, I never understand why people do that. You heard me the first time, so why ask?"

"That's easy. I wanted to hear you say it again."

"Silly." She tried not to gulp her wine, but it was good and if her cheeks were going to flush red, which she was sure they were, they might as well be a bit numb too.

"Probably. So back to your incredibly cool dad."

"Cal alumnus and an insane Golden Bears fan. My whole family actually, except for Hollis. She went to Stanford."

"In a family of bears, that's brave."

"That's Hollis."

"Doesn't she know what bears do around trees?"

This time she couldn't hold back the smile. "That's a good one. Can I use that?"

He was looking at her as if she were a puzzle, something that needed to be figured out. She could have saved him the trouble, shut the conversation down, but she found she didn't want to as his eyes glinted in the dim light of the room. "Sure. It's all yours. Just be careful she doesn't come back with the changing-the-tire joke."

Anna must have looked confused.

"How many Golden Bears does it take to change a tire? One, unless it's a blowout and then they all show up." Dane shook his head. "Stupid joke, but they're trees, what do you expect?"

They stood watching the crowd, in full networking and bragging mode by that time. Anna played with her glass and noticed his watch, the way his hair barely skimmed the top of his ears. Every sense was heightened.

"So how'd they end up with you, your exceptional parents?" he asked.

"Not sure, but I too have pictures. Probably the same way your brilliant mother raised a football coach. Flukes. We're both flukes I guess."

"Look at that, something in common."

"I'm sure it stops there." The clear bottom of the glass peeked at her on that last sip and she told herself to pace the wine.

"I'll bet we can find a few more patches of common ground. My dad died, but he was a huge football fan too. USC, but I think it still counts as something in common."

"I'm sorry." The thought of her father or anyone's father dying seemed raw. Anna occasionally thought about losing someone close to her. It was personal, and he shared it as if he were telling her his favorite dessert. *Did he have to go to a funeral for his father? Was he little? Oh God. Was it some tragic accident?*

Anna tried to shut off her heart, but that was how she worked. Darn it, now he seemed human. She set what was left of her wine down. It wasn't helping. Weren't most people associated with football more about action and less about talk? You know, pad-wearing knuckle draggers? Where the hell were his pads when she needed to get her head on straight?

"When did your father pass away?" she asked, unable to squelch her curiosity.

"I was nineteen. Heart attack."

"That's awful."

"It was for a while, but that's life, right? People die."

The air between them changed and suddenly in the middle of what almost felt like casual conversation, Anna knew she'd hit a nerve. He kind of recoiled at the question about his father as if he only had the one set response and further inquiry was not welcome.

"I suppose they do," she said, a little more careful now.

His eyes returned to playful within a blink, and even though they were both standing in a room full of people, colleagues, they could have been at a tiny table for two. He wasn't looking around, schmoozing, or gesturing to other people during their conversation. He was talking with her, and even more heart jumpy, he was listening. Oh, how Anna loved people who listened.

"Careful, Professor Jeffries, it appears we are getting along."

His eyes twinkled, and the way he looked at her seemed different now. As if he'd noticed something she felt certain wasn't there.

"I need to get going."

He took another sip. "Yeah, I figured that was coming."

"What does that mean?"

"In my limited experience, you seem a little jumpy. Always checking the watch, going somewhere."

"I made my appearance. That's all I needed to do. I hate these things. Have a lovely evening, Coach Sivac."

"Dane."

She turned, and God help her, that gaze landed on her again. "Right. Dane. Good-bye."

"Goodnight. By the way, that makes three things in one night." He leaned in and Anna could smell the soap on his skin, the wine on his breath. "I hate this stuff too, but none of the other coaches had the balls."

She nodded. "Well, good for you and your..."

Dane quietly laughed. Anna shook her head and did not finish the sentence. She felt foolish, out of her sexual banter league. It was a feeling with which she was well acquainted. Without another word, she walked out of the exhibit hall and took in a deep breath of cool evening air.

"Oh no you don't." Cynda hooked her arm. "I just spent what felt like an eternity with some guy telling me all about his trip to Budapest. He ate Pörkölts for a month and washed his socks in a sink."

Her friend looked wide-eyed and probably a bit traumatized.

"Did you tell him you lived in that area for a semester?"

"Hell no. I was slowly wiggling away. There are some scary clowns in there. You, on the other hand, were talking, quite closely I might add, with Coach You-Can-Practice-On-Me-Anytime."

Anna laughed.

"So, we're going back in there for a few minutes because you owe me."

Anna looked at her, pleading. "I have an early morning." She wasn't sure why she tried. Cynda was relentless.

"Uh huh. It's Friday night."

"I know, and I just moved into my new house. I have a million things to do."

Cynda shook her head. "Not going to work. Talk with me while I have another glass and try to wash the Pörkölts off my brain."

She didn't wait for an argument and pulled Anna back toward the bar.

Throughout his high school years, Dane worked as a counselor at Pinewood Summer Camp. Before starting junior year, he was in charge of The Chipmunks with his friend Chris, whose parents owned the camp, and a girl named Noel, another counselor with long wavy hair that seemed to be ten different shades of golden. For two weeks, Noel sat doing arts and crafts and reading what Dane thought at the time was the thickest book he'd ever seen, all while he and Chris swung the campers on huge ropes and set up endless games of capture the flag. Every now and then Noel would look up and notice Dane before turning right back to whatever she was doing. He shared beautiful summer memories with some of the other female counselors, but unlike them, Noel did absolutely nothing to make herself noticeable. She was self-contained and untouchable. There were days when the sunlight hit her a certain way and she almost appeared ethereal in his teenage eyes.

For fourteen days they barely said two sentences to one another, but at the End of Camp Dance, he'd asked Noel to dance. She agreed and when he took her in his arms, she smelled like campfire and her shirt was open in the back so his hand touched her bare skin. Dane thought he was going to lose his mind. She was so soft, and somehow her indifference completely lit him up. The next day, walking her to her car after all the campers had been sent home and they'd cleaned up the grounds for the incoming group, he felt like a bumbling fool. She lived two hours away and when Dane asked for her number, she simply said, "What's the point? This was fun, but we have nothing in common." That was it. She kissed him on the cheek and climbed into her car.

He never saw Noel again but did catch that the book she was reading was *The Iliad*. Yeah, they probably didn't have anything in common, but when Dane looked up from a conversation with his mother and saw Anna back and mingling with the flirty woman from the English lounge, he could have sworn he smelled a campfire.

Professor Annabelle Jeffries was something else and he was pretty sure, like Noel, he should probably leave her alone.

"So, I think Jess is going to try out the new sitter because that's nuts, don't you think?"

Dane knew his mother was speaking. He also knew as long as she was talking about his sister or her grandchildren, he had time since it was often a one-sided venting or gushing session. But right as he was trying to figure out if Anna told him she was leaving to blow him off or had changed her mind, his mom grew quiet and said his name again. It was time to answer.

"I... agree. Yeah, a new sitter is good."

His mother leaned to the left, tracking his line of sight, and then looked at him. "Who is that?"

"Who?"

"Oh, come on. I'm your mother."

Dane put his hands in his pockets. "There are a lot of people here. You're going to need to be a little more specific."

She shook her head. "Okay, who is the beautiful, unassuming woman over there in the black dress with the pink cardigan and perfect strappy sandals. The one with the silky dark hair and eyes barely tolerating Professor Yardley while he tries to entertain her."

Dane's head snapped toward Anna, and his mother laughed.

He closed his eyes. Anna wasn't talking with anyone.

"Works every time. Who is she?" His mother sipped her sparkling water.

"I met her a few days ago. Annabelle Jeffries. She's an associate professor. Shakespeare."

"Oh, I've heard about her. She's quite well-known around here. Have you seen her blog?"

Dane shook his head slowly. His mother was rarely impressed and never read blogs. He suddenly felt out of his league, although that was far from new for him. Rachael Sivac was, as Anna had put it, an accomplished woman and a great legal mind. His sister Jessica was a ridiculously well-paid defense attorney currently juggling five-year-old twins, and Dane was... a football coach. Albeit a football coach with one of the most important programs in the country, but he usually clocked in as the least impressive Sivac. There were moments growing up Dane wished he'd still had his dad, a fireman, to help him out, but that wasn't his life. Besides, what the hell did he mean he was out of his league? He had no interest in Annabelle Jeffries, and she ran from him like the plague. It was this event, these people, that explained why his mind was traveling into areas it had no business going. Christ, he needed to hit the gym or go for a run before he started thinking turtlenecks were cool.

"Well, from what I hear, she's very progressive. Studied at Oxford and Yale. She's brilliant. And in these circles, that says something, don't you think?"

"I do." He looked over his shoulder at Anna. "Listen, this has been a real cerebral blast, but I need to go."

"Not yet, mister. I'd like to meet your new friend."

"Believe me, Mother, she is not my friend."

"You sure about that? She looked over here twice."

Dane did not have the energy to argue, so he took his mother's arm and led her through the crowd of people. Anna was standing with her friend. She smiled but did not meet his eyes. She did that often. Sort of drifted past him, but rarely landed at full eye contact.

"Professor Annabelle Jeffries, this is Dean Rachael Sivac. She's apparently a fan of yours already."

"Really? Well, that is unbelievable. It is a pleasure to meet you, ma'am. Berkeley is so lucky to have you."

His mom looked at him. "I like her."

Dane's eyes betrayed him and fell to Anna's face, flushed and uncomfortable. He'd guess she'd rather be reading a book. What he had not planned on noticing was that she was, as his mother had pointed out, beautiful. Roses and early morning sunrise beautiful. *What the hell is that?* He needed out, now, before the mushy feelings took over his normally rational brain.

Anna, her friend, and now his mom were all in animated conversation about something Dane had no interest in knowing.

"Okay. So you three enjoy. I'm leaving."

"The night is young," his mother said.

Dane shook his head, his dumbass eyes falling on Anna again. Before he made an ass out of himself, he kissed his mom on the cheek and said goodnight.

After climbing into his car, he flipped through his phone for someone—anyone—he'd admit only to himself, who wanted a good time. A woman who was fun, warm, and happy to be in his league. It had been too long. He needed sex or something because there was no way in hell he was ever going to tackle the mountain of attitude that was Annabelle Jeffries. Christ, even her name was doing things to him now. Dane thought of calling Jeb. He always had an extra woman. All time low, he thought as he rolled down his windows and drove home. Trey better get his act together and soon. There would be no more coach-teacher meetings.

Chapter Five

*A*nna spent Saturday looking for a new reading chair. She had donated the one from her old apartment because the cushion was so deteriorated, she could feel a spring when she sat down. She needed a good chair but didn't want to spend a fortune. Her mother offered to order one online for her, but Anna needed to shop in person, to sink down into her potential reading chair, and decide if the feel of it was right. She'd woken up early Saturday morning to work through the list of secondhand shops she'd made but found nothing. Then Cynda called and wanted to see a movie. At the time, it seemed much more exciting than looking for a chair, so she went. Although unexpected, as they were walking out of the theater, Anna found her chair. It was in the window of a small accessories store across from the movie theater called Juxtaposition. Cynda told her it was fate.

"It's too much money," Anna replied, already attached to the chair.

"Eh, buy it. No one I know gets more out of a reading chair than you, my friend."

Anna ran her hand along the nubby fabric with subtle twining roses and yellow doilies along the bottom and decided she had to have it, and the ottoman too. They delivered it the next morning, and

Anna spent all Sunday in her pajama bottoms and T-shirt reading *The Lake House* in her new chair. She hadn't been this excited since she sat on the counter in the kitchen of her little one-bedroom piece of paradise almost five months ago and made the first of many midnight peanut butter and jelly sandwiches.

But Sunday was over, Anna thought, grabbing her lunch box off the passenger seat of her car. It was time to get back to work. As she made her way to her classroom, she realized she'd never viewed teaching as work, nor had she looked forward to going home. Prior to becoming a homeowner, she'd spent most of her life perfectly happy in a classroom, office, coffee shop, or the library. As long as she was studying or learning, that was all she needed. Her little house, just over 1,000 square feet, and now her new chair, spoke to something in her that whispered there was more to life than books. Having a place off campus was changing her somehow. Anna knew she'd need to tackle her outside landscaping eventually, but for now she was happy.

Less than two hours later, she had concluded her summary for the final scene of *Macbeth*, complete with some of her favorite film clips. Her students had been excited and engaged, with the majority of them agreeing that Judi Dench "nailed it" as Lady Macbeth. They were able to see the nuances, the subtleties, that made Dame Dench's performance so spectacular, and Anna had laughed and loved them even more. Right before she began her lecture, she'd noticed two tenure committee chairmen sitting in the back of the classroom. She wasn't sure where the curriculum group left off and the tenure began. Maybe they actually overlapped. When she saw them, for a split second she considered leaving out the film clips, toning down her final day of *Macbeth*, but now, surrounded by chatting students with hands raised for questions, she knew she'd made the right decision. The committee guys had, of course, left halfway through class, with notes chockful of judgment, no doubt. Anna would have liked to brush it off, say that it didn't matter, but it did.

This job was her crowning achievement. She wanted full tenure. Her parents were so excited when she told them she'd applied, they sent her a congratulations card and a leather-bound copy of Shakespeare's sonnets they'd ordered from Rare Editions, a bookstore in the city. She had a long way to go in the tenure process yet, but her parents always loved to encourage or put the pressure on early; it all depended on how Anna chose to look at it. Midway through her lecture, when she saw the doors of her classroom swing closed, it started to feel like pressure. She wanted to give the committee what they wanted, or at least she thought she did. But the truth was she simply didn't know how to teach any other way.

As she wrapped up class and her students began filing out of the room, she took a seat next to Trey Duncan. He was shoving his laptop into his backpack, the frustration spilling off his massive shoulders.

"How's it going?"

"It's not. I have an appointment to change my schedule tomorrow. I'll be out of your hair next week. This was a stupid idea."

"You're not in my hair."

"Sure about that?"

"Actually, I'll be sorry to see you go. I love that my class is out of your comfort zone. It's pretty brave."

He snickered.

"What? It is. Not many guys I know, especially star football players, would even step through that door."

"With respect, Ms. Jeffries, how many football players do you know?"

She nodded. "Good point. Well, I don't want you to leave. We start *A Midsummer Night's Dream* next week and believe me, you'll be missing out. And... your last quiz was a vast improvement. Why are you bailing now?"

"Fifty percent is participation. No way I'm ever getting up there and doing all that moaning and crap like those other kids do. Sorry, with respect."

She laughed. "Oh, wait until next week. There's dancing too. I'm not asking you to act. Participation can be reading or interacting with other students. Did you read *Macbeth*?"

"I did. Understood about half of it. I get all of it now, after your lectures. You're good, by the way."

"Thank you. What is it going to take to make you stay?"

Trey shook his head. "This isn't my scene. I went too far out of the comfort zone and these... brainy types are waiting for me to get up there so they can laugh at the big stupid football player."

"You're not stupid."

"Oh, I know, but they don't. It's all about perceptions, right? Who people think you are, or what role they decide you can and can't do?"

He was wise beyond his years, and Anna genuinely liked Trey Duncan. She wanted him in her class. That was the only explanation for what she did next.

"Tell you what, let's recast some of those roles, shall we? I'll step out of my comfort zone if you agree to get up with me next week and start *A Midsummer Night's Dream*. We'll do it together. However, I have to warn you, there's glitter in this one. But it's a comedy, so I promise no brooding. I'll even let you make up some of the participation points you've lost so far."

Trey crossed his arms in front of his massive chest and considered her offer. Anna could tell he was waiting for the catch. "What makes you uncomfortable?"

Oh dear, where to start, Anna wanted to say.

"Lots of things."

Trey nodded. His brain seemed to be spinning with ideas. "Okay. Okay, yeah, this might be fun. You promise you'll hold up your end of the deal?"

Anna extended her hand, which was quickly engulfed in his large dark palm. She was certain she'd never seen a hand so big.

"I'll think on it."

"And cancel that appointment to drop the class?" Anna asked as they both stood.

Throwing his backpack over one shoulder, Trey nodded with a smile. Anna felt her heart warm in a way she had not felt since becoming a teacher. He was almost to the door when he turned. "I've got it."

"That was quick." She started packing up her things.

"You said you don't know any football players. Come to a practice."

"I'm sorry?"

"Yeah, that's out of your zone all right. You stay for a full practice, and I'll get up and dance around with you."

"You want me to play football?"

"Nah, just come to practice, maybe run a little. I'll throw the ball to you. I can't seem to catch it. Maybe you can."

Anna shook her head.

"Come on. We don't bite. Besides, you shook on it."

She should have said "No." or "Pick something else," but she was asking him to take a chance, and it wasn't fair unless she went with him. "That I did. Don't you have a game tomorrow?"

"Yeah, but we practice at five-ass-dark thirty in the morning on Monday, or four forty-five Monday afternoon."

Anna laughed. She was grumpy if she had to wake up before five and thought Trey's five-ass-dark thirty would look perfect on a coffee mug.

"I'll take four forty-five," Anna said and mentally scanned her calendar as Trey watched her with that look kids often gave adults when they thought they were humoring them. She wanted to prove him wrong. "See you Monday afternoon."

"Seriously? You'll do it?" His huge hands slapped together.

"I will, but believe me, you will dance a jig up here on Wednesday, so ready up and be prepared to become Puck."

"The little goat guy? Hell no."

Anna raised her eyebrows, thrilled that he'd at least started reading the next play and having fun challenging him. "Absolutely. If you want me to break a sweat, then you will definitely be bringing out your inner fairy. I think you're going to like him."

Trey mumbled something under his breath that might have rhymed with Puck, but Anna pretended not to hear.

"So, we have a deal?" she asked, shutting off the lights and walking out of the classroom with him.

Trey nodded.

"Glitter, so much glitter." Anna patted him on the back.

He let out a rumbling laugh that was so warm Anna felt like she'd been given a glimpse of the child inside most grown men. They parted ways at the grass, Trey off to another class and Anna retiring to her office. She could handle one football practice, couldn't she? Of course she could, Anna thought as she threw her stuff on her desk and opened the blinds to her office.

It was a beautiful day. She'd reached a student.

As she sat in her desk chair, she thought of Dane. Were all the coaches at every practice? She turned toward the window and knew for certain he'd be there and he'd have one hell of a time mocking her. That was the nature of things anytime she put her tennis shoes on. Anna shrugged. She could handle it. Heck, it might actually be fun.

She chuckled and shook her head. Not a chance. But if it motivated Trey to participate, it would be well worth it.

"So, that first win last week against Hawaii was kind of a given, right? And it seems everyone feels pretty good about San Diego, but man, you've got the Longhorns coming. Between you and me, even with Birch and Trey, there's still a talent discrepancy," Jeb said.

Dane could smell the bubble gum he was chomping on.

"Yeah? Did your fantasy football team tell you that?"

"For reals." Jeb batted his eyelashes with his hands on his hips, drawing attention to his Muscle Milk T-shirt. The guy was a walking billboard most of the time because he scored more free stuff than all the rest of the coaches put together. And he was the biggest smartass.

"But seriously, did you see Trey working the backhanded catch? Palms up, right into the chest like he'd been doing it his whole life. Some of those extra exercises are paying off."

"I did." Dane's eyes didn't leave the field as the receivers moved to the tap dance drill. "Still fumbling, though, even with the shrink's help," he added quietly.

"Yeah, well, that's all in his mind because those are fine-tuned arms, my friend. You're welcome."

Dane shook his head. "Isn't that your job? You know as assistant strength and conditioning coach, shouldn't you be... strengthening the players?"

Jeb nodded and popped his gum as they both watched the field. "Yes, it is my job, but I'm so good at it, sometimes I amaze even myself."

"Uh huh." Dane blew his whistle and his guys started laps. Another practice down and Trey only fumbled four passes. Progress, Dane thought, grabbing his clipboard.

Jeb was stretching his arms, swinging from his hips side to side. "You wanna grab a beer after we meet and discuss how we're going to get our asses handed to us by Texas?"

"You should be the team motivational speaker."

"Just telling it like I see it." He reached over his head, more stretching.

"According to the sports psychologist, success lies in the mind."

"Probably, but truth conquers all. Hey, want to know a secret?" Jeb dropped his arms and walked next to Dane.

"No. The last time you asked me that question, it took me days to unhear what came next."

"Aw, no, this one is good. The shrink"—Jeb leaned in—"I slept with her. It was a while back, but yeah."

Dane's brow furrowed as a reflex, but he wasn't exactly shocked. He'd known Jeb a little over a year and the man had a way with women. How he managed all that sickening, sweet talk, Dane had no idea, but his friend was a bit of a legend. "I'm not surprised."

"You're not?"

Dane gestured for Brinks to talk less and run more. "She's your type."

"I don't have a type."

"Sure you do, everyone does. She's pent up. Says she tolerates guys in sports because that's her job, but she has no interest in dating them. You like helping those types of women change their minds. It's like a hobby."

"Damn right. I'll tell you one thing, though, don't let those suits fool you, she's a—"

Dane blew his whistle. "You're a sick man. You do realize you're pushing forty, right?"

Jeb's face scrunched. "In like seven years."

Dane shook his head as the guys ran one more lap and started heading toward them.

"So, beer, no beer?"

"No beer. I bought a rice maker this morning, and I still have game films to watch."

Jeb stared at him as if Dane had just dropped his pants. "What the hell is wrong with you? A rice maker? What man with a perfectly functioning dick owns a rice maker? Oh, oh, is that why you never grab a beer with me and you never take any of those women I try to send your way home?" He leaned in. "Erectile dysfunction is not something to be ashamed of."

Dane laughed and flipped him off.

"I mean you can get the little blue pill. Don't turn to the rice maker yet, my man."

"You're an asshole. My... everything works fine. I'm not looking for that right now. I've got a house, and there's some pressure here. I'm working on being an 'emotionally complete' coach." Dane put his thumbs and middle fingers together, copying a meditation pose from his sister. "I don't have time for your... adventures or anything else right now."

"Except rice."

"Except rice. Hey, don't knock it till you try it. According to the box and the stuff I read online, this thing is incredible. Rice, a little bok choy. That's where it's at." Dane rubbed his stomach for effect.

"Uh huh. Okay, well, Leroy and I are grabbing drinks. We'll be at The Wheelhouse if you change your mind."

"Thanks for the invite," Dane said, feeling a little guilty he'd only gone out a handful of times with any of the other coaches. It wasn't his scene anymore.

Trey ran over as the team and coaches walked toward the locker room.

"Better out there, Trey. How'd it feel?"

"Thanks, Coach. Good, I guess. Mitchell all but handed me that first one. Hell, it was so soft I felt like we were drinking tea, not that I'm complaining."

"Just take it easy. Going from high school to college is a big enough adjustment. Football is a whole other thing here. Before you know it, you'll be dancing in the end zone." Dane tried to remember everything Crazy Eyes had said. Be positive, celebrate small accomplishments. Yeah, while he was tucking this kid in with a blanket, the other team's defense was going to flatten him come Sunday, but for now Dane had to admit he liked Trey.

"Speaking of dancing around, I need to bring someone to practice on Monday night."

Dane was intrigued, but the rules were pretty clear.

"I know, practice is closed, but this has to do with my grade, and it's important."

"Okay."

"Professor Jeffries is trying to get me up in front of the class. Turns out she's a really cool teacher. I was going to drop the class, but she made me a deal. She'll step out of her comfort zone if I fully step out of mine."

"So you're bringing her to practice?"

Trey nodded, and Dane wasn't sure what the hell was racing through him. It started out annoyed and quickly moved to "yes, please."

"You okay with that? I mean, it's for my grade and all. She says I can make up some of my missed participation too."

"That's fine. What do you need to do if she comes to practice?" Dane was asking questions, but he was actually thinking if this worked and Trey upped his grade, it would be one less thing for Coach Hall and Crazy Eyes to focus on. That would be nice. It would also be nice to see what Anna's hair looked like with the wind messing it up, but no way in hell that thought was leaving his brain.

"Yeah, the deal is she'll come to one practice and then I have to get up and read for Puck, a fairy, and jump around."

"Wow, can I come and watch that?"

"No. Closed class on that day. Bad enough I have to do this in front of a bunch of nerds who are waiting for me to fall on my ass."

"There's no such thing as a closed class, my friend, but nice try. And the other kids, screw 'em. I think it's terrific you're still in class and giving them hell. Yes, Ms. Jeffries is welcome to come to practice."

Trey high-fived him. "Great."

"Just make sure you tell her to dress out. Might want to remind her to bring a book and a chair, maybe a pot of tea."

Trey laughed and ran toward the locker room.

Dane grabbed his iPad and followed close behind. The sun had set and despite all logic, he grinned. Maybe he'd pay Professor Jeffries a visit in the morning. *In the name of open communication, of course.*

Chapter Six

*A*nnabelle sat in her office the next morning. Unlike the rest of the world, she wasn't a fan of Fridays. She didn't hold a formal class, only an optional discussion, and even the kids who showed up to that seemed distracted by social media or anticipation of weekend parties. Fridays lacked structure, and they didn't have the excitement of her regular class either. They were willy-nilly, as her mother would say anytime Anna couldn't make a decision.

Friday was usually the day Cynda would pop into Anna's office and declare she needed pizza for lunch or a liquid lunch depending on how her week had gone. That part was fun, Anna supposed, but the rest of Friday was too easy for her busy mind.

Another upside, she thought, now sitting at her desk, was that she was able to spend most of Friday in her office. She tried to maintain a positive view. Her sister Sage was forever texting her quotes on positivity from Pinterest, and Anna was trying to improve.

On the surface, her tiny office probably didn't look like much to most people, but like an often overlooked hallway painting, Anna saw the details of her work space. It wasn't much bigger than the bedroom she had as a girl and was almost as drafty. She was tucked into the old section of the Hearst Annex and the minute she walked through the door three years ago, she knew she never wanted to leave.

It was late afternoon, she remembered now, by the time she'd been given the keys to her new office. She carried her tea in a thermos back then, settled in, and carefully placed her books on the same shelves as all those professors who came before her. The first time she sat in the musty red crushed-velvet guest chair, looking at her big and battered desk from a student's perspective, Anna imagined herself growing old between these walls. Among her books. She was someone here, she recalled thinking. Her family had congratulated her and sent a plant and text messages. They were all so proud. Anna was still enjoying her memory when she heard the knock on her door. It was a little early for Cynda.

"Come in."

He walked into her very specific and private space as if it were open to the public. He didn't look awkward or out of place; he simply stood in her doorway, arms above his head as he held on to the doorframe above.

"Mr.... Coach Sivac. Just dropping by?" Anna steadied her breathing.

His long arms fell to his sides as he walked farther into her office with that smile that made her a little dizzy. Suddenly the quiet comfort of her office felt charged with something that belonged outside.

"Well, I was just hanging out with some of my poetry-reading contemporaries, and I thought I'd drop by and see how things are going in Medieval Land."

Anna felt her lips curve, which seemed to happen a lot when he was around. "Will was quite a while after the end of that particular period, but you're funny."

"You think so?"

Anna was in a flexible mood today. It was Friday after all. "Yes, that was clever."

"Right. Well, since you refused to give me your number, I had to drop by in person to tell you that I spoke with my boss and Crazy

Eyes. Trey did go to Student Services. I guess one of your former students works there and gave him some pointers on Shakespeare performance."

"Cassie, that's right. She's wonderful. Who's Crazy Eyes?"

"Oh, sorry. That's… it's a little joke."

"With who?"

"Myself, mostly. She's Trey's sports psychologist. You're not supposed to know about her because that creates a stigma, I guess. So if anyone asks you, play dumb. Do you even know how to do that?"

Anna nodded. "I could give it a try. Is something wrong with Trey?"

"Yeah, he can't catch the ball."

"I see." Anna wasn't sure what that had to do with a psychologist, but she wasn't going to get involved. "You could have e-mailed, by the way. I'm in the directory."

He smiled at her again and took a seat in the chair across from her desk, the crushed-velvet one.

He licked his lips quite a bit, which Anna found both an interesting character trait and incredibly distracting. It wasn't creepy, more like his tongue wasn't satisfied simply resting in his mouth. It wanted to glide along his bottom lip when he seemed to be searching for words, or it stuck out a little when he laughed. Maybe it was a nervous habit, although Anna doubted it. Nothing about Coach Sivac, Dane, came across as nervous. The man made her body hum with a mere lift of his gaze.

"Was there something else?" Anna asked, ignoring the hum.

"Nice office. How long have you been here?"

"Teaching?"

He nodded.

"This is my fourth year."

"Wow, you're young."

"I am."

He laughed. "How old are you?"

"Thirty-two."

"Do you want to know how old I am?"

"No." She did, but what the heck was going on? This had nothing to do with Trey. Oh wait, maybe it did. He must have asked permission for her to attend practice.

"Sure you do. I'm thirty-four."

"Wonderful. Well, again, it was... interesting seeing you, but I have papers to grade and I'm sure you have important things to do out there on the grass." Anna gestured toward her window, which didn't overlook the sports fields, but he'd get the message. Come to think of it, she had no idea where the football team practiced. She should probably figure that out before Monday.

"On the grass?"

"Yes, exactly." Anna looked back at her desk, suddenly unable to read one word. He filled the room, smothered her with those eyes that were a color she still couldn't place. Everything about him was a question or distracting. He was too male, that was the problem.

"So football practices are closed."

Here it comes, Anna thought.

"Rarely are parents allowed, and never friends or we'd have groupies every night." Dane leaned forward, resting his forearms on his legs.

Anna kept her head down, eyes shifting from one side to the other as if she were comparing... something.

"Seems Trey is bringing a guest on Monday. He has a professor who wants to come to practice. Do you know anything about this, Anna?"

"I never said I *wanted* to go to practice." She glanced up quickly. He was looking a little dangerous, and she lost her nerve and focused back on her desk. "We made a deal and I'm keeping my end of it."

"No way," Cynda said, entering Anna's office. Of course she was eavesdropping at the worst possible time. *Great.*

Anna shook her head.

"Wow, this kid must be pretty special." She took a few steps forward.

"He is," Dane and Anna said in unison. Their eyes held and she quickly stood from her desk, trying not to toss papers everywhere.

"Cynda, are you here because... it's time for us to go to lunch?"

"It's only 10:30."

"We could have an early lunch."

Cynda caught her eyes and Anna was clearly pleading for an out, a reason to reclaim her normal. Her friend should have helped, but instead she waggled her eyebrows and shook her head. It reminded Anna of that scene in *The Lion King* when Scar pulls Mufasa's paws off the cliff and lets him fall. Maybe not that cruel, but it was close.

"Okay, so no lunch."

Cynda looked like she might join them, have a chat with Dane. Anna could not allow that train wreck to happen.

"Cynda, please leave."

"Got it." She waved at Dane and casually walked out.

Anna came around her desk, hoping she could muster up some sort of intimidation. This needed to stop. She was helping Trey, holding up her end of the bargain. That did not include... this! Whatever *this* was.

"Mr.... Coach Sivac."

He rose to his feet, dwarfing her physically, which was to be expected. The fact that he had recently been climbing into her head was another thing altogether. Anna's mind space had always been her own, but he tended to crowd there too. Maybe it was a coach thing. Anna wasn't even sure what a receiver coach did, but she'd seen some sports movies. The coaches in fiction were usually grumpy and never looked like the man currently too close yet again.

"Could you not... please back up."

"What?" He looked down at the small space between them and must have seen something in her face because he took three steps back. "Better?"

Anna inhaled. "Yes, much, thank you. What were you saying?"

He grinned. Why was he grinning all the time? She was probably entertaining him in that way jocks enjoyed watching less... coordinated people stumble over their books or get all flustered trying to catch something. God, she couldn't stand guys like him. They'd made her nervous ever since high school. She was a grown woman now and made a point to surround herself with like-minded people. This sort of absurdity didn't happen anymore.

"Sorry about that," Dane said.

"What?"

"The space, I'm sorry."

"It's fine."

"I guess it's a sports thing. I'm usually in someone's face or trying to be heard over a crowd. I tend to... well, crowd."

"I noticed."

He took two more steps back.

"I... please stop. I'm not afraid of you. I'm just not on a football field. We're in my office and I'm... private." That sounded creepy, but again she didn't have a script for these situations, so she had to work with her reality.

"Me too."

Anna was almost safely back on the other side of her desk, but she stopped. "Really?"

He nodded. The charming swagger was replaced with a genuine expression Anna was not expecting. She grabbed her bag from under her desk and stacked her papers. He didn't seem to be moving closer to the door, so she thought she'd help him along. Putting her bag on her shoulder, she grabbed her lunch box. She would stop by Cynda to see if pizza was on. If not, she'd eat lunch outside and head to the library. She had been meaning to pick up her books that were on hold anyway.

"Is that a lunch box?"

Anna felt the warmth creep back up her neck and no matter how hard she fought the urge, her hand pulled her lunch box behind her back as if it was something to hide. *What the heck are you doing?* Meg's voice asked.

"I'm sorry. I wasn't... can I see it? I just bought a rice maker and I was thinking of bringing my lunch, but I'm looking for something cool. Apparently guys don't bring their lunch. Everything I saw at the store had polka dots or flowers. That one's good, though. Can I?" He held out his hand and Anna, a bit stunned at the thought of him wandering the aisles of Target looking for a lunch box, handed over her lunch.

"Oh, yeah." He held the box in one palm and ran his other hand along the leather handle. "This is perfect. Where did you get it?"

"The Container Store."

He nodded and gave it back. "I should have thought of that." There was the tongue again, and now he was biting his lip.

Was that his thinking face? *Dear Lord.*

"There's one right by my house," Dane said.

"You have a house?"

"I do. Is that surprising?"

She nodded.

"Why? Do you think I live at the gym? Maybe I camp outside and shower off with a garden hose like an animal?"

Anna was stuck for a minute as her mind entertained him and a garden hose with such clarity that she felt it all the way down her legs. His laugh thankfully broke her free.

"I..." Anna shook her head clear. "I was just thinking since you've only been here a year that maybe you didn't have a permanent place yet. That's all. No hose."

"Ah, right. Well, I got lucky. This summer I found a perfect place in Fruitvale. Actually it's not perfect yet."

"Me too." If it were possible to smack herself, she would have.

Dane looked as surprised as she was at her suddenly cheerleader-friendly tone.

"In Fruitvale?"

"No. I'm in Elmwood, but I just got it. Four months or so."

Dane had other questions. She could see them as he leaned on her desk in a familiar way that made her jumpy. She needed distance, and she was adept at creating it. "So you think you'll be here a while? Don't coaches move around a lot?"

Dane laughed. "Is there something you know that I don't?"

"Oh no, I didn't mean it that way. I'm sure your job is secure."

"I was joking. You're right, actually. I'm only as good as last season and our jobs are always in flux."

Flux, I love that word and it's not used often enough. Please stop. We do not play the word game with guys like him.

59

"Anna?"

She looked up.

"You know, I never asked. Do you prefer Anna or Belle, or Annabelle? Your name is a compound word and you have two first names. That's very belt and suspenders, don't you think?"

Her insides went a little mushy when she met his eyes. They were the most unassuming eyes she'd ever seen. Not intense or imposing. They were these soft curves, thick lashes, and just a hint of blue, deep blue, maybe a little purple. It was a familiar shade, something about it made her think of swirls. *Belt and suspenders?* Had she actually seen him play football because he spoke like, well, not like a football coach. Y*eah? Because you talk with a lot of coaches, sis.* Meg was back in her head and had she been alone, she would have reminded Meg that she was the older sister and that little sisters needed to shut their traps. At least that's what she used to say when Meg would burst into her room, often dirty, asking if Anna wanted to catch frogs or crying because Hollis had put salt on her garden snails.

"Salt?" Anna would ask, usually annoyed to be brought out of whatever book she was reading or movie she was watching.

"Yes, salt!" Meg would exclaim, hands flailing. "It dissolves them. Hollis has murdered my snails and no one cares. This is the problem with our world. We don't care about the littlest animals. We've lost our humanity."

"Not now," Anna said softly. She was quickly shaken out of the memory once she realized she'd said something out loud.

"Not now?" Dane looked confused.

"I didn't mean that. What were you asking? Oh right, you can call me whatever you want."

Her eyes fell to his mouth just in time to watch the slow curve of his lips. His mouth, that's where the trouble lived. She saw that now.

"Anything?"

"Stop. You know what I meant. My family calls me Anna, most of my colleagues call me Annabelle, so go with that."

"I like Belle, but it reminds me of *Beauty and the Beast*," he said, as if on his own train of thought.

"Pfft. Is that one of your favorites?"

"Sort of, well, she's my favorite Disney princess. Sidney and Claire are Mulan and Ariel, respectively. Although there has been considerable debate over whether or not Mulan is actually a princess because she's such a badass."

Floored. The man was a hulking mass of gorgeous and he had a favorite Disney princess?

"Nieces," he said, clarifying. She must have been staring too long.

"Pardon?"

"Sidney and Claire are my sister's kids. I babysit sometimes. As Uncle Dane, I'm well versed in all things princess."

"I see."

"Yeah, Belle is my favorite."

"Right. I got that. Well, like I said, most of my colleagues call me—"

"Anna it is. See you on Monday." He turned to leave.

Obviously he didn't think they were colleagues. What did that make them? They certainly weren't friends.

"Monday?" Anna asked.

"Practice."

"Is it too late to request you call me Ms. Jeffries?"

Turning back, the smile was still there. "Ms. Jeffries has appeal, but it feeds the schoolteacher fantasy, unless you're into that sort of thing?"

Sweet Lord. She scrambled for something, anything to keep him from getting the upper hand, but she who hesitates is lost and by the time her brain clicked on, she was looking at nothing but the expanse of his back walking away as he laughed. Anna sighed and realized her palms were once again sweating.

After three hours of pulling weeds on Saturday, his days of renting an apartment were starting to look good. The inside of Dane's house still needed paint and he should probably figure out what was wrong with the washing machine, but his priority was the yard. It wasn't much to look at and when the realtor was showing him the house, it seemed pretty low maintenance. What a difference a couple of months made. Had every weed in the neighborhood decided to relocate to his place for the fall?

Dane propped the rake on the side of the house and decided to leave the last pile for tomorrow. He needed a shower and lunch before he e-mailed out the last game clips of the Longhorn defense. Coach Hall wanted the team to watch and "pay attention." Those were his exact words when he'd cornered Dane after practice. He'd send out the clips, but there was never a guarantee anyone would pay attention, not that he told Hall that.

At least they had Texas at home, so if Jeb's prediction was right, Dane could crawl back to his house and sleep it off until Monday's practice. God, he hated losing. Did anyone enjoy losing? Maybe that was a question for Crazy Eyes.

As the spray of the shower hit Dane's face, he decided there was no reason to be a defeatist. What the hell did Jeb know? There was always illness, injury, or hell, maybe Texas's wall of defense would step aside and allow those running passes he'd drilled until his eyes crossed. Maybe they wouldn't put two guys on Trey. It could happen. And Jeb could become a monk, but Dane doubted that was going to happen anytime soon either. No, in less than twenty-four hours, "emotional completeness" or not, the Golden Bears were going to come face-to-face with the realities of what football was often about—pain and disappointment.

Dane wrapped a towel around his waist, sidestepped three still-to-be-unpacked boxes, and went to the kitchen for more rice. He added the broccoli he'd roasted this morning. He considered eating rice for lunch and dinner. The damn thing was so easy to use. Dane laughed at himself and pictured Jeb smacking him upside his head.

Not that he cared. Jeb called Dane an "old man" even though they were a year apart, and Dane enjoyed texting him information on STDs. That was the basis of their friendship. Dane didn't really do friends. He had his mother, his sister, and her husband, The Saint.

They were family, and he had some old friends from high school and college he tried to keep in touch with, but these days he strived to keep things light. Friends had a way of creating complications. His main focus was on his job and finding some stability for himself.

It was nice being close to his mom. As his sister often reminded him back in the days when drinking and acting like an asshole were his priorities, "she's not going to be around forever." Dane knew that all too well. She was part of the reason he'd spent years getting his act together or pushing his mental mess under the bed like he used to do with his toys when he was a kid. His mom turned out to be one of the strongest people he knew, and his sister was a ballbuster who called every Sunday whether he wanted her to or not. If he didn't answer, she'd call over and over again until he picked up.

Dane was a lucky man. Now that he'd made it to thirty-four, he was ready to be the man his father expected him to be. That is, as long as he could keep things under the bed—he'd tried to deal with his feelings before and that got him nowhere. This time he was working on not feeling, and so far he was happy. So, while Jeb was not the deepest guy on the planet, Dane liked him, and someday soon he'd figure out how to have manageable fun again. For now, it was probably best to stick with his rice maker.

Dane pulled on some clothes and stood in the kitchen eating lunch. Looking through the window at all the cleanup still to be done outside, he thought of Anna. He wondered what her yard looked like, if she had a landscaper, or if she planted roses in front of her windows. He guessed she probably did some of the work herself, but somehow it was hard to picture her dirty. Well, that depended on which definition of dirty his mind wanted to work with. He could probably come up with some things that didn't involve gardening. Shaking his head at his own thoughts, he sat and started sending off clips to his players.

Would she actually show up to practice? Hell, did she even own anything athletic? More importantly, was he nervous? No. That wasn't possible. Her opinion rated at exactly zero. They might as well be different species, right? Right, he told himself.

Maybe her opinion rated higher than zero. She was Trey's professor after all and a smart woman by all accounts. So maybe he cared like a two or three, no more. *Rice maker, Dane. Focus on the rice maker or your job. Be about the job, man.*

What the hell was going on? His favorite princess? Is that a lunch box? He barely knew her, but somehow standing in her office was comforting. He felt safe around her, which was ridiculous.

When he was a kid, he and his dad used to wake up early on Sunday mornings to watch cartoons, eat dry cereal out of the box, and eventually, once his mother and sister left for church, watch football. It was their thing. The day before Dane left for college, his dad woke him up early because he had to be at the station by nine. When Dane stumbled out to the kitchen half asleep, his dad had yelled, "Tada!"

In the center of the living room was a small flat-screen television and a case of tiny boxes of cereal.

"I figured you'd need your own setup now that you're off to college. We'll have to do that video chat thing now on Sundays." His dad patted him on the back, clean-shaven and already in his standard navy-blue T-shirt.

Dane was eighteen, and the emotion in his throat was too much to swallow.

"Thanks," was all he managed to get out.

His father nodded and took him by the shoulders. "I'm gonna miss you, kid."

"Me too." Dane had started to tear up, so his dad slapped him on the back and shook his head. "Okay, well, enough of that. Your mom needs you to pick up the dog crap and mow the backyard, so I'll see you when I get home."

"Stay safe out there." That's what they always said when his dad left for work.

"I'll do my best," he'd always said back.

Dane sat, a grown man now, fatherless for more years than he even counted anymore, and wiped his eyes.

Why did she feel warm like that? What was it about her that made him want to share, pull things out of his memory like some adult version of show-and-tell? Christ, he needed to back this whole thing up because no matter how much he was drawn to her, Anna was all about feelings. He could practically see them simmering there on her surface. If he didn't cut this out, those feelings would break free, probably in breathtaking honesty, and where would he be? Dane suspected Anna was the type of woman who cleaned under the bed.

No way he was tackling those kinds of feelings. Hell, he didn't even eat breakfast anymore.

Chapter Seven

*A*nna finished her three-thirty class and went back to her office to change into clothes she could move in—that was the advice Trey offered as he left her morning class.

"Didn't change your mind, did you? You're still going to be there?"

Anna had nodded and confirmed she would be there and also that she would be picking up extra glitter on her way home. Trey laughed and gave her a high five. Anna already felt him opening up, but as she pulled on one of her favorite Cal T-shirts, her stomach jumped at the idea of being on a football field. She was always braver in her head. As she sat to put on her running shoes, Cynda knocked on her open door.

"Do you want to get dinner later? I have to be home by seven to feed Bowzer, but we could get Mexican."

Anna stood and waited for Cynda's reaction.

"Oh, do you have a new gym membership?"

Anna shook her head and pulled her hair back with an elastic she had around her wrist.

"Why are you feeding Bowzer? Did you and..." She looked at Cynda.

"Yup, another one bites the dust. I just couldn't handle all the nudity. The man wanted to eat dinner at the table in the nude. I'm just not about that."

When Cynda didn't seem too disappointed, Anna laughed.

"You got the dog?"

She nodded. "Can't have our little guy growing up in that weirdness. So, what's with the workout wear?" she asked, throwing herself into Anna's desk chair. "Oh, I know. I forgot for a minute there, but you have football practice tonight." Cynda pretended to throw a football and catch it.

"You're hysterical." Anna let out a deep breath.

"Are you nervous?"

"I don't like being outside."

"Um… that's not exactly true. You ride your bike. You go to the farmers market every Sunday."

"Those don't count."

"I think they do."

Anna sat in the red crushed-velvet chair. "I don't know what I'm doing."

"For what it's worth, I think it's great. You are teaching by example. That's like one of the first things we learn. It's powerful, and you're putting it into practice." Cynda's beaming face spoke volumes more than her little pep talk.

"What?" Anna sat up.

"Nothing. I'm just going to point out that it's not a complete hardship—you will get to see Dane." She fluttered her eyes.

Anna shook her head. "You are a child."

"I am. Come on, you can't say that you're not the least bit curious what he looks like all… sweaty and barking orders."

"Cyn, do you have some pent-up fantasies you need to discuss?" Anna was joking, but her word choice brought back Dane's challenge the last time she'd seen him. Unless you're into that sort of thing. She could kick herself for not having the last word on that one. Ugh, her sisters would have had a field day if they knew she'd let that comment slip by. Is she into that sort of thing? "What a stupid, asinine, and quite frankly inappropriate question."

"What was?"

Anna's face bloomed with warmth and she put her hands to her cheeks. This was ridiculous. She threw her phone into her bag and grabbed her water bottle.

Cynda looked at her watch. "Where are you going? Isn't practice at five?"

"Four forty-five, but I'm listening to a good book in my car, so I'll take the long way to the stadium."

"Do you want to meet for drinks after?" Cynda asked in a final tease, trailing after her.

"No." Anna shoved the door to the building open and could still hear Cynda laughing as she stepped into the late afternoon.

It was one practice. How long did these things last, an hour tops? She would make an appearance and that would be that, just like any other school function. Trey would see that she kept her word and stepped out of her comfort zone, and he would finally participate in her class. His grades would go up and all would be right with the world again.

Anna turned on *The Lake House* and sat for a minute in her car listening to the lilting British accent of the narrator. Closing her eyes, she tried to picture vines and long winding roads, but instead she was stuck with Cynda's words, "sweaty and barking orders." Anna hit pause on her audiobook. *Sweet Lord, please give him the flu or at least make sure his shirt stays on.* Anna wondered why so many other people were in her head lately. Wasn't that supposed to be her private space?

True to what she told Cynda, Anna took her time driving to Memorial Field and when she arrived, Trey and the team of guys were in long shorts and sleeveless T-shirts. Those are muscle shirts, she told herself getting out of the car. *See, I know things.*

An hour had come and gone and so far football practice was sort of fascinating, although she wasn't ready to admit that to *him* yet.

Anna enjoyed watching the different drills. There was no denying these young men were talented. Not in the ways she'd appreciated all her life, but talented nonetheless. Trey told Anna where she could refill her water bottle and when she returned, Dane was standing on the sidelines. She'd noticed him earlier grouped with other men in the same navy-blue collared shirts with a gold Nike swish on one side and the Cal logo on the other. Anna assumed they were other coaches. How many coaches did a football team need? Or players for that matter? Anna had seen football on various televisions during her life, and she didn't remember seeing this many players in a game. There was no way she was going to stand there all wide-eyed and ask Coach Sivac, who was looking particularly stern, his face all but hidden under a baseball cap, to explain the big complicated game of football to her. She knew it was him under that cap because, well, she simply did and left it at that as she approached the field. Anna stopped and stood behind the sidelines.

"Have you ever played a sport?" Dane asked, attention still on the field.

He knew she was there? That startled her a little, and Anna wondered if she'd be perpetually uncomfortable in the presence of Dane Sivac, not that she would let that show.

"I have of late—but wherefore I know not—lost all my mirth, forgone all custom of exercises," flew off her lips before she had a chance to stop herself. It was a habit. A tolerated, even revered, habit among her friends and family, but not here, not with him.

Dane turned to look at her, brow furrowed.

"I... mean, does it look like I play sports?" That wasn't the right thing to say either because his eyes slowly traveled the length of her body, lingering in that way that probably sent most women up in flames. Not her, though. Her mind commanded order right as heat slicked across her neck.

"Maybe horseback riding. You carry yourself like an equestrienne."

"I... how did you know that?"

"Your thighs are bigger than the rest of you and your posture is very... erect."

Anna looked down. "My thighs are not big, and there is nothing wrong with good posture."

"Huh, so you don't ride." He turned back to watch the field.

"Did."

"Knew it."

Anna slowly let out a breath.

"I wasn't trying to insult you. Although it seems that's all I manage to do around you. The reason I asked was to confirm you know what it means to work hard physically for something."

"No, no, I do not know anything about that, nor am I interested. I quit riding when I was thirteen."

"Why?"

"None of your business."

Dane laughed, eyes still on the field.

"I understand," he said, after yelling something to a group of players setting up cones.

"Understand what?"

"You're comfortable being indoors, teaching instead of doing. Getting dirty makes you nervous. Makes sense. A lot of women are that way. You don't really like to sweat."

He was messing with her and she should not entertain him, but she did. "I sweat every day." She had to fight the instinct to cover her mouth.

"Really? That is impressive."

"Not every day, but I recognize the need for exercise. I walk to places. I have a bike, and I used to have one of those things that kept track of my calories and steps until it broke."

Dane looked over his shoulder again. "Fitbit."

"Yes, that's what it was called."

Anna took a step forward as two guys in pads crashed into one another.

"How'd it break?"

"I forgot to take it off before my tub, and then I had a glass of wine and was reading," she said, eyes glued to the field and clearly not watching her mouth. When she looked at him, Dane's eyes were on her again and if she hadn't known better, if she hadn't seen the almost permanent dents between his eyes, she would have sworn he had an active imagination too.

"Which play was that?" he asked, eyes back on his players.

"I'm sorry?"

"The line you rambled when I asked if you played a sport. That was a play, right?"

Anna nodded, forgetting she'd let her nerd shine through only moments before. They were talking about Fitbits now, weren't they? She had been trying to stay on his level, talk physical things, and he somehow brought them back around to her. It was beyond unsettling.

"Yes. *Hamlet*," she said and returned to her natural self. "Did you want to know where in the play? The context?"

"No."

She laughed, so spontaneous and loud that she shocked herself. The corner of Dane's mouth quirked upward. He shook his head and walked onto the field with one blow of the whistle hanging from his neck.

Anna put her hand to her chest to quiet the laughter. He was different. Surprising. She should probably be careful because she'd always had a weakness for surprises.

She was adorable. There was no way to share that without sounding condescending so he kept it to himself, but she was. Like one of those free calendars his sister had on her pantry door with kittens and puppies. If those puppies liked to bite and roll their eyes a lot.

"So who is our cast of characters here?" she asked when he returned.

"I'm sorry?"

"The players. Seems like there are a lot of them. Which ones are yours?"

"Three freshmen straight out of high school, two sophomores, one junior, one redshirt junior sitting out this season because our star flanker is a senior. Ben wanted a full year of play since he is most likely next in line. One redshirt freshman who's working with our trainer to get some more weight on him and learn the playbook. One redshirt sophomore struggling with grades, and the last one is out with a broken collarbone." Dane was doing his best not to notice her and she helped him out by asking about the roster. Nothing silenced a guy's imagination quite like a list.

"Do I want to know what a redshirt is?"

"Think of it as an... understudy. They attend regular practices but for various reasons, they don't play in the games."

"Ah, interesting."

"Is it?" He looked back at her, which was a mistake. Now that she was closer, those legs were... Damn it. *Alpha, Bravo, Charlie—*

"It is interesting. Why don't they wear red shirts?"

"Because they don't."

"Okay, straightforward. That works. What's with the last names?" she asked, now standing next to him so every time the wind blew, he caught a waft of flower and... oranges, maybe? *Delta, Echo, Foxtrot. Forget the list, just be a man for God's sake.*

"They're unique. You could have five guys named Mike on a team, so last names are best."

"Two people could have the same last name. There are a lot of common last names."

"True, but it's rare. Those guys usually get a first initial too or a nickname."

"Why not just give double first names a nickname then."

"Because it's... I can tell you think there's something more sinister going on here. Do you have a conspiracy theory you'd like to share? College football using last names as a means of mind control?"

She laughed then caught herself, but not before the sound of it grabbed him around the neck.

"I was trying to make... appropriate conversation."

"Yeah? Any time we discuss football, the conversation takes a nasty turn."

Anna shrugged. "I'm not a fan."

"I can see that. Any particular reason why?"

"I don't like the culture."

Dane nodded and turned his attention back to the passing drills on the field and tried not to react as Trey fumbled every other one. Bad enough Texas had "handed them their ass," as Jeb had so helpfully predicted, but now Crazy Eyes was asking that Trey have a "week-long buffer of kindness." The look on Dane's face must have communicated, "What in the hell are you talking about?" because she explained that he needed "time to absorb his disappointment." Yeah, okay. Sure. Let me get him a lollipop too. Again with the feelings.

"Not enough feelings? The culture is changing, haven't you heard? We are all about feelings these days," he said, trying to temper the edge in his voice.

Trey dropped another pass.

"If by that you mean feelings for women being treated as objects or feelings for the young men who are injured and left without an education, then yes. Not enough feelings."

"Christ!"

He took his sunglasses off—it was dark and well past time to remove them. The lights on the field were bright, and he'd kept them on as a barrier because the minute she walked toward the field with Trey, Dane was sure "Holy hell" was plastered all over his face. At least the shades hid his eyes. He'd managed to stay busy but eventually found himself wanting to talk with her, so there he was sparring again and loving every minute of it. In spite of the feelings. There were moments he thought she might be enjoying herself too until he remembered she was Trey's teacher, and helping him was obviously important to her. She didn't need some dumbstruck coach noticing the way that Cal T-shirt, vintage, he might add, stretched across her small frame or that she didn't appear to have a trace of makeup on and was still stunning. When Dane's thoughts faded, he looked at her and even though her mouth was spouting things he'd heard at least a hundred times from so-called "intellectuals," he still wanted it, wanted her, though that made no sense.

"Oh, I'm sorry. Too much thinking and feelings now?"

Dane smiled, truly smiled for the first time all day. Her hands were on her hips now as if everything she was saying was an original thought, as if he'd never heard the arguments against the violent sport of football before.

Anna sighed. "It's just as well. I'm sure you know opposing teams never get along."

Well played, Professor Jeffries.

"Eh, that's not always true. A lot of teams can learn to respect one another, and the heat of competition is always... stimulating."

She might have stuttered or made a sound, but the new freshman quarterback was hunched over and the rest of the coaches were on the field. Dane needed to do his job instead of playing make-believe with a woman way out of his range. "Hey, Trey wanted to get you something for being a good sport. Suit up, Jeffries." He threw a jersey at her and walked out onto the field before she could start another argument.

Anna held up the jersey, noticed her name was on the back, and yelled after him, "How did he do that?"

Dane held up his hands, shrugged, and kept walking.

After clearing up some confusion about when a quarterback should be sacked in practice even if the opportunity was available, Dane walked back to the sidelines and almost tripped over his feet. She'd put on the jersey. While he wasn't often prone to sports fantasies, there was something sexy about all that education wrapped up in a game he loved.

"I never thought I'd see the day," he said, hoping for sarcasm as everything started to tilt.

"You don't know me." Anna fixed her eyes on the field, arms crossed. She was nervous or uncomfortable. She was right, he didn't know her, but he was starting to figure out some of the signals.

"What the hell was that?" she suddenly yelled, and Dane quickly looked to the field.

"Did you see that? I mean Trey was about to catch the ball and that guy came out of nowhere. He looked so graceful jumping in the air. I just—"

She was breathing a little heavier now, and with her lips parted and her chest moving in and out, he about lost his own breath. He was comfortable with Ms. Jeffries in her cardigans and carrying her reusable lunch box, but this Anna, the one with the flush of color across her collarbone and eyes practically ignited with challenge, was something else. Something dangerous.

Dane made a point to never go for what Jeb liked to call "cerebral" women. He'd grown up with more than his share of "women in the know," as his father liked to joke. Dane didn't want that for his adult life. If and when he ever chose a partner, he wanted no drama. Someone who wanted to hang out on the couch, go camping even. He certainly had no intention of spending his life feeling like every conversation was a quiz. His body might want her, but he could control that, he told himself, until she covered her mouth after her outburst and he wanted to haul her up against him, dying to feel everything spinning in those eyes. She may, in fact, be all up in her brain, but there was something else panting from those perfect lips and God help him, he'd always been curious.

Dane found his words. "It's part of the drill. He's fine. You should probably take that jersey off because that outburst was almost coach-like. It wasn't very Shakespeare proper."

Anna's eyes glinted. "No. I'm not taking it off because it was a gift from my student. The one you just allowed to be clobbered out there. Oh, and you'd be surprised how bawdy Will can be."

"Will, right. Isn't this year the four-hundredth anniversary of his death?"

His eyes met hers and even though he would swear on everything in his playbook that he hadn't just dropped that piece of information to impress her, he had and it worked. She blinked and for the first time since he'd met her, she held and he broke eye contact first.

"I'll have you know that my love affair with Will transcends death. We go back long before... well, probably before you ever picked up a football."

He raised a brow. "Eh, I don't know about that. I won my first-grade spelling bee after my mom promised I could play Pop Warner if I brought home the trophy."

Anna shrugged. "I read *Comedy of Errors* and *Much Ado About Nothing* by the end of first grade."

"Are you shitting me?"

She shook her head. "I don't do that. You won a spelling bee?"

He nodded. "I'm an incredible... speller." He said that last part slowly on purpose. Her cheeks flushed a little deeper at such an obvious innuendo. One minute she was complicated and then she was so simple. Annabelle Jeffries was almost as confusing as the plays she adored.

"A rose by any other name would still smell great."

And there was Jeb, Dane thought without taking his eyes off the field. He knew it was only a matter of time.

"Pardon me?"

"I love that line. Best romance ever written," Jeb said, clearly not knowing he was in the deep end.

"A rose by any other name would smell as sweet," Anna said, gently correcting Jeb and sounding downright sultry to Dane's ears. He'd clearly lost his mind.

"That's what I said. I mean when Romeo looks into her eyes and says those words. It gets you right here, you know."

Dane had to look now and turned just in time to witness Jeb with his hand on his chest. *Oh man, she gave you that one. Quit while you're ahead.* As Jeb, hand still on his chest, transitioned to showing off his pec, Dane waited for Anna to administer what he was sure would be a smackdown.

She tilted her head in a gesture Dane hadn't seen yet and seemed to be looking to him for advice. She could have easily flattened Jeb by now, but she was surprisingly generous.

"*Romeo and Juliet* is a tragedy. So many people mistake it for a romance. I love how you chose that line. It's a famous one, but also important. When *Juliet* utters those words, you can see she's at a precipice and, well, we all know how that ends, right?"

Dane held in a laugh, but it wasn't easy with Jeb blinking at her as if she'd spoken a different language. Here he was trying to hit on Anna and she managed to smack him without so much as an easy tap.

77

Dane would have felt sorry for him, should have warned him, but the idiot brought it on himself.

"Exactly," Jeb said and immediately looked toward the locker room. "It was good meeting you, Anna. I gotta go."

"Lovely to meet you too, Jeb."

Anna turned to face the field and Dane's eyes followed Jeb, who was now shaking his head and making kissy faces like a six-year-old stuck in the back of his parents' minivan on a long road trip.

"Yeah, lock your lady down, Coach." Dane knew it was Birch before he looked over. When he did, he noticed Trey run by and smack his teammate on the back of the head. They both stopped and exchanged words.

"Oh, sorry, Professor Jeffries. I was... being an ass. Sorry ma'am," Birch said and quickly joined the others for another lap.

Trey grinned and nodded toward Anna.

In that moment, Dane couldn't care less if the kid ever caught the ball.

Anna nodded back at him and turned to show him the back of her jersey.

He flashed a grin and nodded his approval.

"You running with us?" Trey asked.

Dane tried not to snicker but knew he must have when she glared at him.

"You have no idea how much glitter is waiting for you, Mr. Duncan," she said, joining Trey and the other guys.

Trey shook his head, and she laughed as they ran off. Dane tried not to notice that her ass didn't look like that in those English department skirts. Did she wear shorts during her off hours? *Why, asshole? Are you thinking you two should spend some off hours together? That's a stellar idea.*

After a few laps, Anna said good-bye to Trey, complete with a kiss to his cheek. The woman was one big surprise.

"Okay, well, this was almost fun, Coach. Thank you." She lifted her bag from the bench and Dane gave up pretending he wasn't sorry to see her go.

"I'm impressed, Professor."

"With?" Anna was still a little breathy, fishing around in her bag.

"You. I don't know many college professors, male or female, who would stoop to join a student on the football field."

She glistened with sweat and all he could see was this new dimension to her. It had nothing to do with what either of them did for a living or how they related to Trey. She was a woman and he sure as hell felt like a man.

"True, but like I said before, you don't know me. Have a pleasant evening, Coach Sivac."

"Dane," he said before his ego engaged.

She looked almost playful. "Very well, Dane."

"It wouldn't be the strangest thing if we became friends."

"Yes, it most certainly would," Anna said over her shoulder as he watched her walk away, somehow making a jersey at least two sizes too big for her look like she belonged in one of those glossy magazines Dane only read in the doctor's office. "By the way"—she turned back—"it was Act II, Scene II. Hamlet is explaining to Rosencrantz that he's lost all interest in things, even exercise."

"Is there a hidden meaning in there somewhere, Professor?"

"Nope, just making sure you know the context," she said, and she was gone.

She could hide behind her words all she wanted, but Dane had always been good at hide-and-seek.

Chapter Eight

*A*nna hadn't slept well. A little after midnight, she'd turned on *27 Dresses*, which always worked. No one died in that movie, no one even got sick, and it usually made her laugh. Then, she would fall asleep thinking about James Marsden's beautiful smile.

Not last night.

Last night it didn't work even a little bit. Which was why she found herself at the waffle shop near campus when they opened at 5:00 a.m. With a ginormous waffle and strong coffee on board, Anna stopped at the gas station and bought three sticks of banana Laffy Taffy. She would need them when she hit the Wall of Tired, as she used to call it in college, right before her three o'clock class. In her sleep-deprived fog, she'd forgotten to make her lunch. That never happened.

She was set to pull into the school parking garage when she changed her mind. She made a quick, some might call it erratic, U-turn and drove to Memorial Stadium. She was going to "grab the bull by the horns." That always seemed dangerous, but Cynda said it all the time when she meant business, so Anna was going to grab the bull too.

"Okay. I give up. What's wrong with you?" she asked, bold and confident as she walked into the coaches' offices and found Dane standing behind his desk, writing something on a whiteboard that took up the entire back wall. Yes, she'd looked up his office location online last night. He didn't need to know that.

"Sorry?" He put the cap on his marker and turned as if he'd expected to see her.

That irked her, and the caffeine was now in full force.

"You're... you." Her hands flew back and forth. "You're not a misogynistic idiot. You have a favorite princess for crying out loud. Stop it. Stop being the way you are because there's no way that you... are the way you are, and I don't have time for games. I'm tired. I forgot my lunch. Stop."

"Anna, is this your way of saying you like me?" Dane quirked a brow.

"What? What are we, twelve? I don't... *like* you. I'm simply putting you on notice that I am not susceptible to your whole hot-smart-guy-who-loves-kids routine. You're a football coach, you *are* football, so... this isn't my first rodeo. Play your games somewhere else, cowboy."

Oh wow, that sounded much better when Cynda said it. Anna had slipped into crazy town and suddenly the waffle, along with the extra whipped cream and strawberries, was not sitting well.

Dane, to his credit, seemed like he was actually trying to sort through her babbling, but she knew better now. He was gearing up, getting ready to strike.

"Is that your original material, or do you have a fight writer?"

"What?"

"This isn't my first rodeo? Not exactly your style, Professor. Just to clarify, is this our first fight?"

Anna shook her head, frustration building. He looked so damn smug and well-rested. "Cynda says it, the rodeo thing. Thought I'd try it out. Who cares? The point is that you—"

"Cowboy? I've never been called a cowboy and considering I'm not a fan, that one kind of hurt."

What was he talking about?

"They're a football team. The Dallas Cowboys?"

"I know that! Just stop. Okay. We don't need to launch into some clever banter and no, this is not our first fight. We will not be fighting. I just want to go back to the way things were three weeks ago before you showed up and started poking your nose into my classroom."

"How is he doing by the way? Trey told me the quiz went well, but I never know what that means."

"Eighty-five. Huge improvement. Again, not the point."

"Hey! That's fantastic. Did he come to your office hours? I know Crazy Eyes wanted him to take advantage of that."

"Yes, but like I was saying, I'd like to create some distance so we can—"

He stepped from behind his desk and moved toward her as if he wasn't listening to what she was saying. She hated that, and she'd already pegged him as a listener.

"You're doing it again." Anna froze at the realization that she wanted him closer, wanted to touch him. Oh God, there went the waffle again.

"Sorry."

"I don't think you are."

"You're right." He stepped a little closer. "You have my attention, Anna. And for the record, you poked your nose into my practice. We were even, but now you're here in my office. Did you have trouble sleeping last night?"

She shook her head. He was too close.

"I can't seem to figure you out," he continued. "Can't seem to stop wanting to."

"Try."

He laughed.

"The only game I play is on a field, Anna. I'm obviously not what you expected. You're a surprise too. Maybe we should get to know each other better."

"You... what? No. That is not going to happen."

Dane stepped back behind his desk. Her thoughts were jumbled and she felt completely out of control. She should have never had that waffle. Petrified she was going to finish off this absurd visit by getting sick all over his office, Anna grabbed the doorframe, white-knuckled. Something must have registered on her face because Dane looked as if his charm was slipping.

"Are you okay? We don't need to get to know each other, that's good too if you're not feeling it."

"Feeling what?"

"Me."

She was going to pass out. This was it, she was going down like the girl tripping over her books in just about every romantic movie flashback. Where the hell did this guy come from and why did he need to upset her balance? She forgot her lunch. *Go back to the stupid court or field or wherever it is you came from.* At this point, she was willing to give Trey an A just so she could return to her corner where she belonged.

"I'm sorry if I said something that gave you the impression—"

He held up his hands. "Really, we're good. No harm, no foul. I must have misread."

She shook herself free of her swirling thoughts. "Right. Good. Okay, so you misread. Glad we figured that out. Send me an e-mail if you have questions about Trey and... good, this has been good."

"I hate e-mail. I'm sure I'll see you around. We don't need to re-sort to e-mail, do we?"

"I like e-mail. It allows me to stay organized. I use the flags. Do you use those? You should try them." Anna blinked rapidly. Was it possible to overdose on thick, waffle shop coffee?

"I'll have to try the flags." His eyes were playful now, as if something funny was happening or about to pop up from around the next corner.

"Great." She turned to leave.

"Hey, are you seeing someone? I didn't even ask, and I should have."

Well, something funny and scary at the same time. Reality was twisted, Anna thought and then realized she needed an answer quickly.

"I... yes. I am... currently seeing someone. It is recent, but yes."

"Oh, nice. Who's the lucky guy? Where'd you meet?"

Was this twenty questions? She hated that game.

"He is... we met at a house party. A housewarming. He strolled right up the walkway and I was... smitten." *Dear God, scriptwriter please. Someone throw me a line.*

Dane nodded, eyes still a tad mischievous, but she couldn't tell if he knew she was scrambling.

"That sounds serious. What's his name?"

"His name is... Brad. Yup, Brad and I are dating." She was going to fall down and die right in front of him. *Did I just say "Yup"? Were house parties still a thing? Stop it, waffles!*

Anna didn't know Dane well enough to tell if he was buying her ridiculousness, which made everything feel all the more ridiculous. He looked a bit like one of those judges at the dog show every Thanksgiving morning. Assessing but not giving anything away. Anna took a deep breath.

"Brad. Well, good for you." He smiled, and Anna felt something deep in her stomach. It wasn't the waffle. It was a bit like disappointment, but that wasn't possible. She'd achieved what she wanted. He would back up now because she had a boyfriend. He was that kind of guy. A decent, respectful guy. She knew that about him, which was... *Quit thinking, Anna. Now is not the time for thoughts.*

"You said you wanted to be friends. We could be friends at least. Don't you think?" she asked. *What. The. Heck. Is. Wrong. With. You? You were in the home stretch, and there is no way in all the thatched roofs of the Globe Theater that you can be this man's friend.*

He stood and put his hands in his pockets. Christ, even that was sexy. "We could do that. Sort of a truce. For the children?" Those lips curled upward, and he licked his bottom lip as if it was the most natural thing in the world.

Anna felt the room turn, not exactly spinning, just a turn and a jolt like a sudden train stop. He was obviously looking for a response.

She nodded. "Sounds good. Have a lovely rest of your day, Coach." She turned to leave before she could do any more damage.

"Professor?"

She should have walked out, her hand was on the door, but she turned and he was so male leaning against the wall of his office that every part of her body was pissed she'd pushed him away. She knew her mind would thank her, but at the moment all reason was drowned out by the buzz in her ears.

He nodded a little and said, "Tell Brad I said 'Hi.'" Then his mouth twitched just a little and there was that tongue again. *Shouldn't his lips be chapped?*

Anna knew her face was red. Knew she was a mess and there was no getting out of it. So, she nodded. Smiled a touch less confident and left the room.

She closed herself into the quiet of her car, rested her head on the steering wheel, and tried to not replay the entire fiasco, which proved impossible. So much for grabbing the bull, she thought as she drove toward her office. It was a stupid saying anyway.

Rachael Mason-Sivac was born in North Carolina but moved to San Francisco when she was eight when her father, a tool salesman, was transferred. She had two younger brothers. Had a thing about which way the toilet paper came off the roll and loved graham crackers with Marshmallow Fluff. She'd been only a year out of law school when she met her husband. Dane used to ask his dad questions about his mother when he was younger anytime they went fishing or camping overnight, just the two of them, and he would get stories that sounded like a biography, sometimes a fairy tale.

His mother was sort of a mystery to him growing up. She always smelled incredible, wore silky blouses, and anytime their dad was on a night shift, she let Dane and his sister have hot dogs for dinner. She was forever surrounded by paper or carrying bulging folders. Dane learned as he grew older that those folders were briefs, but as a boy all he knew was piles of paper kept his mom up late, sitting in her yellow chair in the living room. If he woke up in the middle of the night for water or a snack, he would peek out from the kitchen and see her lit only by the faint glow of the craned reading lap, listening to Aretha Franklin, the volume so low that sometimes Dane thought he imagined it.

She was a character in his childhood. A beautiful woman with the same color hair as his and the eyes of his older sister. She was story time before bed, school paper checker, and every morning before he caught the bus to school, she would smooth his hair down in the back and kiss him on his head. If his dad was the earth—dirty hands, drinking from the hose, and rolling around on the grass—his mom was the sky. A sweet breeze on a Sunday morning and the occasional tornado that whipped through their small house when she was late or someone had left the front door open and the dogs were frolicking through the neighbors' sprinklers.

His mom had always been a bit like a fancy painting or something else decorative in a museum: through his sister's high school graduation to his first day of college, on every holiday and birthday, and in every vacation picture. Even when they moved to a bigger house and when she went from lawyer to professor, his mom's presence in his life was a flutter, but as constant as breathing.

That all changed the day his Aunt Holly picked him up at the airport and brought him home to a house full of family on both sides and his mom on the phone in their kitchen with swollen, red eyes. She'd hugged Dane so tightly that day. It was the same day she'd crashed to earth and had been there with him ever since. Still doing a remarkable job, Dane thought now as he spotted her at the back table of Fino's, their "lunch spot" as she had called it when she set up their every-other-week lunch dates now that she worked at Berkeley too. As he approached, she took off her reading glasses and stood to kiss him before he took the seat across from her.

"Did you read this article in the *Times* this morning about the drought? Look at these pictures." She handed him the folded paper right as the waitress, dressed in all black with a white apron, took his drink order.

"I didn't, but that is awful." He handed the paper back.

"Awful doesn't even begin to describe it."

Dane cracked a smile. "Well, words were never my game."

"Maybe your new friend can help you with that."

"Oh wow. That was a beautiful pass. Look at you go, right from concerned citizen to meddling mother." He laughed and thankfully they ordered.

"I'm not meddling, exactly. I tried asking your sister if she knew anything, and I swear that girl is a man sometimes. There's not a gossiping bone in her body."

"That's because there's nothing to gossip about. Annabelle Jeffries, Professor Jeffries, is an acquaintance at best. One of my players is taking her class as part of some warm and fuzzy assignment handed down from his sports shrink. It's ridiculous, but he's in the class, struggling, but in it. I was assigned to check in with his teacher. That's it."

"No." His mother took off her glasses again and set them on the table.

"No?"

"I think there's more to it than that. I saw the two of you together, and there's something there."

"Huh, well, you may want to tell her that. While you're at it, you can inform her boyfriend." Dane saw no reason not to bring up Anna's pretend boyfriend if it helped distract his mom.

"Really?"

Dane nodded. "Brad. Brad the boyfriend, so like I said, no gossip."

"No. I think she's making that up. Brad. That seems like a fake name."

Dane laughed as their sandwiches were placed in front of them. The woman was uncanny. Like a bloodhound.

"Pretty sure Brad is a real name. Brad Pitt? And if she did make him up, I'm certainly not going to tell her she has a fake boyfriend, so let's get back to the drought. Does the article mention any solutions?"

"Oh, no you don't. No passing."

She stared at him, which was never good because she had an assessing glare, disguised as sophistication, that would put the toughest coaches to shame.

"I think you like her."

"Do you now?" Dane took a bite of his sandwich to give himself time to think.

"I do. And why wouldn't you? She's different and creative. You've always liked different."

"I have? Since when?"

"Since you were in the third grade. Remember you had a crush on that little girl who had the art farm?"

"Morgan Pierce? Mom, how do you remember these things? I was in the third grade. I sure as hell hope my dating choices were not nailed down then."

"I remember everything. I'm a lawyer. Well, I'm not anymore, but details are my thing. What about that one who had the tiny flower tattoo behind her ear? She was... unique, remember?"

Dane shook his head and finished the first half of his sandwich. "If I admit that I have a history of liking different women, can this please stop? I'd like this to end before we get to Julie, the performance artist."

His mother laughed. "See! Wow, she was something too. Your father and I were sweating over that one."

Dane smiled, the same gauzy expression normally reserved for any mention of his dad. It was amazing how time softened the edges of things that once were painfully sharp.

"Fine," his mother said, accepting more iced tea from the waitress. "I'll stop going down memory lane if you admit that Professor Jeffries, Anna, has piqued your interest. Just a little."

Dane wiped his mouth and put the napkin back in his lap. He was stalling in an effort to sort out his feelings. "She is an interesting woman. I'm surprised at all the layers. I expected her to be just like every other holier-than-thou academic."

His mother grinned. "And she's not."

He swallowed some fries and shook his head. "Doesn't appear to be."

"So, you like her."

"I do. Maybe I'll have her and Brad over for dinner once I get the house organized."

"Very funny. You know she has a new home too."

"I do."

"Doesn't that feel like kismet? The two of you putting down roots, brought together by this young man on your team? It feels meant to be."

Dane took in a deep breath because his mother was prone to these "flights of fancy," to use his sister's term.

"I've never understood what the hell kismet is, but whatever it is, no. I don't think it is kismet that we both bought a house around the same time. I'm sure lots of people bought homes on the same day even."

His mother asked for a box for the rest of her sandwich, and Dane stuck his credit card on top of the check left behind by the waitress.

"Well, I think it's something. I'd really like it to be something. She would be good for you."

"How's that?" Dane signed and nodded at the waitress who left her number at the bottom of his receipt. He tucked it in his wallet to be polite but had no intention of calling her. He was going off appearances, but she seemed like she enjoyed partying. He knew it wasn't fair, but he'd learned how to spot a sort of "party level." It was for her own good. She'd be disappointed if he called and couldn't deliver what she clearly thought he was about. He was doing them both a favor.

"She's kind of magical," his mother said.

"I'm sorry?"

"I don't know how to explain it, but there's something about her energy that I like."

"Oh, look at the time. I'm sure you need to get back." Dane stood, looked briefly at his mom, and pulled out her chair.

She swatted his arm and pulled her purse onto her shoulder. "You know, there are only so many trains coming through the station."

"And they keep on coming, these pearls of wisdom." He held the door open for her and was happy to close her and her kismet thoughts up in her car.

Magical. Damn it, now he'd be thinking about that all day. It made him want to talk with her, or fight with her again. He'd take either at this point.

Chapter Nine

Cynda brought tacos and Corona over the following Tuesday night to help Anna paint the accent wall in her dining room and because Cynda wanted to hear all the "steamy details," as she put it, about Anna's first and last football practice. Anna had declined to share her little meltdown in Dane's office. If she didn't talk about it, perhaps it would simply undo itself, like a rewind.

"He had a shirt on?" Cynda said as she set the bag down in the kitchen. "What the hell kind of injustice is that?"

Anna laughed as she cut up a lime and grabbed two paper plates. She had asked the movers months ago to keep all the furniture off the wall she knew would be the accent, which meant the dining room table was in the corner on the opposite wall. After she spread out one of the drop cloths, they ate on the floor while she proceeded to further disappoint her friend with her uneventful story.

"The coaches were in collared shirts and khakis, Cyn."

"And the players?"

Anna shook her head. "Shorts and shirts. Should you have your hormones checked?"

"Honey, I'm thirty-six. One year into my prime. I may not want to eat my dinner in the buff, but I'm perfectly healthy. You, on the other hand, seem completely unfazed by all beautiful things male. Was Trey happy to see you?"

Anna crunched into her taco and nodded. "He was, and I was thoroughly impressed with all of the players. It's not easy getting banged up out there." She squeezed a piece of lime and tucked it into the bottle of her beer before taking a sip.

Cynda stared at her, taco midway to her mouth.

"What?"

"I never thought I'd see the day."

"That's what he said."

"Who?"

"Dane."

"Oh, it's Dane now, is it?" She waggled her eyebrows.

"Stop. When I put the jersey on, those were his exact words. I'm not sure why it's so shocking that I am capable of participating. Look at my class. I'm all over the place in there. Football practice was no big deal." Anna lied. In truth, she'd been way out of her comfort zone when she arrived and even worse when she left, but there was no need to share that. If she did, she'd have to explain why. That was not something she was ready to admit.

Dane Sivac made her feel things she hadn't felt since she was young and riding her bicycle with the streamer handlebars. There was something about him that made it safe to be silly again. The way he looked at her said he found her fascinating instead of barely visible. Anna had spent a lot of years believing she would only find that in a contemporary, a partner who saw value in the same things she valued. Perhaps that wasn't true, though. After all, Dane was so different from her, yet they both recognized Trey's potential. Maybe that was the common ground and once the semester was over, all would be right with the universe and she and Dane could return to their designated corners. Anna felt a twist in her stomach at the thought.

"Do I get to see the jersey?" Cynda asked, grabbing another taco.

Anna pushed up from her crisscrossed position and grabbed the jersey out of her bedroom. She held it up and showed her friend the back.

"Oh, that's so cool. He had that made for you."

"I guess. I'm not sure how he got it done so quickly, but Dane said it was a gift from Trey. My dad is going to freak, and I've already texted a picture to Hollis."

"Of course you have, and I'm sure you got a very ladylike response."

Anna threw the jersey back on her bed and returned with Hollis's response on her phone. It was a picture of her middle finger.

"Good to see pregnancy hasn't slowed her down. And that is an excellent manicure." Cynda laughed and wiped her mouth at the same time.

"It's always fun to piss her off." Anna sat back down.

"Did you tell her where you got the jersey?"

"I told her a student gave it to me."

"Anything else?"

"There's nothing else to tell, Cyn." Anna popped the last bit of taco into her mouth and washed it down with her beer.

"I know this is going to piss you off, but I'm going to say it anyway. You're a little different. Lighter. I think you're having fun with him."

"Trey is a great kid, and it is stimulating and a challenge to have him in my class. He's not typical so I'm finding that I have to get creative, which I like."

"Not the 'him' I was referring to."

Anna broke eye contact. When it came to reading someone, Cynda was a lot like Dane—she had heat-seeking eye contact, although her eyes were deep brown and dangerous in a different way. They knew her, all her weaknesses. That's what came with four years of friendship, and Anna could see into her, much the same way. But right now she wanted to turn that particular superpower off because she couldn't discuss Dane or the way he made her feel yet. She didn't understand it herself and every time she thought about him, she felt foolish. Like those nerdy girls with a crush on the football player. She was a grown woman and well past the butterflies in her stomach phase. Dane had clearly awoken something in her, namely frustration, but that didn't mean she needed to acknowledge or dissect it.

"As much as I would love to feed your need for smut, there's nothing going on. We are both focused on Trey and his success. That's it. Dane is a little less annoying, which is helpful, but that's the extent of it. Should we get started painting?" Anna stood before Cynda could say another word and gathered up their plates and empty bottles.

"Hey, what time is it?" Cynda asked while Anna was still in the kitchen.

"Eight thirty," Anna said, returning to the dining room. "Why?"

She stopped in her tracks when she saw Cynda holding her phone up. "Definitely after school hours."

Anna snatched her phone back and saw the message from a number she didn't recognize.

Our boy didn't drop the ball once during drills today. It meant a lot that you were at practice. Thank you. By the way, don't put the jersey in the dryer. Flat dry, Jeffries.

The smile spread across her face before she could stop it. She looked up at Cynda and realized her hands were shaking.

"It's okay, honey. You're allowed to have fun."

Anna shook her head slowly. Somewhere deep inside, she didn't believe that was true. Why not? All this time she'd thought she wasn't built for fun, for windows down, but suddenly her playful side felt trapped rather than nonexistent. She'd believed the reason she was stuck with the boring Halloween costume every year was because her sisters always barged in and took the best ones first. Or that she'd missed out on seeing the Sistine Chapel because the line was too long. For as long as she could remember, Anna felt as if life, reality, had put her in her place, made her background scenery. Maybe that wasn't the case at all because there was nothing keeping her from Dane or from returning his text.

Anna slipped the phone into her back pocket and turned on the iPod plugged into her stereo. Cynda held her gaze for one more moment as the music filled the room before she dropped it. For now, at least.

"Okay, so I'll tape and you get the other drop cloth." Cynda picked up the roll of masking tape.

Anna nodded and pulled open the plastic-wrapped cloth.

"You thinking about replying to that text message?" her friend hinted as she crouched down to tape the baseboard.

Anna shook her head. "It wasn't a response type of text. It's not like he asked me a question."

"Don't we find that a wee bit snooty or dismissive to not answer at all?"

"No. *We* do not. I'm sure he wanted to let me know Trey was doing well."

"Yeah, I'm sure that's it. Because I often have an overwhelming urge at eight thirty on a Tuesday night to reach out to other teachers. It's a real problem. I've had to hide my phone it has gotten so—"

Anna threw the balled-up wrapper at her friend and they both laughed. There were four more beers in the fridge, and she had a feeling not a whole lot of actual painting was going to get done.

❋ ❋ ❋

This was all his mother's fault.

Dane had told himself he was going for drinks after practice. Jeb asked for what he said was the "millionth fricken time" and Dane agreed to go even though he hated any bar scene. Been there, done that. In his experience, nothing good ever came from mixing beer and football. But he was going, and he would be social even though he couldn't stop thinking about Anna.

That's when Dane decided it was his mom's fault. She'd planted things in his head, and now he couldn't get it on straight. The woman was deadly that way. He was still thinking about her "magical" comment when he came up with the brilliant idea to piss Jeb off again, grab a pizza, go home instead of the bar, and text Anna. Where the hell were the idiot police when he needed them?

It had been an excellent practice. Trey didn't miss one pass. Granted, there weren't many to miss tonight, but Coach Hall was happy, and that meant Dane was happy. He should have been celebrating like a grown man. Instead he was home watching rehearsal clips and texting Anna—who had a boyfriend by the way, real or imaginary—like he was some teenager.

Her number was on Trey's syllabus. When Dane had pathetically asked the kid some random question about lectures, Trey eagerly whipped out his folder and went over the whole schedule with him. They'd spent the last two class periods going over "some boring garbage called the life and times of Shakespeare," and Trey said he'd be getting up in front of the class on Monday. According to Trey, there were two guys in bad turtlenecks sitting at the back of Anna's classroom the whole time.

"Professor Jeffries looked a little nervous," he said, putting his papers back.

Dane wasn't sure what that was about and wasn't really listening at that point. He was too busy noticing the professor's contact information. After Trey left, Dane put it in his phone. There was no doubt now he was losing his mind. *She's not interested, idiot. Let it go*, his brain practically yelled.

Dane didn't bother coming up with explanations. Nothing made sense. All he knew was he wanted to spend more time with her. He moved the film back a few seconds, clipped it, and sent it to Birch. He'd already sent Trey his clips along with a "Way to go!" Take that, Crazy Eyes.

Although practice had gone well, Dane wasn't sure why that wasn't enough, why he'd arrived home restless. He'd shoved the pizza in the oven and even gone on an extra long run. Nothing helped. He was comfortable with winging it in practice, allowing for things to pop up and change the direction of the drills, but he knew better than anyone that a coach lived and died by his playbook when it was game time. There was nothing wrong with sparring, enjoying the heat disguised as ice in Anna, but if he was going to take it any further, if he was going to— Hell, Dane had no idea what he was doing and that should have been the clue to shut down and go to bed, but instead he texted her. Walked right into the game with nothing, and after an hour of checking his phone like a girl, he gave up. Threw the thing in his gym bag for the morning and pretended to go to bed.

Amateur move, Sivac. After another hour of replaying his stupidity, Dane rolled over, shoved his face as deep as he could into his pillow, and begged for sleep. His phone vibrated in his bag right as he was about to fall into darkness and Dane scrambled—that was the only way to explain how his body sprawled across his bed as he reached for the bag. It took his eyes a minute to adjust to the glare of his screen and then he saw Jeb's name. *Aw, hell.*

It was after midnight, which meant only one thing. Dane swiped his phone to reveal a picture of some woman in a *Game Day* T-shirt and take-me-on-the-bar heels. She was looking into the camera, clearly a few drinks in. Below her picture was Jeb's message.

Snooze you lose, grandpa.

Dane deleted the message. There was no point in responding. He'd played drunk texting with Jeb before, and those were minutes of his life he could never get back. He lay back on his bed, watched the ceiling fan make a few rotations, his phone resting on his chest. He closed his eyes, thought of her one last time, set his phone on his nightstand, and went to bed for real this time.

Chapter Ten

*A*nna had arrived early Monday morning to meet Checkers, her favorite maintenance man, in her classroom. He'd offered to bring some ladders and to help out with the lights. They were on the same bowling league, so she'd discussed her plans with him the week before. Checkers was the nickname given to Cletus Jones by most of the university staff because he wore red-and-black suspenders.

"Pretty sure that's it, Miss Anna," he said, plugging in the last extension cord at the far end of the classroom.

Anna clasped her hands and surveyed their work. Twinkling light strands dangled loosely from the ceiling and accented the flower petals and glitter she had scattered throughout the seats. She'd borrowed a fake tree and a couple of foam boulders from the theater department in hopes that when she hit the dimmer switch on the normally glaring and reality-inducing overhead lights, her students would slip into the world of *A Midsummer Night's Dream*.

"Sort of looks like a trippy nightclub," Checkers said as he closed his toolbox and hoisted the extra extension cord over his shoulder.

"Another world," Anna said. "Thank you." She kissed him on the cheek.

"Ain't nothing wrong with this world, Miss Anna, but I suppose bringing dreams to these kids is important to you."

She nodded. "It is."

"You know Imogene says the day she met me was magic. Do you think this is what she saw?" He laughed and Anna joined him.

"Thank you for this," she said.

"Anytime. I'll be back toward the end of the day to help you clean up. You just know the powers-that-be will want things back to boring before too long."

"Aren't you going to watch the opening of *A Midsummer Night's Dream*? Trey and I are performing."

"Trey Duncan?"

"The one and only."

"Aw, yeah. I'll need to see that. I'll hang toward the back in case I have to leave, but I'll be here." Checkers walked out, leaving her alone in her dimly lit classroom.

Even though her room was in LeConte Hall this year and surrounded by the Physics department, the small space had grown on her. The classroom was more intimate than the one she'd had last semester. This room brought her students closer to one another. It was perfect for the way she liked to teach and well suited for both plays this semester. It had been like they were right next to the witches in *Macbeth*, which had been incredible.

Anna always missed the story when it was time to move on to another play. She loved *A Midsummer Night's Dream*, but it was a different kind of experience. Macbeth had been intense, and it was a joy to watch her students' concentration as they tried to figure out each turn of phrase.

Midsummer would be lighter, funny, and all about love. Anna supposed she'd been in love with love all her life, but usually make-believe love. She still got butterflies when she read *Pride and Prejudice* and cried over the last few pages of *A Light Between Oceans*. Love in those stories was epic and sweeping. It wasn't awkward dates and fumbling over words caught somewhere between her head and her heart. Real-life love had never lived up to the hype for Anna, but standing on the grass with Dane as the sun set, learning about him, and allowing him to discover a few things about her had been... simple, almost effortless, and then like a twist on an amusement park ride, it had turned sexy, fun.

She wasn't sure why she was suddenly thinking about him. Their interactions were not the makings of a love story. They were too different, and not in a romantic comedy way. Dane was enjoyable and he did seem genuinely interested during their conversations, but Anna was certain her novelty would soon wear off and he would remember the type of woman he honestly found attractive.

It wasn't that Anna thought she was unattractive, that wasn't it. But, she was "a lot of work," as her mother hinted anytime Anna sat on the stairwell growing up, half-dressed for some event because she desperately needed to finish a chapter or find out the end of some story. Anna knew she was weighted by the things she found fascinating. She knew she talked about things most people glossed over, and she was resigned that it meant she would probably spend her life alone. There'd be friends and family, of course, but men wanted things that took away from what Anna considered her identity.

That's not to say Dane would, but maybe... *Why am I thinking about him again?* Because he texted her, and that changed things one more time. She hadn't given him her number, and yet he'd found her. Anna knew it sounded ridiculous. She had a doctorate; she was accomplished. She wasn't some mooning juvenile, but she had purposely kept herself tucked away from relationships. Women tended to come in second once they were with a man. Her mother, while still an architect and a partner, was second in charge. Her friends from college, including one who had a master's degree in biochemical engineering, were now wives and mothers. Anna was sure there were joys to that life, but not if it meant giving up who she was, what she'd worked for. And yet, like those other women, when Dane texted her she was filled with an absurd flush of feelings. And after that, she promptly panicked. It was fine she didn't answer, right? She was dating Brad. Although she imagined Dane was smart enough to figure out that mess.

She had not responded because he made her nervous. There, at least she could be honest with herself.

Anna took a seat in the second row of her classroom, propped her feet on the seatback in front of her, and admired her sparkly gold ballet shoes. She was certain there was not one person approved for full tenure who owned a pair of gold glitter ballet shoes, let alone wore them. She was in a world all her own. Anna had known that since she was a child begging her sisters to put on skits and variety shows for their parents. She would write the script. Hollis would direct, usually resulting in Meg insisting on some stunt or fight scene, which often ended in tears from Sage. When things got crazy, and they always did, Annabelle would simply slip into her story and wait out the storm.

One summer, Anna tried to put on her version of *Little Women*. It was shorter of course and a little more *Charlie's Angels* meets *Little Women*. Meg was thrilled for the first time in, well, ever. Her character already had her same name so it was one less thing she had to remember. Hollis started off fine but grew increasingly irritated when Meg insisted her character had to be a photographer who hung out under the pier, and Sage was distracted by some robot project she was doing with their dad. Hollis finally called a rehearsal on the pier at Uncle Mitch's place and told them all they were amateurs and she was going on strike. Meg and Sage laughed at her, and she threw them in the water and jumped in herself. Annabelle sat in a beach chair on the dock and after watching her sisters exhaust one another, she closed her eyes and imagined the whole play in her mind.

Eyes closed in her current make-believe setting, Anna brought her thoughts back to her class. A few minutes later, the door opened and light flooded the room. Anna hit the controls and turned on her scene. Students began filing in and to Anna's delight, there were several "oohs" and "ahhs."

She believed teaching was about giving her experience to her students, turning on the light, and letting them see the magic she saw. Her classroom was a safe place for all of them. Suddenly, she could hear her mother in her head. "You have so much to offer, dear," which seemed encouraging on the surface until it quickly spiraled to, "You can't hide in that library forever." Anna never felt like she was hiding as long as no one noticed, but lately things felt off. Perhaps that was the simple explanation, the reason why she could not stop thinking about Dane. He noticed, called her out into the open air, and probably most unnerving, he seemed to *see* her. Past what she offered up to most people and into the corners of her mind reserved only for her.

As class began, Anna felt herself return to her familiar home, except the furniture was rearranged or someone had knocked a hole in the wall for renovations. Yes, that's what it felt like. She was safe within her walls, but someone was putting in a skylight. She didn't need a skylight—didn't ask for one—but the hole, although small at the moment, had the potential to let in all sorts of things. Yet another reason Anna never rolled the windows down. It just might rain.

There was glitter in her hair, and she was still breathing a little heavy after her performance in front of the class. God, she was incredible and he was so screwed. Dane could feel it more and more each time he saw her now. He wondered what else he was missing when she didn't know he was around.

As the students shuffled out and the lights were turned back on, she finally noticed him in the back of the room. The softest smile of accomplishment rested on her lips as she walked toward him. Dane felt the air leave his lungs.

"Hi," she said, finally making her way to him after the last of her students left.

Up close now, Dane took in the glitter on her arms, her neck, and he was suddenly distracted by want.

"Hi. That was amazing. I felt like I was there," he said.

"Great. That's how it's supposed to be. Did you see him?" Anna looked back toward the font of the empty classroom.

He pulled a thin purple ribbon from her hair, being sure not to touch her as he wasn't sure how much more he could take without finding out exactly how those perpetually pink lips tasted.

"I did. Who knew Puck was such a badass?"

"Right? Ah, I'm so proud of him, and the class was on their feet. It's such a brilliant play."

"Beautiful," he said, and it had nothing to do with the play. The woman had this way of making things that should be stuffy sound fresh and fun, at least when she was in this classroom. He wondered what it would take to see the real Annabelle minus the glitter.

"Oh, yes, the room looked beautiful."

Not what he meant, but he quickly remembered his stupid text message and felt less bold.

"Checkers really gets credit for the lights."

"The maintenance guy?"

Anna nodded, looking around her classroom with the wonder of seeing it for the first time. Christ, she was going to kill him, and for some stupid reason he was okay with that.

"That was nice of him, he also works the locker rooms."

"I know. He loves football," Anna said.

"Everyone but you, huh?"

Her eyes sparkled but she said nothing.

"Set decoration is a little outside his job duties, right?"

"I charmed him."

"I have no doubt." He managed to hold her gaze, but then she looking everywhere but at him.

"Not really, he's on my bowling league."

Dane reached back and held on to one of the seats, willing his heart to settle down. She had to stop doing this. She was right when she barged into his office. This needed to stop, or he'd be in love with her by next week and cleaning out all the emotional garbage under his bed by Christmastime.

"You bowl with The Sweepers?"

Anna nodded. "They recruited me after one of their wives said it was chauvinistic that there were no females on their league. Can you imagine? I think it was Imogene. She's married to Checkers. Something like forty years. Anyway, they put up a flyer in the English lounge and I called him. All the guys are charming. Well, maybe not Gus, but he broke his ankle jumping on the trampoline with his granddaughter, so we cut him a little slack while he's healing." Anna let out a deep breath. "Wow, that was way more information than you needed. Sorry. I'm still buzzing from being up there with Trey."

"Didn't they win their league championships?"

"We did."

"Are you any good?"

"Yes. There's no way The Sweepers would bowl with a 'little lady' if I didn't deliver. I was second highest in points last year."

"Unbelievable." Dane grinned and shook his head. "How long have you been bowling?"

"Field trip in eighth grade. I'm a natural." She shrugged, and he loved the confidence and humility that rested on her shoulders in perfect balance. "And I like that it's dark." Her eyes met his, and this time he saw her catch herself. She was in a good mood; her guard was down. She broke eye contact and took a step back.

"I enjoyed your class," Dane said quickly before she made a break for it.

"Thank you. You're welcome back anytime."

"Honestly?"

She blushed.

"Well, not every day, but sure. You can come back. For Trey."

"Of course, for Trey." He moved close and she smelled like sunshine... as though there were just enough clouds in the sky, a perfect breeze, and sunshine.

"Dane."

Holy hell! Had she ever said his name before or was he losing his damn mind?

"Sorry, I didn't get your message until this morning and I was crazy busy. Thanks for the advice, but I'll probably dry-clean my jersey."

Oh right, she wasn't interested, logic reminded the pounding in his chest.

"Are you sure? I think football jerseys are allergic to dry cleaning."

Her lips threatened a laugh. "I'm sure it will be fine. Thank you for coming. I know Trey appreciates the support." She turned, dismissing him again in that way she'd perfected.

"Anna."

She glanced back.

"If you go into the settings on your phone, you can turn off read receipts."

"Pardon?" She blushed even through the glitter, so he knew she understood, but he was happy to spend a few more seconds with her.

"Read receipts. If you're going to brush some guy off and tell him you didn't get his text, it's only polite to shut that feature off."

"I..." She looked to the front of her classroom and Dane walked out. There was nothing left to say. He needed to back the hell up because no matter what signals her body kept sending his, she wasn't ready and probably never would be.

He walked aimlessly toward the center of campus, which was not where he needed to go, but he wanted to sit down. He took a seat on the edge of a planter under one of the massive oak trees on campus just as Sather Tower began playing the carillon. It must be noon, he thought as the bells continued, and the rhythm of it felt soothing. He needed to get things back in order. His family, his job, and his own mental sanity. Those were the priorities. Anna had a boyfriend, and she went to Yale and Oxford. She was all about the turtleneck set and briefcases.

Didn't he spend enough time sandwiched between two smart women to know he would always come in last? Not that his mom or sister meant harm, but harm was done nonetheless. Dane believed people were completely responsible for their lives regardless of circumstances, but some of that crap shaped you. He'd been successful in his own right, but similar to Trey's hands at practice this morning, he often came up short. He knew all of these things, so why did he still want her?

Looking up at the tower as the bells finished and the iconic symbol fell silent, Dane somehow felt so different in the span of just a few weeks. Could be he simply needed a new perspective. He had enough time before his one-thirty meeting to catch the elevator to the tower's observation deck. Maybe the fresh air up there would clear his head. He sure hoped so.

Chapter Eleven

*A*nna watched as the glitter pooled around her feet and down the drain of her shower. She closed her eyes to rinse her hair and could still see his face when he told her he knew she was blowing him off. She wiped her eyes clear and turned off the water. There was no way to tell him he was too much or that she felt out of control. No one put that in a text message. It wasn't possible to type out what he did to her, how he made her feel.

So she simply ignored the text, which was rude, she knew, but she'd spent that night after Cynda left trying to think of a response. Something funny or sarcastic, but the truth was she wasn't that girl. Sure, she'd managed to spar with him for a while, mainly to keep some distance, but she wasn't like her sisters. She was quiet and content. Happy to blend in. At least she was before she met him.

The way he looked at her, the conversations and the questions as if he was fascinated by her, was more than she could deal with right now. She had people monitoring her class. She was on track for tenure. Being silly over some football coach was not going to move her any closer toward anything but a confused heart. He was so unexpectedly genuine.

Anna got dressed and wrapped her hair in a towel. Her stomach growled, so she went to the kitchen to make a peanut butter sandwich. Leaning against her counter and staring at her microwave as the clock flashed to eight thirty, she realized she'd never asked him one thing about himself. After their initial scratchiness, he'd been personable and almost friendly. In return she had been... mean? Was that possible?

She'd been trying to keep her distance, but he came to her class, albeit for Trey. He'd asked about her lunch box, whether she played sports, even her bowling with Checkers and the guys. She'd shut everything down.

Maybe this had nothing to do with him wanting more. Maybe he was just a nice guy and she *was* being snobbish. "You come across as better than everyone else, Anna," Meg had said when she spoke to her on the phone yesterday and tried to confide. "I mean Hollis is a bitch, but people see that coming. Yours comes out when you're scared, and it's isolating. Don't you think?"

Anna had made a quick excuse to get off the phone. The idea that she consciously pushed people away was something she needed to think about. Perhaps she had been defensive most of her life. She had answered questions like, "Why are you always studying?" or "Are you sure you even like boys?" since she was barely old enough to know the underlying meaning of those inquiries.

There was this boy her junior year in high school, a field hockey player, who asked her in front of their entire French class if she was a lesbian. Anna had not been offended by the idea of being gay; it was the intimacy, the closeness of the comment that startled her. She didn't know him and certainly wouldn't share her sexuality with anyone who wore a T-shirt that read "I'll show you my stick if you show me yours."

Growing up, she'd been different: quiet and consumed by her imagination and books. That was where she wanted to be, and she never felt the pressure to be anything else except for the few times people felt it necessary to call her out on the fact that she wasn't running around like the rest of them. Maybe that's where her reaction to

Dane's text came from. She simply wanted to be left alone, but she wasn't better than anyone and the idea she might have made him feel that way bothered her. Her response to him, the jump of her pulse, were her issues, not his. She wasn't a child anymore, and hiding was ridiculous.

Anna wiped her fingers and threw away the paper towel she'd wrapped around her sandwich. She grabbed her phone from the charger on her desk, her thumbs hovering over the screen. A mixture of relief and hesitation filled her when she pulled up her text messages and saw she still had his number.

"Friendly," she said to the dark space of her living room.

Hey. She typed and then deleted it.

Maybe she should start with casual, maybe *What's up, Coach?* Anna deleted that too and threw the phone back onto her desk.

Dear God. She collapsed on her couch. She was a misfit. Words were her life, and yet she was right back to some twisted adolescent at the thought of a simple text message. Why was she even bothering? He felt brushed off. Done. There was no need to stir things up. Anna rolled on her back and reached for her remote. *Notting Hill*, she needed *Notting Hill*.

Right after her favorite part, "I'm just a girl, standing in front of a boy," she always said it along with Julia Roberts, Anna hit the pause button and grabbed her phone again. Keep it simple, she told herself. "Be true to you, Banana," her Uncle Mitch used to tell her growing up. Anna took in a shallow breath, typed a few words, and hit send. She quickly turned the phone over and after hitting play to finish the movie, she stuck her phone under the cushion of her couch as if that would somehow soften the feelings racing through her.

Memorial Stadium was built in 1923 and four years ago had undergone a $321 million renovation. No public funds were used, the school loved to say, but the truth was Dane didn't care. Either way, the place was incredible—a nod to history that he felt deep in his bones every time he came to work.

From time to time, people claimed they heard the voice of loved ones who had passed. Dane never heard his dad's voice after he died, which pissed Dane off when he was young. Now, he figured he was filled with such angst and stupidity that he never bothered to listen even if his father was trying to reach him. All of that was a long time ago and mixed up somewhere in those feelings he preferred to avoid. He would admit, though, that being at Memorial Stadium, especially at night, reminded him of his dad. He felt closer.

After practice, Dane stayed behind to run laps and pummel his muscles into exhaustion in the weight room. He wasn't sure what else would help him get his head on straight. He was actually feeling better until he ran into Checkers in the locker room.

"Coach, aren't you supposed to be riding the carriage instead of being the horse?"

Dane laughed and wiped the sweat off his face. He had no idea what that meant, but Checkers often made up his own sayings.

"Just clearing my head. I'm going to grab my bag. I'll be out of your way."

"Not in my way. I'm just changing two bulbs in the showers so I don't have to squeeze it in tomorrow."

Dane should have nodded, picked up his bag, and walked out. Lately, it seemed he rarely did what he should do.

"How's the bowling league going?"

Checkers nodded and sat on one of the benches, pulling up the legs of his pants as he always did. "Good. We're off to a good start. Thanks for asking."

"Glad to hear it." This was ridiculous. Dane was not going to corner the maintenance guy after hours for information on Anna. "Have a good night."

"Aren't you going to ask me about Anna?"

Dane turned and furrowed his brow, hoping it made him look less like an idiot.

Checkers raised his brow. "You never ask about bowling."

"Not true, I've asked about... fine, I guess I haven't."

"Saw you in her class today. Trey did a great job."

"Is there anything you don't know?"

Checkers shook his head and Dane took a seat across from him. "She's special, huh?"

"She is... an incredible teacher."

"When I met Imogene, she was a teacher at the grammar school. Spitfire from the get-go she was, but I was a puppy for that woman."

"I'm not a puppy."

"Not saying you are, but you sure were giving the beautiful Miss Annabelle the look during Trey's performance. I'm surprised you even heard a word the boy said." Checkers laughed at himself.

Dane shook his head. "It was dark."

"I see it all, son."

Dane flinched a bit at what he knew was a term of endearment, but he hadn't been called "son" in quite a long time. His dad always used to call him that, but that wasn't Checker's fault.

"Fine. I think she's interesting. Happy?"

"Be careful with her."

"Why?"

"Because she's special. A guy only gets one shot at special."

"You don't need to worry about my shot. She has clearly shut me right down."

"Eh." Checkers stood up. "She'll come around."

Dane shut off the lights near the sink, and both men walked out of the locker room together.

"I wouldn't hold my breath."

"Maybe not, but I watched her too when your boy was dancing around." Checkers locked the door behind them.

"And?"

The old man nodded, a definite twinkle in his eye that reminded Dane of a Christmas card. "She'll come around."

Dane laughed and patted him on the back. By the time he climbed into his truck, his phone vibrated.

How did the old guy manage to do that? Dane thought as he looked down at the screen again.

Do you have any siblings?

It was Anna. Dane's heart lurched and he felt like a stupid kid. Tired of the back and forth and sick of playing games, he didn't hesitate to respond. What's the worst thing that could happen? He'd been brought to the ground by people much bigger than Anna. He wanted in, wanted to see her, and if that meant she knocked the wind out of him, then so be it.

He texted her back.

Yes. I have an older sister. Would you like to get a coffee?

He hit send and waited. She'd turned her read receipts off, probably in a fit of frenzy after he left her hanging in her classroom, he thought. Dane started his truck and drove toward home.

Philz will be closed by the time we get there.

That wasn't exactly a no, he thought, but she was right. It was almost 10:30 p.m. and nothing was open. He was poised to ask her maybe tomorrow when another text came in.

You could come over. I'm grading tests tonight, so...

Dane pulled up to a stoplight. His heart was pounding as he watched the little bubble blink. She was typing and if it was her address, he was going to kiss Checkers because the man had some kind of psychic power. Anna's address flashed on the screen, and Dane texted her that he would be there in ten minutes. Happy he'd showered in the locker room, he turned around and drove toward something, someone more important than protecting what he'd shoved under the bed.

Chapter Twelve

When Anna was fifteen years old, her friend Margot talked her into auditioning for the school talent show. They were going to do a dance routine. Anna didn't know how to dance, but Margot said she would look good in the costume and all she had to do was stand in the background. Margot would do every-thing—that was the plan. Terrified, Anna was sure it would be awful, and it was.

When the knock came on her front door, Anna felt the same stir of panic, the same certainty that she was heading into a disaster. She wasn't prepared for her reaction when Dane asked her to coffee and certainly wasn't ready for the urge to see him that swept over her regardless of the hour. She rubbed her lips together one more time so it didn't look like she'd just applied lip balm and opened her door.

"Was that a pity text after you blew me off, or have you been thinking about me?" Dane asked with a casual grin as he stood in her doorway.

Thinking about you, thinking about you, her absurd heart yelled. "Neither," Anna said, stepping back and letting him into her home.

Dane looked around her house. In most cases, she would have felt uncomfortable under the scrutiny, but there was something about him, something about the two of them together that seemed normal. And scary, because this was too good to be real life.

"Wow. What's going on in there?" He pointed to her dining room.

"Cynda and I started painting, but the project involved tacos and beer so we didn't get too far."

He smiled. "What kind of beer do you like?"

He'd stopped sounding shocked when she didn't fit his stereotype, and she made a mental note to do the same. "Well, I'll drink pretty much anything."

"That's a shame."

She quirked her mouth and took his coat. "Very funny. I like most beer, as long as it's cold. Corona and whatever some of those craft beers are at the bowling alley. Beer is beer to me. Now if we start talking about red wine, I'll have opinions. That's my drink of choice."

Dane's eyes were wandering, and he gestured if it was all right for him to keep looking. Anna nodded.

"Beer is definitely not beer, but Corona isn't bad." He ran a hand along her bookcase, and the man might as well have been touching her. He moved through her space so carefully. She couldn't take her eyes off him.

"So you asked about my siblings." He turned to her.

"Yes, I suppose I was curious." She went into the kitchen. "Do you want coffee?"

"Please." He followed her. "I have a sister. Two years older. She lives in Santa Barbara with The Saint."

"The Saint?" Anna handed him a mug.

Dane nodded. "That's what I call him. My mother loves him."

"Ah. Cream?"

He shook his head and took a sip of coffee.

"Well, that's nice for your sister. Makes things easier."

"It does." He looked around her kitchen and his eyes lit up.

"What?" Anna sat at the kitchen table in front of her papers and laptop, somehow feeling they would ground her no matter what he said next.

"I like your place." He took the seat next to her, his leg momentarily bumping hers under the table before he adjusted to the small space.

Anna willed herself not to jump at the sheer warmth of him. Dane was a big man out in the real world but appeared bigger sitting at her small, four-seat, whitewashed kitchen table that she'd recently purchased at the same store where she found her reading chair.

He was taller than her father, so that made him over six feet. She had no idea how much he weighed—she was never good at that sort of thing, but he was muscular. Not in a showy, Venice Beach sort of way, just beautifully muscular.

"Thank you." She typed in the password to her computer. "Not what you were expecting?"

"It is. I expected you to live in a nice place, kind of quirky and unique."

"Because I'm such a nice person?" Anna laughed a little.

"I think you might be, Anna."

Their eyes met. "Really?"

Dane nodded. "You've gone out of your way to hide it from me, but I think I see you. Now that I've been to your home, I'm pretty sure."

"Huh, well, I invited you over because I wanted to show you—"

Dane stood, poured himself more coffee, and topped off Anna's. It was the most natural thing. Like they were having breakfast or getting ready to look at new furniture on the Internet. When he was done, he set his cup on the table next to hers and leaned over her shoulder. He rested his hand on the back of her chair, and Anna suddenly felt nothing but that hand barely touching her shoulder blade. Her heart knocked on her chest, begging to get out and leap at him. She swallowed and tried to make her hands work so she could show him Trey's grades.

"Is this where you log all the grades?" he asked, genuinely interested.

"Yes." She clicked on the tab marked *Student Roster* under *Period Two*.

"How many classes do you teach?"

"Three."

"All Shakespeare?"

"Yes."

"Was your mother a professor when you were growing up?" she asked while they waited for the screen to refresh.

"Yes."

Anna was surprised at the brevity of the answer and looked over her shoulder, but that was a mistake. He was looking down at her, not at the laptop screen, and when their eyes met a whoosh of breath left her body and she wasn't sure she could retrieve it. Unable to speak, she returned to her laptop and finally found Trey's grades. After explaining that he'd made up his lost participation points and pulled a B on the *Macbeth* final, she pointed to the paper she'd graded earlier in the day.

He leaned over her shoulder even more to get a better look and *Dear All Things Holy*, the man's body was touching her back, or was he? She had no idea because the feel of him was almost scandalous at any distance. She tried to regulate her breathing and came back to reality just in time for him to point at the screen over her shoulder and ask, "So it's this one here? Is that an A?"

Anna closed her eyes, unsure she could take one more minute of her entire body being so alive. She would have to burn out at some point, right?

Managing a nod, she turned to find those eyes tangled up with hers and right then and there she gave up, completely abandoned everything she believed to be appropriate.

Anna was always the best in their family at hide-and-seek. She was the one who held out until her sisters finally gave up and went to dinner. She was a master at holding the hide and yet there she was, wanting for the first time in her life to be found. She wanted him to see what was swimming through her body. That she was drawn to him for some inexplicable reason. That she didn't care if they had little or nothing in common, although the more time she spent with him, it seemed they did. Anna didn't want to be safe. She wanted to touch him and sink into the sheer enjoyment of a man like him looking at her the way he was looking at her now.

Collect yourself, her sensible mind tried to reason, but she was too far gone. All sense was muffled by the thundering of her heart. Pure and simple need.

Dane appeared frozen. Eyes on her, but seemingly unsure what to do next. As if he were expecting something to fall out of the sky and crush them at any minute.

"I don't know what I'm doing, but do you mind if I just…" Anna lifted her hand toward his face, wanting to touch him in a way that she'd never experienced before.

Dane shook his head, his eyes meeting hers. "Brad is going to be pissed," he whispered.

Anna touched his cheek, stubbled and warm, and his eyes closed as if he were trying to hold back something he knew he'd eventually hand over. She leaned into him.

"Brad is my UPS guy."

It was funny and he should have laughed, but he remained still, arm braced on the back of her chair. Anna ran her fingers down his neck and felt his pulse beating even and steady.

Last year, Anna bought a green dress. It was silk, long, and retro with spaghetti straps. She'd seen it in the movie *Atonement,* which takes place in the thirties. Keira Knightley's character wore it and Anna's body was similar, so she decided she wanted one. She found it in one of Sage's favorite vintage stores and bought it. The dress dipped low in the back and felt so lovely on her legs, Anna remembered. It was so light, she thought of it as a barely there kind of dress. But when she brought it home and looked in the mirror again, she decided it was all wrong. There was too much showing along the sides and her collarbone stuck out funny. She looked too skinny. Buying it had been a bad idea—it should have stayed in the movie, on Keira. She returned the dress the next day, but every time she watched *Atonement*, she still loved that dress and remembered how she felt before she'd looked at her reflection.

Anna was about to make another mistake based on a similar emotion: how he made her feel. It would not be everything she wanted it to be, it would mess with both of them, and it was irresponsible. She could not give Dane what he wanted, and he would surely pale in comparison to her imagination. Men always did.

She was an adult with the absolute ability to put him in his place, back him up. She'd done it before, but now her heart was racing, begging her to please just this once do something stupid.

So she did.

Despite her trembling hands, she turned in her chair and pulled his face closer. Dane bent and rested his other hand on the table. Without a word, her eyes fell closed as her lips brushed across his once. And then again.

Oh my, he was like the silk. Her body hummed and she felt sensual. She didn't want to look in the mirror, not yet. He made her want to do things that made no sense, and there was something exhilarating about the shock on his face right before he pulled her to her feet with one arm wrapped around her waist and took her entire mouth.

She had never experienced anything like it, and when she slid her tongue into the late-night warm coffee of his mouth and gently held that bottom lip that had been driving her stupid between her teeth, his hand slipped behind her neck. It was so gentle it felt like a dream, but then a moan rattled from his chest and she knew he was there. Real and so male. Their lips still pulling, he wrapped her in his arms, which was good because she wasn't sure she could stand anymore. The man knew how to kiss, and that shouldn't have been a surprise. Didn't all men with his degree of... equipment know how to use it? Anna had no idea. She didn't normally play at this level, but the only word currently buzzing through her normally active mind was—more.

Dane forgot where he was. When he opened his eyes, it still took him a minute to figure out how he'd gotten from frustrated in a locker room to this in the space of a couple of hours. He wondered if this sense of a windfall was what it felt like to win the lottery.

Muttering something that sounded like "wow," and "whoa," mixed together, his voice still had her kiss on it. Dane was grateful for her kitchen counter when he drifted back to reality. Without something to grab onto, Little Miss Cardigan surely would have knocked him on his ass. What kind of a woman brushed past a man's lips like an unlit match simply begging to ignite? He pulled his bottom lip into his mouth as if he could somehow keep tasting her.

"I..."

He grinned. There was something gratifying about knocking her out too.

"I'm... sorry," Anna said.

"Don't be."

"No, but I am. You came here to discuss Trey and I... I'm not sure what the heck I just did, but it was nowhere... it was not appropriate at all."

He couldn't shut her up, keep her from turning what had happened into something ordered and scripted, so he pulled her back in and took them both back where things made sense.

The next time they parted, her hands were resting on his chest and it felt so right he didn't want to let her go. He was suddenly full speed on the "feelings freeway," as his mother liked to say when they were growing up. That phrase was usually reserved for his older sister, but right now, standing in Anna's kitchen with her in his arms, it was all freeway. He had honestly only come over to see her, talk to her, but something was clearly building inside her and as gratifying as that thought was, he felt a little out of control. Yet if he thought he was stunned, the look on her face meant she was at least three notches ahead of him, so he loosened his hold on her.

"Anna." He touched her face and lifted her gaze from his chest to meet his. "I can practically hear your mind."

She stepped back and his arms were immediately needy.

"You are... that was good. I mean, that was nice."

She looked like she was going to pass out as she slid back into her chair. The kiss had been her idea first, right? Because for a minute, he was beginning to feel like one of those guys who showed up late at night for a booty call. *Perfect, idiot, let's allow our mind to wander there. Focus.*

"Nice. Okay. Thank you? I practice a lot on the back of my hand," Dane said jokingly and grabbed the coffee pot again. In the game of football, this was called an audible. It was when the quarterback chose a different play on the fly. There was no way to move through something she wasn't ready to share, so he tried a different route.

Anna laughed and *Sweet Jesus*, his heart skipped again as he refilled her coffee.

"Your hand... very cute." She let out a breath she'd probably been holding since she shocked the hell out of him and drank her coffee. Her shoulders lowered and Dane could see she was coming back to him.

"So, Trey got an A on his paper. That is incredible," he said.

She tucked her hair behind her ear and looked down, failing miserably at hiding her smile and her flushed cheeks as she sifted through the papers, seemingly looking to show him Trey's work. She handed him the paper, still grinning, and held her hands to her cheeks.

"Thank you."

"For what?"

"That was an audible, right? Change in play?"

"How did—"

Anna pointed to the paper. "Trey uses it in his paper. A few football terms actually. I had no idea that game of yours had such clever terminology. His paper is brilliant and so fun to read."

Dane read the paper, and she was right. It was great work. The kid was able to explain *Macbeth* and his thoughts in ways that were easy to understand. Dane guessed that had a lot to do with his teacher. They talked about how far Trey had come until Anna yawned and he realized it was after midnight.

"I should get going." He stood and put their mugs in the sink.

Anna walked ahead to get his coat.

"I'm..." Handing him his coat, she opened the door and met his eyes. She seemed to get lost in that way he was sure he could get used to.

"You're something, Professor."

"I know. Like my quirky house. I get that a lot." Her gaze dropped.

Was it possible she had no idea that her eyes alone could bring a man to his knees? "I was actually thinking more like a surprise. A brilliant and sexy-out-of-nowhere surprise."

Anna looked up at him and before she could say another word, he gently kissed her. Her eyes remained closed when he pulled back.

"Goodnight, Anna," he said softly.

She nodded, standing in the doorway, her eyes still closed.

Dane walked to his truck and hoped like hell she understood the concept of the long game because he was positive he was ruined for all other women with one simple kiss.

Chapter Thirteen

*A*nna slept well, which struck her as odd: she should have been nervous or at least anxious. She'd kissed Dane. He hadn't grabbed her, smoldering right before he took her mouth in a rush of passion. No. She had kissed him first, asked him if she could touch him. Anna hummed while she made coffee—it was a great scene and it was hers. Reality. Unscripted. A piece of her own story.

She wasn't sure how she felt about her ability to have an entire story, but that kiss had been... better than anything she'd seen from the comfort of her couch in a while.

Getting ready for work, she was a little giddy and not one bit anxious. She wore her favorite paisley blouse and left her hair down, curled at the ends.

The day Anna was awarded her doctorate from Oxford, she was calm. Even her family had commented that she seemed at peace, and she had been. Comfortable, nestled in her experience and the time she'd spent studying. It was a special time and although it sounded crazy, she felt the same kissing Dane. Being that close to him felt slow and natural, an easy melt into something she wanted. She'd wanted to feel his lips, know what it was to touch him, let him hold her in that intimate breathing space, their eyes locked. And unlike most encounters, it had proven better than she'd ever imagined. Maybe that was because she hadn't seen him coming, certainly had not seen her attraction to him building, and then there it was. She didn't have time to get all worked up or think it into the ground.

After breakfast, it was a short drive to the campus. Once inside her office, she sat, looking out the window. October was almost half over and the mornings were chilly. She inhaled and went to the window. Gently touching the cold glass in between the white-painted panes, her fingers left a mark and her breath a cloud of soft fog that quickly disappeared. She took the heavy metal lever, turned it with some effort, and with the sound of cracking paint pushed open the window. There was some sort of flowering bush right below and her senses filled immediately with the faint scent of perfume, sweet and earthy. She closed her eyes and thought of Dane. Had that kiss changed anything for him?

Leaving the window open, she returned to her desk and checked her e-mail. By the time she reached the second paragraph of the first e-mail, Anna stood and closed the window. It was too cold for fresh air. She finished reading, taking in the detailed "report card" sent to her by the review committee. "Does not seem to have a firm grasp on the responsibility of disseminating important concepts." "Her class was a bit of a free-for-all. Some may even say out of control." Her eyes traveled her computer screen as she read the entire thing again. Anger coursed through her chest.

What the hell is going on?

When she'd been hired by the university, they'd welcomed her and said they were excited about what she would bring to the department. That was only three years ago, and now she was being treated like some sort of deviant. Her heart raced. It felt like a witch hunt. Anna closed her eyes. Surrounded by the memory of the meeting she'd had at the beginning of the semester, she felt her blood boil all over again.

"Your classroom experience is unconventional and while we appreciate creativity, I'm sure I speak for the panel when I say there needs to be value under all that fun. Parents don't pay this institution for their children to have a good time or a 'moment,' as I noticed you mentioned in your writings to this committee."

"Yes, we don't have a huge budget, and yours is one of only two Shakespeare offerings this semester. We need it to be educational."

"This is Shakespeare. He would have hated that treatment, don't you think?"

They looked at her as if she were standing in front of them naked, maybe wearing the boa from the little girl at the costume shop. Yes, definitely a boa. Did they not know anything about Will? The man was all about feeling and jump-to-your-feet experience.

The guy with the bow tie was the department chair with an emphasis on Milton and Greek something. At the time, Anna once again wished she had a scriptwriter. Maybe something like *Dirty Harry* or *Thelma and Louise*.

These committees were the exact reason no one wanted to take Shakespeare anymore. If she'd had a script, she would have been defiant, a rebel willing to pack up her things and walk across that expanse of green lawn. Instead, Professor Roberts had cleared his throat for at least the tenth time, and Anna felt trapped between what was best and what they wanted.

"What are you asking me to do?" she had asked.

"Well, we're simply going to watch your class this year. You're an associate professor, and your aspirations for full tenure rest in this committee's hands. We take that responsibility very seriously."

"Miss Jeffries, the thing is—" some other guy started to say, and Anna interrupted.

"Professor."

"I beg your pardon?"

"Professor Jeffries. I may be an associate, but I am a professor. Please address me as such."

Oh, yes, Anna had thought, and had she been standing in front of her bedroom mirror instead of suffocating under the weight in the room, she might have smiled. As she sat at her desk now, she realized the small correction was the only moment where she'd stood up for herself.

Whoever was next to Roberts had looked down his nose in that way that fed the stereotype of academic snobbery. "My apologies, Professor. I think what Professor Graston is saying is we can't let just anyone become a full professor."

"Certainly not." Anna had acquiesced by that point.

"You do bring a certain... eclectic flair, so to speak, to our department, but we'd like to see substance too. Does that make sense?"

No, she thought at the time, but did not bother saying. She had been in academia long enough to know that she was the only one that would lose if her anger got the best of her. Egos above her needed to be fed, not challenged.

"Absolutely. I welcome any of you into my class periods." She had slid a folder across the table. "As requested, these are my lesson plans and a general scope of the experien— the knowledge base I'm looking to impart."

All four of them had nodded like uptight assholes at an opera who never bothered to understand the music but loved the idea of sitting in box seats. Finding it difficult to breathe, as she did now even in the quiet of her office, Anna had stood abruptly from the meeting and reluctantly shaken their clammy hands.

"So, if that is everything," she had said, feeling more defeated than ever.

"Professor Jeffries."

Anna turned.

"Make us proud out there."

She was going to puke. Instead, Anna nodded and as her hand dropped to her side, she flashed them her pinkie. An insignificant stand considering, but again it was something.

Growing up, she and her sisters modified the middle finger gesture after Anna read that the pinkie was the equivalent of flipping someone off in Chinese. It was probably bull, but it stuck and Anna used it as a way to find humor in a situation that was completely humiliating and out of her control. These men held her chances of tenure in their hands.

When Anna was younger and her parents returned from vacation, they used to say they would spend the next couple of weeks "paying for their fun." That was the nature of being self-employed, they often added with smiles that never rang true to Anna or her sisters. All they saw was that their parents were either working, talking about work, or tired most of the time.

That was how she felt after the meeting. Was she being punished for enjoying what she did too much? Did they know she was living her dream and they somehow weren't going to allow that much happiness for her? Could four guys in bad sweaters slap her on the wrist and demand she stay between the lines? It sure looked that way, Anna thought, closing the email, the report card, and turning toward the now closed window.

For the first time in a long time, she had no idea what to do. It was becoming clear that the only place she was brave was in her classroom. Away from her students, she was a bit of a doormat, at least when it came to her career. She was accomplished and educated and whether the men behind her "report card" knew it or not, this school needed her. See, those were the things she should have said.

"Screw you, pent-up assholes." That's what Hollis would say. Darn it, why couldn't she have said that and march out of the administration building with some kind of kick-ass soundtrack playing P!nk or The Rolling Stones. Yes, again, where had the scriptwriter been when she needed one?

"Life is not a movie," Anna's mother had often reminded her growing up, usually after they'd watched a family movie and she had exclaimed, "Why can't guys be like that in real life?" Her mother never failed to jump in and remind her that the world was a cruel place. She was right, and whether Anna liked it or not, it was her job to teach her students according to the standards of the university. She'd thought she was doing that, but ever since Dean Riley—the man who had hired her—retired, things felt uncertain. As if the new dean of the English department was trying to make a point. Sort of like a new president moving into The White House. She certainly hoped she wasn't going to be cast aside like last season's china pattern. Or maybe it was her application for tenure that had put the spotlight on her. Anna didn't do the spotlight. In fact, she'd gone out of her way to avoid this type of thing, but something was up and she needed to figure it out before she lost her job.

It was the one thing that mattered, that's what she told herself as she grabbed her bag and her laptop. She needed to get out of her office, so she decided to grade papers in her sanctuary—the library.

Dane walked into the Doe Library. He'd been once before when he took the Getting to Know Berkeley tour after he was hired. It still looked like a train station, he thought, standing among the milling students and faculty. After speaking briefly with the circulation desk, he turned into the North Reading Room and remembered why the train station came to mind. High arched ceilings with molding and squares, lots of squares, extended above him. The huge main reading room was filled with tables made of light wood, maple maybe, and matching chairs. Each row of tables had antique-looking lamps that seemed original.

He never understood why these head cases, his mother included, were forever bitching and whining that they never received a fair share of the university money. Although he'd admit it was not Memorial Stadium, nothing but opulence surrounded him. That and the incredible light that filled the room. The windows were the big draw, he decided, right as his eyes found Anna.

She was at one of the middle tables, in a sea of students. Her hair was pulled back and she was dressed in what looked like tights or leggings. A pencil balanced between her lips, and one leg was bent and resting on the wooden chair where she sat. She could have been a student, he thought, but when she looked up, he corrected himself. The years were there in her eyes. He had only begun to understand Anna Jeffries, but she was no child. When she was born, was her mind already filled with so many thoughts? Had she always been smart, or was she simply a hard worker? Dane guessed a little of both and moved toward the edge of the room before she spotted him stalking her. No crowding, he reminded himself as he approached and took the empty seat opposite her.

It was clear she frequented the library and was at home here; she didn't flinch or even look up when he sat directly across from her. That could only come from years of hardcore studying, and for reasons he would need to figure out later, he found her stunning in her solace. Simple, reading, and so engrossed in a world of her own making that she made him almost jealous. What must it be like to live in that mind?

Anna took in a quiet breath, opened the folder next to her, and slid a paper across the table to him. She did know he was there and for some stupid reason, that felt amazing.

Flipping over the paper, Dane saw a large letter A written in dark ink above the title "Midsummer Night's Dream – Test One." First an A on the Macbeth paper and now another A on the second play. *Oh, hell yeah.* This was going to make Crazy Eyes's day. Dane looked at Anna, who was now writing something and smiling. At the thought of Trey's psychologist, Dane was suddenly reminded of their beginning and how he'd first met Anna. It had all started over a grade report, and now look at them. She had been difficult, but he'd also been an ass back then.

"I'm sorry," he said quietly.

Anna looked confused, and Dane was at a loss to explain.

Life was strange, and without getting too feely, he acknowledged that he was grateful he'd been sent to meet with Trey's teacher.

"I'm sorry for the way I treated you when we first met," he said, still trying to whisper.

Anna swallowed back what looked like embarrassment, and Dane couldn't tell if it was because he was talking in the library or because of the things they'd both said.

"Me too," she mouthed silently.

If her intent was to keep him quiet, the silent lips weren't helping. He wanted to kiss her again, but even he knew the code of conduct in the library.

"Are we allowed to talk in this place? I'd like to show you my version of the touchdown dance for Trey's success. This is so good. Does he know yet?" Dane started out whispering, but his voice must have grown louder given that two guys at the next table over turned around.

Quiet place. Got it. Dane winced an apology in their direction.

Anna closed her book and her laptop without a word and stuck them in her bag. She gestured for him to follow her, and Dane nearly knocked his chair over getting up. *Were these made for tiny people? Big guys didn't read back then?* He'd be sure to discuss that discrimination with Anna the next time they were debating the rights and wrongs of the world. Right now though, he was following her deep into the building and into a room that had only four bookcases and two huge King Henry-looking tables. There was a guy posted outside the door. Anna nodded to him. She and Dane entered the room and she locked the door. Dane was going to say something, but she held her finger to her mouth like a preschool teacher and pulled the blinds down on the door.

Quietly she walked over to him, laced her arms around his neck, and whispered in his ear, "I was having a crappy day, but then I graded Trey's test and now you're here. How did you know I needed you?"

"I didn't. All I knew was if I didn't kiss you again soon, I wasn't going to be able to function during practice, so I set out to find you. Cynda was very helpful, by the way."

"I'm sure she was." Anna pulled him over into the bookshelves and kissed him.

The smell of old leather and Anna surrounded him. When he pulled her closer, the pencil dropped from her hair and landed on the aged burgundy carpet without a sound.

"You're not a jerk, Dane Sivac." She was still whispering when they came up for air.

"Thank you." He touched her hair. So soft. "Where are we?"

"Dissertation Writer's Room," she said, picking up the pencil but staying tucked into the bookcases.

"That sounds... important." Dane's eyes widened, and since she seemed determined to keep them out of sight, he took a seat. There was something strangely romantic about being in such a quiet space. Before he could smack himself upside the head for more feelings, Anna sat down next to him and he realized there weren't enough mushy words for the way she made him feel.

"Are we hiding?" he asked.

"Maybe."

"Do you want to tell me why?"

She shook her head. "Not really."

They sat in silence, nothing but the hum of the old fan above them doing its best to pretend it wasn't too old anymore.

"So, did you decide I'm not a jerk because you've kissed me stupid twice now, or was it just something you wanted to share?"

"Probably the kissing and that I'm feeling like these guys watching my class are picking on me." She laughed but quickly went silent. He could see the weight of her day on her face. Maybe laughing wasn't allowed while they were on the burgundy carpet.

"Did you want me to send some of the guys over to roughen them up?" He bumped her shoulder gently.

"I don't think that will be necessary," she whispered and rested her head on his shoulder.

Dane dropped his hand over hers, allowing their fingers to tangle. "So the sweater vests can be jerks too? Maybe you were a little hasty in your prejudice against those of us who enjoy wearing quick-dry material?"

"Oh please, everyone is a victim of stereotype." Anna bumped his shoulder back. "Remember when you were surprised I taught Shakespeare?"

"I do remember the first time I laid eyes on you." That was the understatement of the year. Dane realized he was now running his thumb along her wrist, unable to keep his hands to himself and feeling an awful lot like a kid sitting in a dark corner with the most fascinating girl in school.

"See, so that was a form of prejudice too. I'm not sure when I decided sporty people annoyed me. Maybe it was because they always tried to cheat off me in high school? Besides, they're never very nice in the movies."

Dane rolled his eyes. "Sporty people? Wasn't that one of the Spice Girls?"

She laughed again and, much to his disappointment, she stood. Most likely to tell him she had to go.

"I think so. Yes, Sporty Spice. Let's leave it at the Spice Girls. You came all the way to the library to find me and while it's usually fun to argue with you, not today. Today, I need..." She stepped into him, putting her arms around his waist, and Dane was pretty sure whatever she wanted he'd be willing to give her.

"What do you need?"

"This," she said, and then she leaned into him. Something crashed in the room next to them, as if someone knocked over an entire bookcase.

Anna jumped, appeared to realize where she was, and looked at her watch. "But, I need to get to class, so—"

Before she ran off again, Dane took her beautiful face and fell into another kiss. This time was different, somewhat familiar, but mostly it was more. More relaxed, more intimate, more tongue. The woman knew how to work her tongue, which shouldn't have surprised him. There was something about her touch, as if everything she did was a question, a request for another piece of him and deeper. So far, the intimacy wasn't yet terrifying, so he was happy to answer and oblige. Dane ran his hand down the back of her blouse and came to rest on her lower back. Her hands found his shirt and pulled him closer as if she'd just realized she wasn't ready to leave either.

Chapter Fourteen

B y Saturday night, Anna had responded to the committee's e-mail and provided "report card feedback" as instructed. Hers was a sound and fair response. She was careful to keep the tone neutral and although it felt weak, she reminded herself that they held the key to her future.

Once that was done, she went home and finished painting her living room. She'd even managed to muscle her dining room table into place, and the room looked so beautiful she texted a picture to Cynda, who was on a blind date with a new guy. Hopefully this one kept his clothes on, at least while they were eating.

Anna had just finished a frozen dinner that was supposed to be lasagna and green beans but tasted more like what she imagined the baby food her niece Olive had recently started eating. Trying to muster up the energy to hang some pictures, Anna noticed her phone vibrated.

Have you ever even watched any football movies?

The Bears were away playing Oregon State, and Anna was afraid to ask if they won or not. She'd look at the score later. Instead of dwelling on whether or not Trey was still dropping the ball, Anna contemplated the question and texted Dane back.

Yes. Jerry Maguire.

Cuba Gooding Jr.'s character wasn't a jerk.

Yes, he was! Show me the money?

Well, maybe in the beginning, but the guy was under a lot of pressure. It's a crazy amount of stress to hang on to that level of success.

Please.

Anna sat on her couch with her laptop.

What about Friday Night Lights or Remember the Titans? Both incredible football movies.

Haven't seen them.

Dane sent her the emoji with the rolling eyes, and Anna felt that stupid jump in her stomach. He always managed to make her feel... light. She guessed that's what it was because even when they were disagreeing, she enjoyed talking with him, or texting in this case.

Breakfast Club? Dane texted.

He taped someone's butt together.

Her phone rang and when she answered, Dane was laughing. "I forgot about that part." The sounds of people talking and the familiar airport announcements echoed in the background. "They all made mistakes, though. The nerd brought a flare gun to school." He kept laughing. "But then they all learned, even the jock."

"Oh, yes, and that's exactly how high school works."

"Professor, you sound so... realistic. I thought that was my job. You're supposed to be the dreamer in this relationship." His voice sounded tired and sexy. It was a bit easier talking with him on the phone. His physical presence, those eyes, weren't on her.

"Relationship? Since when is our sparring a relationship?"

"Since you keep kissing me and I keep kissing you back."

"Ah, is that all it takes?"

"Pretty incredible kissing."

Anna exhaled and lay back on her couch. There it was again: the sense of belonging that hearing his voice brought her. "Yes, I suppose it was."

"I'd like to kiss you again, Anna."

"You kissed me in the library. That was what? Two days ago."

"I can't seem to get enough."

Me neither. "How's Trey?"

"Still dropping the ball, but he's flying high on those two As he got in your class, so that's some consolation."

"Is it a consolation for you?"

"Seeing as I'm a coach, specifically in charge of receivers, it makes my life difficult. But lately I'm a little stupid for you, so why not?"

"Has anyone asked him what's going on? Is it mental or is he just not good enough?"

"He's a natural talent. God-given stuff. My boss and Crazy Eyes," he whispered, "they seem to think he has some kind of block. They're working on it."

"Are you?"

"Working on his block?"

"Yes."

"No. Feelings are not my strong suit."

"Really?"

"I know, you're shocked."

"Should I be concerned about our relationship then? I mean a man who can't express his feelings is not the best choice."

Dane was quiet for a beat and Anna suddenly felt awkward. Before she could backtrack, his voice came through deep and low.

"Anna, believe me, I'd have no trouble expressing the feelings I'm having for you right now."

She felt a quick intake of breath and went from familiar to awkward in record time. What was she supposed to say to that? Should she try to be seductive too in some feeble attempt to turn him on? She sure as hell hoped not—no way was that possible without a scriptwriter.

"Too much?" Dane finally asked, rescuing her. "Yeah, I was trying to get you all turned on and hot for me, but that didn't seem to work. Let me try again. I think about you. When I'm with you, I don't want you to leave. I haven't felt this way in... ever. I guess I'm saying I've never felt this way. There, is that enough feeling for you? We can get to the naughty stuff later. I'm pretty good at naughty too."

Anna couldn't breathe. She wasn't sure which was harder to work through in her mind, the overt attraction or the bare feelings?

"You there?"

"I feel... real when I'm with you. That probably doesn't make sense, but things are touchable when you're around. And you make me laugh."

"Okay. I'll take that. Touching and laughter are both great things, right?"

Annabelle held the phone to her ear and the rush of belonging, of realizing another person "gets" her, returned. "Yes."

There was silence for a few beats.

"Anna."

"Yes."

"I think it's time for us to go to dinner."

She closed her eyes, not sure she was ready for any of this, but wanting it in a way she didn't care to think about. "I'd like that," she said before she had a chance to change her mind.

He was quiet, no response.

"Dane?"

"Yeah, sorry. I was just smiling like a complete dumbass in the middle of the airport."

She laughed again.

"Is tomorrow night too soon?"

"Technically I'm supposed to make you wait."

"Haven't you done enough of that?"

"I suppose."

"Good. Okay, we're boarding. Sleep well."

"You too." Anna ended the call. "Cupid is a knavish lad, thus to make females mad," she whispered and tried to get some work done. When that proved no use, she went to bed and for the first time, she doubted her dreams would be as wonderful as her present reality.

The game in Oregon went as expected. Big plays, some of them a mess, but it was all they had because Oregon's defense had some phenomenal guys this year. Dane knew from watching their games this season that they were not giving up one yard without a fight. Birch, who thrived on the big splash plays, managed two touchdowns, one off a running pass he delivered himself; the other was such a flawless play that when he hit the ground with the ball against his chest, "it looked like goddamn ballet out there," said Coach Hall, who was now sitting next to Dane on the plane, replaying the entire game.

Trey ran a few yards, but for the most part still looked like a deer in headlights anytime the ball got near him. They were halfway through the season. Dane was starting to feel the pressure of mediocre and Coach Hall was running out of patience. Conveniently, Crazy Eyes had moved on to other cases now that Trey's grade in her little experiment was better.

Useless, Dane thought. All that talking was absolutely useless. The kid was still in the same boat. Well, not quite. Thanks to Anna, he did seem more confident and a hell of a lot happier, except for right now. Dane looked across the dimly lit airplane and noticed Trey, earphones on, staring out the window into the dark night as if it was the middle of the day. Wide-awake, staring at nothing.

Dane took a deep breath as Coach Hall continued his assessment of what went right, but mostly what went wrong. During the course of the flight, he'd managed to "visit" with each of the assistant coaches and, lucky Dane, his was the last one and the longest.

"So, looks like you're on your own. Dr. Frasier said she's done all she can do. I guess that's how it works. Or someone has lost interest, hell if I know." He lowered his voice, leaned in, and Dane knew what was coming next.

"The thing is, the interest in him has waned, so unless the kid has some kind of revelation, I'm going to cut him."

There it was. *Shit!*

Players were cut all the time. Dane wasn't sure why this one seemed to hit him right in the center of his chest. It's not like Trey was trying and physically couldn't make it happen. Those stories were worse, weren't they?

Trey clearly didn't want to be a receiver and if nothing changed, Coach Hall was going to make quitting a whole lot easier. Dane kept his mouth shut, nodding his head, and when he looked back over, Trey was asleep.

"Maybe you should talk with him." His boss repeated the same words Anna had said on the phone. Maybe he should. It couldn't hurt at this point, but Dane wasn't sure what to say. Or maybe he did know what to say and didn't want to go there. If he was going to get to the bottom of what was going on with Trey, he would need to share some of himself, and Dane didn't know if he could do that. But if it meant this kid was going to be cut and lose his scholarship, Dane probably needed to figure something out and fast.

Chapter Fifteen

The Foreign Cinema on Mission was about twenty-five minutes from campus in light traffic, Anna learned from Dane when he called her that morning.

"I'm not sure I know what light traffic even looks like in this city, so I'll pick you up at five," he'd said.

Anna had promised not to Google the restaurant once he found out she had never been. He'd wanted it to be a surprise, which Anna found charming. In truth, she was already surprised by the excitement in his voice. Dane wasn't exactly brooding, but since she'd met him, he'd never sounded like he did on the phone. He was downright jovial, tired and jovial since he'd arrived late from Oregon.

Anna couldn't remember the last time she'd been on a real date other than the sort-of-but-no date with Steve from the bowling alley, and the hilarious blind date she'd had with one of Nude Paul's friends after Cynda had won a bet that Anna couldn't name all the kings and queens of England in order. She'd been close, but she forgot about Henry III, which was crazy because he rebuilt Westminster Abbey for heaven's sake. Anna had skipped right over him and found herself on a date with Nude Paul's friend Jacob. He was a sculptor, not a very good one based on the pictures he'd showed

Anna on his phone, but he kept his clothes on the entire date, so that was a plus.

As Anna dressed, she couldn't remember who came after she'd politely agreed to drop Jacob off at his mom's house after their date. Apparently he believed "sons belonged with their mothers." He must have registered the stunned look on her face because as they sat in her car, he asked, "Don't you think?" Anna did not, and that was the last time she saw Jacob.

Surely she'd been on other dates, but at the moment, she couldn't remember anything over the buzz of her nerves. She smoothed her dark purple dress, the wraparound one with the perfect sleeves, and took a deep breath. Nothing mattered more than somehow finding a way to relax, to get out of her neurotic head, and to enjoy her date with Dane. She'd spent months bantering back and forth with him. They'd both kissed each other practically within an inch of their lives. A simple date should be easy, but it felt surprisingly more difficult with him. So far, their conversations had been texting and witty banter. Granted, kissing him had been the real thing, but what if under normal dating circumstances, things fell quiet or turned awkward. It wouldn't be the first time reality paled in comparison to her imaginings, she thought as she slipped on her silver hoop earrings.

Get out of your silly head, Meg's voice whispered as Anna checked her mascara and her breath. She walked around her house straightening pillows and right at five, the new doorbell she'd put in over the weekend rang.

Anna opened the door to Dane in dark pants that looked like they were made for him and a denim-colored shirt, collar open, under a dark blazer. He was clean-shaven and so beautiful it almost didn't seem fair. He grinned, leaned in, and kissed her softly.

"Why the hell am I so nervous?" he whispered in her ear and stepped back. "Oh well, that's why. You look incredible."

"Thank you. I like your shirt," Anna said, somehow a little less nervous herself. Meg was right. It wasn't just his body or his lovely face, it was all of him. With one kiss, one sentence, he'd managed to take the pressure off and relate to her in a way no one, male or female, ever had before. It was as if he somehow understood who she was and why she'd spent so much of her life on the sidelines. Anna locked her door and climbed into Dane's truck.

"Are you going to tell me about this place?" Anna asked as traffic slowed to a crawl about three-quarters of the way across the Bay Bridge.

Dane shook his head.

"Hmm... awfully mysterious."

"I am incredibly mysterious. Haven't you figured that out yet?"

She laughed. "Okay. Do you want to talk about the game?"

He shook his head, a little more animated this time.

"Right. Let's see what I can come up with for pleasant first-date talk." Anna thought for a minute as they rode in silence. No radio, just the sounds of traffic, and somehow they didn't seem to need anything else.

"So why football?" she finally asked.

"Aside from the obvious answer?"

"You don't seem to ever give me the obvious anything, so okay. What's the real answer?"

She smiled and ran her hand along the door of his truck.

"I like the history, the knowledge that all of these other men have come before me. I suppose there's a sense of pride in that, being part of it all. Playing started off as a way to do something with the kids in my neighborhood, and I guess we grew into it."

Anna hadn't expected that answer or the vulnerability that her question seemed to bring onto his face. Dane was softer somehow when he talked about football, which struck her as intriguing considering the sport.

"So it's not about wanting to smash into other guys and screw all the cheerleaders?"

"Not for me, no. I guess it was when I was young and stupid, but football is strategy and tactics. There's an intelligence component to it."

"Come on."

"I'm serious. Look up any discussion about the game on the Internet or look at plays. These guys, and women, are not what is promoted and advertised all the time in beer commercials. That hype is what sells tickets, but there's more brain than muscle behind the scenes. Maybe it's not what you're used to, but they know their sport. It can be intimidating."

"Really?"

Dane nodded, and she wasn't going to argue. The traffic finally started moving again. He rolled down the windows and she looked out over the bay as the sun set. She relished the breeze on her face. This was going to be a good date.

"Favorite team?" Anna asked, her eyes sparkling as they finally moved off the bridge.

Dane quirked his brow. "What's with you and the football questions?"

"This is first-date conversation. I'm expressing an interest. Enjoy it while it lasts."

He laughed. "What was the question?" He changed lanes and hit traffic again.

"Favorite team?"

"Seriously?"

She nodded, seemingly oblivious that the answer was a given based on where they lived.

"I grew up here. In San Francisco."

"Okay."

"We have a great team. Well, maybe not always great, but they're up there," he hinted.

"So they're your favorite? What are they called again?"

Wow. She didn't even try to impress him with her Google search knowledge. She was genuinely clueless when it came to professional football and to his surprise, he found it refreshing.

"I prefer college ball, but I support the 49ers," Dane said.

"What does that mean, you support them? You buy their T-shirts or you have a bumper sticker?"

He laughed. "Neither. I watch them play, appreciate their talent. I'm not a fan, I support them."

"So fans are those ridiculous people who paint their bodies, and you're not that?"

"Hey, your snob is showing. Fans are important, and they're only having fun. It's harmless and had I not been on the field at USC, I might have painted my chest."

"Okay. And I'm not a snob. I honestly don't see the point of pouring money into sports and getting so pumped up over a ball and some guys chasing after it."

"I could say the same about the theater."

"No, you could not." Anna's expression was adamant disagreement glossed over with a heavy dose of snob.

Dane nodded. "It's all the same, Anna. Different packaging. Boxed wine and black dresses versus tailgates and a keg, but it's all watching, cheering, and getting into something. Yours is simply more... refined or bullshit. Depends how you look at it."

"I'm not going to argue with you. You have your thing, and I do find sports good for children. There's a sense of team and community that is admirable, but I don't get the grown men dancing around or being nasty to their wives all in the name of some game." Anna raised her voice, and Dane found the rise even more fascinating.

"Being mean to their wives? Is that some kind of statistic?"

"Yes, actually. More men beat their wives on Super Bowl Sunday than any other day of the year."

Dane laughed. He didn't mean to, but coming from an educated woman, the statement was ridiculous.

She shook her head and now that he knew her, he recognized the tension, the pissed-off energy.

"How exactly do they measure something like that? What day of the year do more men who go to the opera beat their wives?"

She looked out the window, and Dane realized he even enjoyed debating with her. So much for nice first-date conversation.

"Before you start freaking out on me, I'm not saying domestic violence isn't a big problem, nor am I saying it is funny. What I am saying is that statement makes no sense to me and it seems to say that men who watch football beat their wives more than say, men who watch tennis?"

Anna said nothing; she was watching him.

"Come on, you have to see that." He turned onto Mission and drove past a few unassuming flat buildings, one that looked as if someone had placed a piece of a museum front on top of a garage. They were close. Now if he could coax her into the restaurant before he managed to piss her off even more...

"I believe football creates a culture of drinking and aggressive behavior. Maybe the statement is inaccurate, but professional sports is dripping in misogyny. Funny, when I go to the opera, the ushers aren't walking around with their bottoms hanging out."

He guffawed. "Bottoms?"

She pulled on the sweater she'd been holding in her lap, and Dane could have sworn the thing was her armor.

They'd pulled into the lot across from the restaurant. "Hey, I'm sorry." He reached out and touched her hand, but she pulled away.

"You're mocking me."

He held back a laugh with all his strength because he wanted to kiss her more now than when he'd picked her up.

"I am not." He turned off the car and was surprised when she leaned over and kissed him. Maybe being pissed off turned her on? *Noted.*

"We are not going to agree on this. I don't see value in sports and you think I'm an uptight snob. There's not much left to discuss."

Dane held his hands up in surrender. "Can we agree to disagree?"

She was still glaring at him when she kissed him again. It was like there was some kind of internal struggle going on. He guessed it had something to do with that thin line between love and hate. Wasn't that how the song went? She pulled back from the kiss, took off her sweater, and draped it over the passenger seat. When he walked around and opened her door, her eyes softened and he realized she wasn't only sunshine. Her eyes were also the ocean on a rainy day. She was mesmerizing.

"I suppose. As colleagues, both responsible for young and impressionable lives, we should be civil."

"Colleagues, huh? Come here, Professor Jeffries." Dane wrapped his arm around her waist and pulled her close as they crossed the street.

She turned to him right before the door. "I like you. I haven't figured out why yet, but when I'm with you I'm... I don't look at my watch anymore." There was a strange experience hidden behind the innocence in her eyes. He had no doubt the full force of the woman would take him to the ground.

"I like you too, Anna," he barely managed to get out as he reached for the door like some kind of lifeline.

"Did I tell you we are up to Bottom's scenes in *Midsummer*?" Anna asked as they approached the hostess. It was a direct effort to move off her moment of vulnerability out there in the sunset. Dane recognized the pullback.

"Bottom? You teach about bottoms in your class. Professor, what about the children?"

She looked back over her shoulder as they stood waiting to be seated. She was going to say something. He could almost see it on her soft pink lips, but she held back. Maybe it was that they were out in public now. As he watched her eyes widen once they walked farther into the restaurant and she saw the huge outdoor movie screen, he would have taken a two-game penalty to know what happened when Anna held nothing back.

Their table was small and off to the side while still within viewing distance of the huge outdoor screen. Movie or no movie, the place was cool, but when the Disney castle splashed on the screen, Anna beamed. Dane felt like he'd pulled off a good first date. When she sighed as the French music that began *Ratatouille* played, he was certain things had gone from good to great.

"Have you seen this one?" she asked, giving him a glimpse into the little girl she must have been. Curious and interested.

He nodded, looking more at her than at the screen. "Nieces, remember?"

"That's right. I think this might be one of my favorites. It's such a clever concept. A cooking rat in a restaurant."

They ordered crab cakes and some bread. Anna selected the bottle of wine after Dane finished talking with the owner about how the place came to be. It had started as a foreign cinema and evolved into an incredible restaurant with a different movie each week.

"I'll bet you like foreign films," Dane said once they were alone again.

"No." She spread butter on her bread. "I like movies and I like reading, but not together, so if I do watch something foreign, I shut off the subtitles."

"Do you speak other languages?"

She shook her head and took a bite of her bread. "My sisters do. Hollis speaks four now, I think."

"Wow."

"Yes, it is impressive."

"So how do you know what's going on if you don't have subtitles?"

"You can get the basic plot with most of them. I usually only watch romance so... I guess I speak the language of love because I get gushy and weepy even though I don't know the words."

At some point their dinner arrived, but Dane was too busy watching her watch the movie. It was a cartoon, albeit an incredible one, but the way she was drawn in, it could have been a documentary. She was open to it, intrigued by the simple just as much as the complicated. Dane had a hard time looking away.

"There's a little romance in this one if I remember."

Anna beamed. "There is." She looked up at the night sky peeking through the strands of light that hung between the open courtyard above them. Dane had to admit it was a romantic place and somehow, being here with her made simple gestures seem even more important. They ate, laughed, and enjoyed the movie. He walked her to the door a little after one in the morning and when she whispered, "Perfect first date," in his ear, he felt everything shift.

What had started as fun and physical was turning down a road he'd sworn he would steer clear of for the rest of his life. His sanity depended on keeping things at a distance, not getting too involved. When he kissed Anna goodnight in the moonlight, her beautiful face looked up at him in a way he'd never seen before—like she was letting him in on a secret. She closed her eyes, rested her head on his chest, and without a word, went into her house. Something changed. They both knew it, and they both seemed equally terrified.

Dane started his truck.

It was one date, he told himself on the drive home. There was no commitment and he could pull back at any time.

Sure, you keep telling yourself that, kid, said a voice he recognized, but hadn't heard in years.

Chapter Sixteen

When Anna arrived at her office the next morning, there were flowers on her desk. Snapdragons and lilies. The beautiful glass vase spilled over with purple and white, soft pink, and waxy green. She dropped her bag and her lunch box right where she stood and slowly walked toward the desk. Her hand ran across the polished wood and up toward the small ivory-colored envelope perched right above the blooms. Closing her eyes, Anna knew they were from him. He'd sent her flowers of all things, and not grocery store flowers. Not that it would have mattered, but these were gesture flowers. Like the difference between saying "Hi" and "Hello." As her fingers touched the card, she leaned in to smell the soft fragrance. There were lilacs in there too.

Her thumb flipped the card open and her chest stuttered, just as a child's might at the surprise of a birthday cake blazing with candles being brought to the table.

There's no way I'm quoting Will, so I'll stick with what I know.

The Avett Brothers sing about a woman with eyes that shine like stolen dimes.

That song reminds me of you, Anna.

I had a great time. Hope you did too.

Dane

She pressed the card to her chest as if it would somehow help her breathe.

Who are you, Dane Sivac? She found her phone and called him, completely ignoring the manila envelope also on her desk. She recognized the handwriting and would deal with that later. Right now, she was going to be happy.

Sending flowers wasn't exactly the best way to pull back, Dane thought on his way to practice that night. She deserved flowers, though, and he wanted to buy them for her, so he did. Simple as that. The rest would sort itself out, or it wouldn't. Aw, hell, he was tired of thinking.

He finished practice with seven-on-seven and hoped to God Trey figured his stuff out soon because after his conversation with Hall on the plane, the pressure had become worse. No one cared anymore about Trey's potential. The vultures were circling, and Dane wouldn't be surprised if they cut him right after the Big Game.

Dane didn't want that to happen. In fact, he had not wanted to see something turn around so bad since he was the one on the field trying to figure out why at his own peak shape he could never get his head together. Trey's father was absent too. Maybe that had something to do with it, but he had brothers and uncles. The kid was loved and supported. There was no reason for him to hear the footsteps, and yet there was nothing Dane could do to fix him. Trey needed to do that all on his own.

Dane watched the drill, prickly with impatience he tried to ignore. Trey came out of the slot and knew his route. Honestly, the kid could track a ball in the dark. The ball hadn't even been snapped yet and Dane could see Trey tense, looking around. If he could put blinders on Trey's helmet, he would. After the snap, Trey followed his route. Redding, second quarterback, fired. It was too high, but catchable. Trey was right *there*. From a strictly physical standpoint, the play was in the bag, but Dane saw it probably before Trey even felt it and when Trey's feet left the ground, Dane blinked. The jump was so small he thought something must have happened. There weren't even fireworks, no big hit, nothing except a weak shoulder whip.

Come on, Trey!

Dane threw his clipboard on the chair in a fury that had been building for weeks. He wasn't sure he'd be able to reel his frustration back in even if he wanted to. He stormed onto the field, and the players cleared a path as if he were a locomotive about to blow. Trey stood there, head low, frozen in place. Dane wanted to feel for him, throw his arm around the kid and tell him yet another motivational story or let him know there would be a next time, but that's not what happened.

"Duncan." He was right in his face, could see the beads of sweat across his forehead. "Do me a favor, could you check your damn pants and make sure there's something down there because I swear to God I'm beginning to wonder."

Trey said nothing, but his breathing faltered and Dane, seeing no other way to reach him, reverted to old school trash talk. "If"—Dane bent to catch Trey's eyes, which were glass and looking right through him as if he knew what was coming—"if and when you find something down there, you can get the hell back on my field. Until then"—Dane shook his head in disgust and walked away—"stairs!"

Lively, a freshman that talked way more than he played, must have found his balls because he stepped into Dane's path and said, "Coach, are we all doing stairs, or just Duncan?"

"Get the hell out of my face, Lively." Dane turned and saw Trey begin stairs as the field lights went on and the sun began to set. "We're done. Back tomorrow morning at five," Dane said to the rest of the guys and stormed toward the locker room. That scene wasn't the answer, Dane knew that, stairs never fixed a player any more than talking about his feelings did. But the kid wasn't screwing himself without a fight and somewhere, probably under that bed where Dane shoved all of his other messy emotions, it pissed him off to no end.

✳   ✳   ✳

Almost thirty minutes later, Dane walked back out to the field lit now only by the overhead lights. He picked up a left-behind water bottle and someone's black T-shirt. As he approached, he heard the tapping of Trey's cleats first and looked up to find him dragging but still making his way down in the rhythmic cadence of an athlete at home with fatigue. Dane sat, looking out to the field.

"Done, Duncan. Take a seat."

Trey grunted, turned, and went back up for one more lap before throwing himself onto the metal bench next to Dane. It was an act of defiance, a "screw you, I can do this all night long," and Dane almost smiled.

They sat in silence for a few minutes, nothing but the guzzling sound of Trey emptying a water bottle and the sprinklers kicking on somewhere.

"I don't know what else to do, man. Help me out here?"

"It's getting better."

"No." Dane pivoted to face him. "No, it's not. Your hands aren't there in practice, forget losing the ball in the game. I can't even get you there against our own guys."

"Fine. I'm letting everyone down. Cut my ass and let's be done with it." Trey slammed his helmet on the railing.

"Is that what you want? Is that what this is about? Self-sabotage?"

"Aw, Coach, don't quote the shrink lady or we'll have to check for your balls next."

It was disrespectful. Dane should have said something, but he didn't. He was running out of energy. What else could he do to get through to the kid?

"They're there, asshole. If that's not it, then what is it?"

Trey sat, his face in his hands. "I don't know. Don't you think if I knew I would fix it? The shrink lady keeps trying to get in my head about my dad leaving, and maybe that's it. Maybe she's right."

"Your dad?" Dane was suddenly aware of his blood rushing under the surface of his skin. Like one of those science films where the camera zooms in.

"He left. It's been like two years now, so I'm not sure where she comes up with this stuff, but I do worry about my mom, so maybe."

Dane swallowed. "You've talked to the shrink about your dad?"

Trey nodded.

"What did she say?"

"Oh, you know, that I have abandonment issues, that I'm fearful because my family unit is broken. Blah, blah, blah. None of that tells me how to keep the ball, so I'm not sure why this school is paying for me to lie around on a couch."

"Because you're talented. The kind of talent we haven't seen in a long time. You were picked by Head Coach Hall. He sees what you have, Trey. Now you need to see it."

"All I see when I'm at the end of my route is my bone sticking out of my leg or my head being bashed in. I tried the visualization and the damn mantras, but I can't get it out of my mind."

Dane was quiet. He was trying to regulate his breathing as a flood of emotions crashed over him. The sky was darker now.

"I'm all they have and what if I get hurt, you know? I read those articles, reports. I'm not some dumb bag of meat. I know what happens to us, to guys like me when our heads are slammed around too many times. It's not just the defense. I don't want that, and what if my mama ends up having to take care of me? She's already lost my dad. I don't want that either, so I bring all that crap up there with me."

"No wonder I can't get your ass off the ground."

Trey snickered and bumped Dane with his pads.

Dane knew how he was feeling, the weight and responsibility, even though their situations weren't the same. He knew what it was to lose a father, to feel the world shift. He wanted to help Trey, but he wasn't sure how to offer advice. Then he thought of what Anna said on their date when the conversation shifted to teaching and how she dealt with different students. "I try to get through, and occasionally that means sharing a part of myself and letting them see that I'm human. Sometimes nothing works, but all you can do is try, right?"

Dane took in a breath. "I lost my dad when I was nineteen."

Trey looked out over the field, clearly not ready to deal with his feelings either.

"It's tough. Mine didn't leave, he died. I guess it's the same thing. I didn't handle it the best way. I basically lost myself for a few years."

"Yeah?"

Dane looked at him. "Yeah. I put my mom and sister through some trouble. At least you're worried about your mom, but you're also angry at your dad, so I'm sure the shrink is saying you need to deal with that."

Trey nodded.

"You don't have to play."

"Oh come on, I'm black. Full scholarship to Cal. This is a big deal."

"It's a big deal for anyone, any color, Trey."

"Said the white guy."

"Why does this need to be about skin? Most receivers are black. True statement. But I was a receiver in college, one of exactly one white guy catching the ball. That means there's color all over the field."

Trey shook his head. "Fine, I'll give you that down there in the trenches, it's dark." Trey gestured to the empty turf in front of them. "But up here where the decisions are made, it's pearly white. Sometimes it reminds me of the coliseums. You know, the Greeks letting the less important guys, the poorer guys fight to the death while they sat up high eating grapes?"

Dane couldn't argue, so he didn't. "You're right."

"I am?"

Dane laughed, probably for the first time all day. "Yeah. The people in power, the guys handing out your scholarships or deciding if you play or don't play are probably white. But that's changing. Slow as a grandma with a walker, but it is."

This time Trey laughed and pulled off his pads.

"What does any of this have to do with you catching and holding on to that ball?"

"I'm scared," he said, loud enough that there was a slight echo. "I don't want to be a statistic. I want a whole life, not just what's offered to me because I can catch a ball. Maybe this isn't worth risking it all. I only get one neck."

Dane nodded.

"I'd say it's a little more like chocolate milk. We have some flavor now. Bro, brother..."

Trey laughed, his full chest rumbling. "Stop, please..."

Dane joined him and was thankful for Anna's advice.

"Why'd you quit? The pressure?" Trey asked.

"No. I was good under pressure and for a while, I didn't care if someone brought me to the ground. I was in so much pain, there were times it felt good. I gave up my junior year because I couldn't control my drinking after I lost my dad."

"Oh, sorry."

"Don't be sorry. It was a long time ago. I'm telling you this so that you can do things differently. You don't need to be an adult right now, Trey. Your mom seems more than capable of raising you and your sisters. Maybe let the shrink help you figure out your feelings and fix it. Because you're good. Without even trying, you're better than I would have ever been. You could catch that ball in your sleep, but if you don't want it, then it's time to pack it in. For what it's worth, I'd be as happy watching you dance around Ms. Jeffries' classroom."

Trey bumped him again, this time hard, and Dane wobbled. They sat in silence for a couple of minutes, nothing but the bugs zapping in the lights and Trey's helmet bouncing on his knee.

"That sucks that your dad died."

"Yeah. It sucks that yours left, but we need to take care of our own lives, right?"

Trey nodded and when Dane stood to leave, Trey stayed behind. Right before Dane entered the locker room, he looked back and saw Trey with his face in his hands.

"There you go. Cry," Dane whispered to himself.

Dane had never cried unless he was drunk, which he was quite often in college, now that he thought about it. At the time he'd make sure he was alone. He hated the weakness, thought crying was a waste of time, but now, with some distance from himself at that age, he thought it maybe it had helped him find his way back.

Crying was a release, even if he'd locked himself in a room at some stupid party and cried until he had nothing left. Every time, he must have left a little of the pain behind because he eventually stopped doing it, stopped doing things to numb the pain, stopped feeling guilty he'd let his father down. There must have been something to the crying—it led him out of a place he never knew existed. A place where his being was wrapped up in another person so tightly that the pain of loss all but consumed him.

"Love does that," his mother had said one night, crying herself when he showed up at her doorstep.

"Not to me, it doesn't," he'd said. "Never again."

Dane had an almost ominous feeling that if his feelings for Anna grew any more, if he didn't find a way to put the brakes on this thing, he would eat those words in the near future. Probably choke on them.

Chapter Seventeen

*A*nna eventually opened the manila envelope. It was a copy of a complaint from two students in her class as well as a request that she meet with the dean to discuss her side of the story. Anna felt the anger build at the back of her neck. She had never had a complaint, had never even seen this type of paperwork before. Her class was an open place. There was always room for debate, disagreement, but this felt cheap.

Apparently, Mr. James Swift, freshman and only son to the Swift Produce family, and Mr. Thomas Granville, also a freshman and middle son to the San Rafael Granvilles, whatever that meant, were insulted during the second month of Anna's class. They didn't come forward then because they "didn't feel anyone would listen," according to the complaint.

More like they weren't failing her class back then, Anna thought a few hours later as she sat across from the dean. She made an effort to focus on the painting of a ship that hung in the dean's office. Something seemed off about the perspective, either the ship was too big or the waves lacked dimension. Anna wasn't sure which it was. All she knew was the painting was bad, but it was a distraction that kept her from screaming.

"The point is, Professor Jeffries, that Jimmy and Tommy have not felt comfortable in your class since day one and they feel that you give preferential treatment to athletes. Do you feel there is that bias in your class?"

"No," Anna said. *How is this happening?*

She didn't deserve this. Those students were spoiled, entitled shi... *Deep breath. Be the ugly ship.* They were failing because they both received zeros for cheating on the *Macbeth* final. She should have reported them. Berkeley had zero tolerance for cheating, but she had given them a second chance. *And look where that got you.*

She wanted to say something, but she'd spoken to her father when she received the complaint and he, of course, had called his lawyer. Her family was pretty sure he had that guy on speed dial. Mr. Tom Stranham had advised Anna to speak as little as possible and to forward any deposition or notes to his office. If Tom felt she was in any real danger of losing her job, he would be on the next plane.

Lose her job? Anna had felt everything spin in her tiny kitchen when she had hung up with her father. How had things gotten so out of hand?

"Why were both boys singled out that day when they were simply trying to engage in discussion?" the dean asked. "According to them, you only wanted to hear from Mr. Duncan, is that correct?"

"They were not singled out. They were asked to refrain from making inappropriate remarks. Mr. Duncan had been called on and was going to answer a question, and they were rude."

"I see." The only other woman in the room was sitting next to Anna and taking notes. The dean held up his hand to her, and she stopped typing. Dean Bradley closed the folder in front of him and placed his clasped hands gently on top.

"Professor Jeffries, as with a lot of these complaints, it's a matter of he said, she said. Both of these boys are decent students in their other classes, and both sets of parents are very good friends of the university."

Friends with their parents' money, Anna thought.

"It is suspicious that these young men didn't step forward immediately, but at the same time, it is... unique that the only football player in your class is getting an A in Shakespeare."

Anna motioned to speak, and he held up his hand to her too as if she were a dog. She remained quiet.

"I'm sure you have better things to do with your time than go back and forth on this, so here's what I would like to see happen. Let's give these two boys an assignment that will allow them to raise their grade above failing, provided, of course, they meet whatever criteria you put forth, and finish out the year without incident."

Anna nodded. She was livid, but there was nothing she could say.

"At the same time, I have received some reports from the tenure committee. I'm sure you are aware they are observing your classes as part of your application."

"I am."

"They have sent you report cards and observations?"

"They have."

"Good. Okay, so let's give Mr. Swift and Mr. Granville a fair shake and at the same time, please review those comments from the committee. A... vibrant classroom can be exciting, Professor, but let's make sure things are under control."

Anna gave a tight smile. Her head felt heavy as the room swirled a bit. She wasn't sure she could stand until she actually did. She thanked the dean for his time and promptly walked to the entrance. Placing her hand on a cold stone wall, she tried to regain her balance.

After a few breaths, Anna left Wheeler Hall, got in her car, and drove home. She didn't have class until three thirty and if she still felt the way she did in that moment, English 117 Shakespeare would be canceled for the first time since she started teaching at Berkeley.

"It's two weeks before Thanksgiving. So you received a complaint. Isn't that the sign of a kick-ass teacher? Remember when Robin Williams stood on the desks in that movie? He got all kinds of complaints from uptight parents and students." Meg was calling from their parents' house. Although Anna wanted to be excited that her sister was finally home and she would see her in two weeks, for the first time in her life, the movie analogy was not working.

"*Dead Poets Society*," Anna mumbled as she looked through her front window at the hedges that still needed to be trimmed.

"Yeah, that's the one."

"This isn't a movie, Meg."

"Oh well, excuse me. I've definitely been gone too long. When did you turn reality on me?"

Anna warmed at the sound of her voice. It was good to know she was so near. Meg had a way of making even the big stuff seem small. She'd been to the principal's office more than all of her sisters combined, and Anna supposed that gave her the sense of "no big deal" she needed at this particular moment.

"I have to give them some assignment so they can bring up their grade."

"Maybe you should give those little twits *King Lear,* or who's the guy with the hump?"

"*Richard III*?" Anna laughed.

"Yeah, that guy. Make them write a… recipe book as if they were Richard III." Meg snorted. "Oh wow, remember when I had to do that in like fifth grade. Write a recipe book as if you were Betsy Ross?"

More laughing, and Anna could see her sister's mocking face in her mind. God, she'd missed Meg.

"It has to be related to the two plays we're doing in class: *Macbeth* and *A Midsummer Night's Dream*."

"Okay, how about they have to dress up like Lady Macbeth and… sing. Yeah, make them sing."

Anna shook her head and looked at the clock on her microwave. "Okay. Well, thanks for all of this advice, but I need to get going or I'll be late for class."

"So you are going. See, I made you feel better. Sometimes you have to laugh these things off, sis, or you'll lose your mind. You know?"

Anna leaned against the wall, taking some of the weight off her legs. She was tired. So tired of explaining herself. But Meg was right, laughing did help. For now.

"I do. Thank you."

"Anytime. I'm going to see you in no time unless you need me to come down there and kick some sweater-vest ass?"

Anna laughed. Meg was right—it felt good. "I'll take care of it, but thanks."

"You're welcome. I'm going to go help Mom make pie crust now, so if one of us is missing when you get here, you know what happened."

"I love you, little sister."

"Me too." Meg ended the call.

Anna felt like she was going to cry, but she didn't have time. She needed to show up to her class, needed to look Mr. Swift and Mr. Granville in the eyes. She was made of much tougher stuff than she often realized. Maybe she *would* make them sing, she thought as she grabbed her keys.

Dane was covered in sweat. They'd won against Arizona State, which was saying something because their new quarterback was a hybrid. The kid threw and ran. It was incredible to watch but not so great for ASU as a whole, Dane guessed. It didn't matter—Cal took the game by twelve points, all twelve in some way thanks to Trey. He was still not what Dane had seen from his high school footage, but he was better. He'd scored a touchdown, ran countless yards, and while there was still something missing, Dane felt like their little heart-to-heart had helped. At least the kid was off Coach Hall's chopping block. For now.

Yesterday, Dane had woken up in the middle of the night, bolted right up in bed, heart pounding because of a dream.

He had dreamed only once about his dad two weeks after he died and never did again. In that dream, they were in some maze and no matter how fast Dane ran, he could only catch glimpses of his father. When he reached the end of the maze, there was nothing but an empty dirt field with a fishing boat in the middle. There was no water. His father was gone. Yeah, the shrink his mother sent him to had a party dissecting that thing. Dane had dismissed it all as stupid in his storm of anger that his father had left him behind.

But the dream he'd had last night was different. Dane was at a diner he didn't recognize, and a trucker came in and sat across from him. The guy was holding up a newspaper, or maybe it was a map, and Dane couldn't see his face. Specifics were a little fuzzy on that now that he was awake. The guy was silent for a long time, until he said, "You know where you're going, kid?" He lowered the map or newspaper, and Dane found himself looking into his father's eyes for the first time in over fifteen years. It woke him up, breathless and immediately sad that he hadn't stayed in the dream.

So, that's why he had once again told Jeb to go have fun while Dane hit the gym. It was all these feelings. That's what was bringing everything to the surface.

Of course Anna topped his list of feeling inducers. He hadn't seen her in three days. He'd talked to her briefly that morning, but she was short and stressed about something to do with her students. Dane found out she had a meeting with the dean, but that was about it. He'd heard her voice, but he had not seen her since their date, which was fine. Totally fine. Except that he started wanting her the minute he opened his eyes in the morning and that didn't go away until he finally fell asleep at night. Yet another reason why he stopped by the gym, why he was sweaty and disgusting as he pulled up to his house a little after ten.

He was tired of thinking and when he wasn't thinking, he was feeling. He went into coaching in an effort to avoid all things warm and fuzzy. What the hell was wrong with the world?

Chapter Eighteen

*A*nna had read Act V of *A Midsummer Night's Dream* hundreds of times. She knew it was filled with latent sexuality and innuendo. That's why she was carefully going over her lecture to make sure she had appropriate responses when they read it in class in two weeks. She had not taught *Midsummer* at Berkeley yet and while most of her students would barely understand some of the more obscure references, Anna wanted to be sure. The lecture wouldn't take place until after Big Game Week, so maybe everyone would be too tired to notice, especially the tenure committee. All she needed was for them to stop by while she was discussing Pyramus and Thisbe's dirty talk.

Preparation was key, but her immediate problem—as she stood in her kitchen eating snap peas and waiting for her tea water to boil—was why something written as a comedy, in the language of the late-1600s, something she'd read and dissected so many times, was suddenly turning her on. Clearly she was losing her mind. She could not stop thinking of Dane or the things she imagined doing to him. Imagination was the key word there because Anna was pretty sure if faced with Dane in her kitchen, she would not even know where to start.

That's not true. But it was. She was out of practice, not that she was ever that comfortable in the saddle anyway. Anna laughed at another

Cynda phrase and tried to return to the lecture notes, but it was no use. She wanted to find out. She wanted him naked and even though she had no idea how to go about that, stopping by his house at a quarter to eleven at night suddenly seemed like a good place to start.

Anna pulled off her socks. Even she knew they weren't sexy, but she left the sweatpants and the tank top on. He was into sports, she told herself as she grabbed her keys. This was a mistake, some voice, probably her mother's, whispered, but Anna, most likely fueled by her anger at the complaint, didn't care. She was tired of playing by the rules, tired of answering to other people and cowering to authority. She wanted sex, and she wanted it with Dane.

Honestly, what woman wouldn't?

As she turned onto his street, she of course had second thoughts, but she dismissed them. She had been waiting in the wings her whole life, allowing others to go first, stepping aside. For one night she was going to take what she wanted and if she fell on her face, if he didn't want her, then she'd blame it all on Will.

Dane had showered and eaten rice for what felt like the tenth time this week. The novelty of the rice maker was wearing off now. He'd stopped grilling vegetables and was now eating it right out of the machine. Grabbing a bottle of water, he hit the lights in his kitchen when the doorbell rang. Glancing at the clock on the rice maker, he opened the door to find Anna in tight sweatpants and a tank top with... no bra. The late-night chill had confirmed it even as she folded her arms across her chest. Professor Anna Jeffries was at his front door a little before eleven at night with no bra on. Dane was waiting for one of those booming sports announcer voices to chime in and exclaim, "That's right, ladies and gentlemen, Christmas has come early for Dane Sivac."

"Anna." He tried to direct his attention back to her eyes, but there were some things that were damn near impossible.

"You have a lovely yard. Who does your landscaping?" she asked, clearly freezing, as if she were a neighbor borrowing sugar.

"I do." He gently pulled her into his house and closed the door.

"I never pictured myself with someone like you, someone who looked like you," Anna said, turning on him as he locked the door, as if she suddenly needed to clear the air.

He laughed. "What does that mean?"

"I suppose I thought I'd find a quiet, smaller guy. You know? Maybe someone who wore vests."

Dane couldn't take it anymore. He kissed her. Her lips were cold, but he fell into a warmth he had not realized he was missing. When she eased back, a little less chilled now, Dane moved to her neck.

"I took Latin in college."

Latin? Okay. He stopped kissing her neck but still held her close.

"It was a tough class, mainly because I wasn't good at it."

"Anna." Their eyes met, and Dane was drowning in the reasons he wanted her.

"I'm not going to be good at this. It's not my priority. I focus on other things and you are built for this, your body is... well, it's impressive. Like a master's thesis in touchable yum."

Dane held her hand as it reached for his chest. "Cynda?"

"Yes, but I think she has it right. You are yummy."

He laughed. "Let's stick with your words. I can't concentrate when you say yummy."

"I'm more in my head, you know, and I'm sure you are more..."

"I'm more what?"

"Physical. Touching you, being here, is like Latin. I have no idea what I'm doing or where to start." Her hands fell to his chest. "I was at home reading and it's kind of a sexual part in the play and I found myself so—" As if lost in thoughts he wanted in on, Anna's fingers gently woke up every nerve in his body.

"Turned on?" he asked, and when her entire face went bright red, he should have registered she was sweet or innocent, but he couldn't get the idea of Anna home alone and turned on out of his head. He needed to slow down or he was going to take her right up against the wall.

"If I ask you something, could you not get pissed or offended?"

"I guess."

"Sex. Are you comfortable, have you ever?"

"Oh. My. God. I'm thirty-two, Dane. You think I'm some kind of old spinster virgin? Yes, I have had sex before. I just told you I was getting all hot and steamy at home."

"Often?"

"I am not telling you how many times I've had sex."

He laughed. "I'm not asking you to tell me how many times, but you seem nervous. Turned on and hot as hell, but nervous."

"This was a bad idea." She squirmed in his arms.

"Can I get you to give your mind a break?" He ran the back of his hand along her neck, across her collarbone.

"I'm not good at that."

"I know, but I would really like to have sex with you, Anna. Is that why you're here?"

She smiled, not meeting his eyes, and nodded. There was something incredibly sexy about a brilliant woman simply wanting sex.

"I have no doubt that anything you'd like to do with my body will be... appreciated," he continued and lifted her chin until their eyes met. "And, I'd really like to learn what drives yours crazy. I'd like to taste you, slide inside, and start all over again. Do you understand what I'm saying?"

She nodded and for once seemed at a loss for words.

"And you want that too?"

Again, a nod.

"Great. I can't do all of those things if you are talking and thinking me dizzy."

"Oh, teach me how to forget to think."

When the hell did Shakespeare get so sexy?

"Comedy?"

Anna shook her head slowly, eyes still on him and mind still whirling. "Tragedy. *Romeo and Juliet*. Act I, Scene I actually. Before he even meets Juliet. It could be said that one line caused everything else to unravel. You know a lot of people think *Romeo and Juliet* is romantic, but it's the opposite. It's a cautionary tale against romance and blind love."

He couldn't stop listening. Couldn't care less about Romeo or Juliet, but she was so beautiful when she talked about things that flew right over his head.

"So, Romeo stopped thinking and that's how he ended up on the balcony?"

Anna nodded. "Neither of them were paying attention. Are you asking me to stop thinking? Because I'm sure you read it in high school, or at the very least, saw Leonardo DiCaprio in the movie. It doesn't end well for them."

He kissed her and was rewarded when the softest moan escaped her mouth as his lips traveled down her neck again. "Keep thinking, Anna. I'm guessing you have a pretty active imagination, so use that. Think about me, think about what you want and tell me."

She laughed, her head falling back. "That's not going to happen. I'm not a talker."

Grinning, he took her hands, kissed them, and led her toward his bedroom. She squeezed his hands and he was again taken by how delicate she was, at least physically. He had been playing or involved in football his whole life and was always middle of the pack weight and height wise, but next to her, he felt like a giant. Anna kept talking.

"I mean not like that. I don't say things like that."

He kissed her shoulder. "You're beautiful, Anna."

Her chest seemed to be begging for breath. "You are too."

Oh Christ, he was in trouble. Big trouble.

"I like your house," she said right before he scooped her up and carried her the rest of the way down the hall.

He was sure she would see it as a romantic gesture, but the truth was he couldn't wait one more second.

Dane lay her on the bed and gently lowered himself on top of her.

"I'm not going to lie. I've thought about this." His voice was low and mischievous against her ear.

Anna's skin warmed and she touched his shoulders. "Something else we have in common."

She leaned up to unbutton his shirt and when he threw it aside, she made a sound she barely recognized. He was more beautiful than she could have imagined and so incredibly real at the same time. He wasn't some guy in a movie or some perfect specimen described in a book. His skin was smooth, except for a scar on the right side of his chest. His stomach was flat and firm, but not photoshopped. He was her own private fantasy, sexier than anything she'd ever seen or read. "Do you have a game plan, Coach?"

He pulled her sweatpants down her legs and gently ran his fingers along the exposed skin of her side. She couldn't breathe.

"I'm already turned on, Anna. You can save the football talk for next time."

She laughed, and so did he as he pulled her on top of him. "Next time, huh? You seem pretty confident." She was straddling him now, looking down into those soulful eyes that softened in a way she'd never seen before as she moved across his body. "Maybe this is a one-and-done thing for me, you know? A booty call."

His chest rumbled as he gently lifted her tank top over her head, which was good considering her hands were shaking. His eyes went dark and it was as if he knew talking helped calm her nerves.

"You've been hanging out with Trey too long. One and done? Where else would you have heard that?"

"I'm telling you, it's fascinating. Do you know what 'goals' means?" Anna asked, bringing a hand up instinctively to cover herself, but Dane stopped her hand and gently placed it back on his chest.

"Yes. They say things like 'girlfriend goals' or 'arm goals.' It's annoying," he said.

"I think it's clever. Did you know Shakespeare made up words too? Lots of them."

Anna, stop talking, please. Are you looking at that chest? Look down, big sister, and shut up. Meg climbed into her head just in time because a moment later Dane flipped her back on the bed and kissed her as if it was the most important part of making love.

Making love? Were they in love, is that what this was? *Shhh.* Anna could never shut off her brain, but she could quiet it. It didn't matter if they were in love yet. They cared about each other and she'd said she wanted sex. *Kiss the man, Annabelle. Kiss the hell out of him.* Anna wondered if there were many women who heard the voices of not one but two sisters in their heads. Thanks, Hollis. Her older sister's raunchy advice would certainly show up during a booty call. Seemed about right.

Anna ran her hands along the strength of his shoulders and fell back into the kiss. She loved kissing. The kiss was always her favorite part in movies. It was often more intimate than sex and while her sex life up until this point had been pretty uneventful, she'd had some lovely kisses. None like this one, though. As they twisted and undressed one another, the difference hit her square in the chest. This one was different—every touch, every caress seemed as though it were her first—because she did love him. She loved him with every part of her romantic heart. Dane held her face, kissed her slow, deep, and she suddenly felt like she had a secret she wasn't sure how to share. She'd always been good at hiding, but never at keeping secrets.

Dane stood and grabbed something off his dresser. For a moment Anna wondered how many of those he had or how many women he'd had. She thought about asking, but the bathroom light cast a glow over his strong and resplendent body, and her chest swelled, searching for air. There was a moment of panic when her mind returned. How was she ever going to recover when whatever this was played itself out? When he realized he wanted a cheerleader, a little wife who would take their kids to practice and barely crack a book before falling asleep exhausted? When he figured out what he truly wanted and she was a phase or a booty call? What then?

Dane's warm and naked body slid next to her and by the time his arms wrapped around her, she listened to Will's words and gave up thinking. Gave up the game of hide-and-seek and allowed herself to be found.

Moving the hair off Dane's forehead, she was once again struck by his lovely face. The angles, the curve of his mouth, and the depth of his eyes that would forever remind her of the darkest blue paint, the paint in...van Gogh's *Starry Night*. That was it. That was the color she'd been searching for since their eyes first met. The color was familiar, a distinct rich purple-blue. She'd spent the last few months trying to place that color. Now, as he moved inside of her, their bodies in rhythm with one another, Anna realized it was van Gogh. Sweet Lord, what kind of man was given *Starry Night* eyes?

She made him feel cherished; that was the only way to explain it. She was intelligent and intense, but the way she looked at him made him feel like he was more than enough. No one looked at him like that. With her hair splayed out on the pillow and her lips raw, Dane wasn't sure he could take much more. He kissed her again, fiercely. Her body strained beneath his and watching her let go was the most erotic thing he had ever seen. There was something about watching complete order and discipline come apart. She'd chosen *him* to do that to her. That thought alone made him lose it.

He would never be labeled as a cuddler, but he couldn't stop touching her. They lay face-to-face, saying nothing, touching one another in that way that somehow brought them closer. Her hands were small and so gentle it was as if she knew every nerve in his body.

"What were you like when you were little?" she asked, her voice thick as she ran a finger along his jaw.

He sifted through a lifetime of memories and tried to find the safest thing to say. "I was a typical boy, I guess."

"Hmm. Were you close with your sister?"

"I was. You seem to be interested in my family." He kissed her in a desperate effort to distract.

"I think we are shaped by where we come from. I guess I want to know you."

"You do know me."

He could see her consider pushing, then deciding to let it go. Dane was restless. It wasn't that he didn't want to share. Well, maybe it was, but mostly he didn't know how. He honestly couldn't figure out a way to show her pieces of himself without giving her the whole thing. And he wasn't ready to give it all. There would always be a piece he kept for himself.

"You have van Gogh eyes." She changed direction.

Dane sighed quietly in relief. "Were his eyes blue?"

"No. Well, no one knows for sure because he always painted them in different colors. They might have been green." She leaned up on her elbow, animated and so gorgeous he had no idea how he was ever going to get out of the bed and go to work.

"Yours are the same blue as his painting *Starry Night*."

"Is that the swirly one of the sky? The famous one?" He tucked his arm behind his head so he could see her.

She nodded. "The first time I met you, I knew I recognized the color."

"I knew you were checking me out."

She sat up, the white cotton of his sheets pressed to her body, and laughed. Dane couldn't look away. It was too much for him, his heart racing way ahead of his brain as their eyes locked. She felt it too. He saw it on her face: the moment she realized how deep they were. Anna defaulted to what she knew best, words.

"My eyes aren't actually blue."

He couldn't speak because the only thing left to say to her was that he never wanted her to leave. That he could listen to her talk for hours. That she was the only woman he thought about and that were he at all capable of giving himself to her, he would. The only thing rushing through him was that he loved her, and since that was definitely not possible, he stayed quiet.

"I know. They're silver. Like dimes. That's why I wrote that when I sent your flowers," he said once he pulled it together.

The truth was silver didn't quite cover it. He knew exactly what color they were, but he had no way to describe it. Deep gray, but sometimes in the sunlight they sparkled blue, sort of like the ocean when it's overcast and the sun peeks through and skims the surface with light. Christ, he wasn't a poet, but that wasn't half bad. Not that he was going to spout that gibberish to her, not while she was looking at him like she might want him all over again.

"That's right. The Avett Brothers. I bought that song by the way." She lay back down on a sigh and looked up at the ceiling.

"Dimes don't do them justice. Maybe pewter or steel."

"Hard," she said.

"I... I'm speechless."

"Sorry, that was probably an after-incredible-sex metaphor. I can't help myself." She looked at him and beamed.

He laughed because she'd done it again, surprised him. He ran his thumb along her wrist, felt her pulse. It was like one of those things the teacher used to put on the piano during his weekly lesson. Steady and knocking. Metronome, that's what it was called. *Why am I thinking about a piano lesson?*

"Beautiful."

Anna blinked, her eyes growing heavy.

"That's what they are. Your eyes are beautiful, whatever color they are. I could look into them all night, Anna."

She sighed, kissed him softly, and turned away, her body curved in front of his. She pulled his arm around her.

"I think I'll stay," she whispered, barely awake, and fell asleep in his arms.

Dane kissed her shoulder—"That's your best idea yet, Professor"—and closed his eyes.

Chapter Nineteen

The entire campus was in the throes of Big Game Week. Their Golden Bears were set to play Stanford this Sunday as they'd done for hundreds of years. Anna respected the tradition. She would probably even go to the Bonfire Rally tomorrow night. Cynda would drag her there and she might as well—she hadn't seen Dane more than once all week.

For now, it was only Thursday and Anna was droning on about the year Shakespeare was born and every other useless fact she promised to include in her curriculum. The two men in bad V-neck sweaters were in the back of her classroom, which was perfect—they seemed thrilled with the mundane drivel of a thousand other Shakespeare teachers. Her students were barely awake. When time was finally up, she met the committee members briefly to inform them that she'd assigned Mr. Swift and Mr. Granville their projects. They were to work independently. One would create a timeline of Shakespeare's life from birth to death and the other would create a diorama of The Globe Theater. Two stupid projects for two obnoxious young men.

That wasn't very generous, she heard her sister Sage's voice. Anna didn't care. She was anxious again about the constant observation and for the first time in her life, teaching wasn't fun. It wasn't her free-and-safe place. In her quest for tenure, she'd allowed them to turn something she loved into what felt like her first pair of ballet slippers. Too tight, digging into her feet, and cutting off her circulation. She'd hated ballet as a kid, and maybe that was the reason why. Nothing was fun if it cut off a person's circulation.

By the time Anna unclenched her jaw and turned to pack her things, she noticed Trey was still sitting in his seat. Maybe talking with him would help bring her back around to normal, although she needed to be careful not to show favorites. *Ridiculous.*

"You nervous?" she asked, taking the seat next to him.

"About what?" He gave her a sideways glance.

She bumped his shoulder. It felt like a wall, and she wondered how big the guys who kept him from playing his game were. They must be huge.

"I heard you kicked Arizona State's ass."

The corner of Trey's mouth twitched up. He continued to gaze toward the front of the class.

"Some are born great, some achieve greatness, and some have greatness thrust upon 'em," Anna said.

"Hey, my sister loves that movie. I like it too, but if you tell anyone, I'll deny it." He shifted in his seat and looked at her now.

"You've seen *Twelfth Night?*"

"That's from *She's the Man.*"

Anna laughed. "That's right. It is. See, Will is all around you."

"Uh huh. Have you seen the guys on Stanford's D? If they want the ball, they're going to be all around me too. Let's just say I don't want anything thrust upon me Saturday night. If I fail—"

Anna raised her eyebrows. She knew he would remember. Maybe he would need a little help, but that's what she was for, wasn't it?

"If we should fail?" she prompted.

Trey smiled, all teeth and insecure youth. It was amazing how in only a couple of months she'd come to care so much about him.

"Wait, isn't that my line?"

"I'll be Macbeth. What's the rest?" Anna asked.

"Then we fail, but screw your courage to the sticking place and we'll not fail."

Anna instantly felt herself return to normal. "There's power in those words, Trey."

"She was batshit crazy."

She laughed. "True, but the words, listen to the words. For a second, she feigns acceptance of failure, but before he thinks that's okay, she tells him to screw his courage to the sticking place. It's brilliant manipulation."

"Yeah, it really is. I mean she's kind of a badass."

She nodded.

"It's all in your head. You can change what you're telling yourself. It takes practice, but I do it all the time."

"Yeah?"

She turned to face him. On the outside, he looked like he didn't need a thing, but when she looked into his eyes, she saw the things they had in common.

"Courage is tough stuff. It's not a commercial or one of those football movies. It's sweaty palms, Trey. Shaking and about to puke. Courage is ugly and so hard to find when you need it."

"Is that our man, Will?"

Anna grinned. She'd somehow managed to find her own lines. Maybe with some practice, she could be her own scriptwriter. She shook her head and put her hand over her heart.

"You said that? Huh. Well, I'll do my best," Trey said, standing up and throwing his backpack over his shoulder.

"I know you will. Just remember you have one thing those guys don't, no matter how big they are."

"What's that?"

"You have knowledge. You know what it is to be a crazy badass. There's strength in that, the kind of courage that creates success, good or bad. Now go out there on Saturday and—How did you say it in your paper? Oh yes, go make those guys Lady Macbeth's bitch."

He turned, a mountain of wonderful young man, and laughed all the way out the door.

Anna would need to tell Sage when she saw her at Thanksgiving that she was right. People could change their minds any time they chose to.

❋ ❋ ❋

Dane convinced Anna that Twin Peaks at sunset was a much better idea than a bonfire she was never going to enjoy, whether she was dating one of the coaches or not. It was selfish on his part too because he wanted some peace and quiet before the game the next day, and he wanted time with Anna. She brought the sandwiches and Dane brought the blanket. As they lay in the back of his truck taking in the stars above and the view of the bay below it, Dane was pretty sure he'd never had a better idea.

"That's what he said. He quoted Lady Macbeth?"

"I swear to God. I felt a bit like that coach in *Friday Night Lights*, or maybe it was the other one."

Dane pulled her closer. "We're not a bad team, Professor."

"I know. We're like the odd couple. Maybe we should go around motivating athletes through Shakespeare." She laughed and sat up, looking out at the night sky. "I never get tired of this city. I've been here my whole life, except for when I was in school, and it never gets old." Anna hugged her legs and took a deep breath.

Dane hung his legs over the back of his truck. "We're not that odd."

"Oh, I think we are."

"Why?"

"Because I'm... I don't know. We're different."

He wasn't giving her enough to hold on to. He knew he wasn't and yet somehow couldn't give her more. But Anna solved that the same way she seemed to with everyone else: she helped him share.

"Do you like lasagna?"

"I... do. Yes. As long as it has meat sauce and isn't good for me. Do you?"

"I did when I was little, but right around college, I lost the taste for it. I think it's the cheese or the consistency," she said. "My mom uses a lot of cheese."

"Does your mom cook Thanksgiving dinner?"

"She tries." Anna laughed.

"Mine gave up trying. My sister cooks."

"So you'll go to Santa Barbara?"

"No, she'll bring the kids and The Saint up here. She will complain the entire time that my mom's pots aren't copper core and once we've stuffed ourselves, we'll crash on the couch and watch the movie *Uncle Buck*."

"Really?" She scooted up, draped her legs over his, and he fought the urge to pull her into his lap and stop talking. She was good at getting him right where she wanted him.

"Every year?" she confirmed.

"Every year."

They sat looking out over the city. Quiet.

"It was my dad's favorite. I guess it's our way of sharing the holiday with him."

"Huh, that's nice." She squeezed his hand. "All we do is play Pictionary. I always lose."

"Seriously? Well, I'll have to stop by one year because I think we need to fix that losing streak. Who's your partner?"

"I'm not sure how it will go this year. I'm usually paired up last."

Anna seemed miles away as she looked out over the city. She'd started off wanting to know more about him, but now it seemed like they'd hit something she wasn't ready to share.

"Did you know this is a big make-out spot?"

Anna's lips curled in amusement. She'd come back to him, and whatever pain had drifted into her eyes was gone. "Is it?"

Dane nodded slowly and leaned in to kiss her. She climbed into his lap and he lay back on the blanket.

"Are you worried about the game tomorrow?" she asked when they came up for air.

"No. Trey is at about eighty percent now, which means he'll stay on for another season and keep his scholarship. My boss is happy and Crazy Eyes is gone. I get to spend nights like this with you. Life is good."

Anna bumped his shoulder. "No way you're that calm. The coaches in those movies you made me watch were outrageous. Burger eating, smoking, stress balls, and you're just 'Hey, life is good.'"

He smiled at her attempt to mimic his voice, although she made him sound a little more surfer dude for effect.

"I'm not the head coach. There's less pressure. Of course I want to win, but it's one game. Life doesn't pivot on one game or one season even. I'm kind of a long-view guy."

They stood and folded the blankets.

"That's very Zen of you," Anna said.

"What about you? Are you nervous we won't win? That's probably a bitch dealing with your sister, right?"

She shrugged. "I think I'm going to tell her what I said the last time she gave me a hard time: We ran out of time."

"Lombardi."

She nodded. "You posted that in the English lounge your first year."

"I did. I had no idea how interesting the English lounge was at the time."

"Maybe it was kismet." She laughed and jumped in the cab of his truck.

There was that word again.

Chapter Twenty

They'd lost. Played much better according to a text from Dane, but "still sucked," according to a text from Hollis. Anna prepared herself to endure Hollis holding up seven fingers, now adding one more to Stanford's current winning streak against Cal.

"Yes, I know Stanford has won the last seven games," Anna's father would most likely argue. "But you're looking at a tradition that dates back to 1892, one hundred and eighteen games," he would continue, and Hollis would eventually roll her eyes and give up gloating. Gloating was difficult in the Jeffries family because their father tended to know things most people never bothered with, so he had this way of whittling most egos down to size. The thought of her father, of all of them, caused a stirring in her heart specially reserved for family. She was looking forward to going home this year.

If she were honest with herself, she was also a little excited that she had something going on in the real world for once. What was it she had? A date. Sex. *Don't be silly, Anna. It was one date and sex. Your sisters have husbands and babies. Sit down.* She wasn't sure what voice that was, but it occasionally popped up and was rarely nice. Maybe it was her inner voice or her inner child. If that was the case, someone needed to teach that kid some manners.

When Anna walked into The Married Widow, Cynda was already at a corner table near the door. Through the sea of people both at the bar and filling the tables, she waved and Anna joined her.

"This place is packed. These are the cheap seats," Cynda said. "I already ordered you a beer since you hated their wine last time we were here."

"I remember." Anna hung her purse on the back of the chair and opened her jacket right as their beers were dropped off by a frazzled waitress in a referee uniform, modified of course to show more of her body than any male referee would dare.

Cynda raised her bottle in a toast. "Last class on Tuesday and then... here's to eating our weight in stuffing."

They cheered and drank.

As the bottle traveled past her line of sight and back down to the table, everything seemed to shift into slow motion. There were people everywhere and yet somehow her eyes found him.

Dane was leaning over the bar, and behind him was a woman holding the back of his belt. He had four beers, two in each hand, and as he turned, the woman in the short skirt put her hands on his chest, her lips stretched wide as she looked up at him as if he were some kind of celebrity. Anna was pretty sure she could see the woman batting her eyelashes all the way from their cramped corner table.

The breath left her body and as Anna's gaze traveled the bar, the crowd, she wondered what the hell she was doing there. She still had laundry to do, bags to pack, and a class to get ready for. Why was she in a sports bar?

"Why are we here?"

"What do you mean? It's close to campus and you said—"

Anna was no longer looking toward the bar, but she knew the moment Cynda's eyes found him.

"That's... probably his sister," she said after an odd silence and the sound of a woman with incredibly long nails yelling at her boyfriend from the next table.

Anna laughed and sipped her beer. Twice. And then she looked back toward the bar.

Dane walked through the crowd, arms held high, and handed two of the beers to Jeb, who had his arm wrapped around another short skirt while he grinned from ear to ear. The bar, the push-up bras, and dangling earrings all seemed to fit the scene. It was all very *Friday Night Lights*, which Anna knew now because she'd watched it. That made her the most gullible woman on the planet. Dane had mentioned *Friday Night Lights* and instead of dismissing it as a stupid football movie, which she should have, she'd watched it. Trying to rationalize her lapse in judgement, Anna decided she was thrown by the unexpected invitation to dinner while he was still at the airport and even more so by the flowers that followed. Excuses didn't work. She was angry with herself.

God, the guy must be some kind of professional fantasy for women too stupid to tell the difference between real and fiction. There was the nasty internal voice again.

Anna put her hands to her face. "I am stupid."

"That is certainly not true. Are you getting pissed about this? Because nothing is happening over there."

"Cyn, can you not? He is clearly on a date with a very tiny skirt. That is not his sister and just because he doesn't have his"—Anna looked over in time to see Dane's date climb up his chest on her tippy toes and kiss him on the neck—"tongue. Just because he doesn't have his tongue down her throat, not yet anyway, doesn't mean this is some new take on a book club. I'm stupid when it comes to men. That's why I don't do this." Anna finished her beer. "I don't know how to manage my expectations."

"Oh Lord, you sound like a suit in a conference room."

"It's true. You're right, I'm not stupid. I have my own life and up until recently, people seemed to like what I did for a living. That's enough."

"Is it?"

"Yes. A person only gets so much good in one life."

"You've said that before. Did you read that somewhere? What about the phrase, 'My cup runneth over?' I prefer that one. There's no such thing as too much good in life."

"That's the Hebrew Bible," Anna said, suddenly feeling like she needed to leave.

"Well, there you go. That many generations of Jewish people can't be wrong. I'm looking over there, Anna, and the man is not on a date. Please don't limit how much happy you let in."

"I need to go."

"I figured."

"Stop doing that."

"What?"

"Stop saying things he says. I am not always leaving. This is a specific case where any woman, real or fiction, would get up and leave."

"You could go over there and say something."

Anna snorted, grabbed her purse, and leaned over to kiss her friend on the cheek. "I'll talk to you later."

Cynda seemed at a loss for advice, which irritated Anna even more. What was supposed to be drinks to celebrate the coming holiday had turned into something awkward, all because Anna had let him into her world. They were different, she'd said it before and tonight was the confirmation.

Anna's freshman year in college, Meg tried to convince her to go bungee jumping. Meg had showed her brochures and built it up so much that Anna freaked herself out and ended up watching her sister instead. Walking out into the cool evening air, Anna remembered why she hadn't tried it herself. She didn't like the idea of mixing euphoria with the shock of snapping back. The shock looked painful. She preferred a smooth and clear path. Things were either good or bad, happy or challenging. The idea of two polar opposites existing so close together scared her.

Anna didn't like being scared. She pulled up to her house, grabbed the clippers out of the shed on the side yard, and decided under the glow of the full moon and her newly installed front door light to take out her frustration on those walkway bushes once and for all.

The front of Anna's house looked different, somehow. *Christ, who was her landscaper?* It looked like someone hacked the hell out of her front bushes. Not that now was the right time to bring that up. Dane could tell the television was on, and he wondered if Anna watched romantic movies even when she was pissed off or if she shifted to something more sinister. He sure as hell hoped not.

Parking, he sat there for a minute in the dark. It had been ages since he'd been in deep enough to have the argument that was only minutes away.

How to proceed?

According to Cynda, who almost threw a drink in his face, Anna had seen the whole thing from their corner table. Weren't there like one hundred bars near campus? What were the chances? Not that he was hiding anything. It was a bad situation. He had been backed into going with Jeb because they'd lost the Big Game and he was a "boring old man." It was all stupid now that he was outside her house, but even though he sounded like some PSA for peer pressure, it was the truth.

The woman Jeb's latest conquest had brought with her was... affectionate. *Damn it!* It looked bad. There was no way around it, and of course Anna had left minutes before Dane squirmed himself out of Tina, Terri's—see, he couldn't even remember her name—arms and decided to call it a night. He was planning to go by Anna's house on the way home, optimistic he might climb in bed with the only woman he ever thought about these days. That was before Cynda approached him on his way out and told him he was in "deep shit."

Dane took a breath, drummed his hands on his steering wheel, and climbed out of his truck. She should plant some rosebushes under her front window, he thought. Maybe he'd lead with that, some gardening tips. *Turn around. You are clearly not equipped for this.*

He wanted to run, head home and pretend what she'd seen, or thought she saw, was perfectly fine. They weren't exclusive. He hated that word. It was what douche bags, as his sister termed them, used when they'd screwed up. So, maybe it *was* his word.

Dane knocked on the bright yellow door. He saw a small shadow rise behind the front window, and Anna peeked through the sheer curtains. She didn't look mad. *Oh man, you're dumb too.*

A few rumblings at the front door, the turn of the lock, and there standing in the entryway of her home, arms folded across her chest, was Anna. Anna with dirt smudged on her face and leaves in her hair. Christ, the woman got him every time.

"Coach Sivac. What brings you by? Keg run dry?" She flicked something out of her hair.

Oh, hell!

"Hi. I wanted to come by and see if we could talk." Not bad, slow and steady. Just like that time when he was eleven and a bear came into their campsite. Dane had left his Doritos on the table even though his dad had told him twice to put them in the box. Yeah, it was sort of like that.

"I'm not sure there's anything to talk about, and it's late."

"Can I come in?"

"I don't think that's a good idea. We can talk on Monday if you have something—"

"It's not what it looked like."

She said nothing, only held herself tighter. He noticed dirt on her other cheek too.

"If I'd known you were there, I would have come over and explained."

Anna scoffed. "Oh yes, I'm sure that's how it would have played out."

"I get that it looked bad. I'm sure from a distance it seemed like that woman was... well, whatever, but that is not what was happening at all. Can I please come in?"

"I'm tired, and you don't owe me an explanation. It was awkward, but you had a big game and I know all of that goes along with your world."

"What? That is not what goes along with *my* world and... this is ridiculous. I'm not standing out here." He carefully moved past her and into the entryway. It smelled like her, and there was popcorn on her small coffee table. He loved everything about this woman.

Anna closed the front door. "I have nothing to say. I don't understand why you are making such a big deal out of this. You don't owe me—"

"Anything. Yeah, you said that, but I think you're lying."

"Do you?"

"Yes. You saw me in a bar with some other woman, and I think you're pissed. You have feelings for me. You had sex with me and we are together. I have feelings for you and it seems like I was cheating on you, or at least screwing around when I didn't think you were watching."

She said nothing.

"Am I close?"

Anna shook her head.

"Anna, please. I'm trying to clear the air here and tell you that Jeb made me feel like I was some ogre, so I agreed to a beer. He brought along his girlfriend and her friend. I'm not interested in her and I get that she was... all hands, but it was not returned. You must feel—"

"No," she said pretty loudly, and it seemed out of place in her peaceful home. Wrinkling her brow and brushing a leaf out of her hair, she tried the dismissive attitude she'd perfected in an effort, he suspected now, to keep herself alone. "I don't do that."

"What?"

"Feel. I mean, I do, but I tend to feel too much so it's a bit like chocolate for me or Hugh Jackman. Do you understand?"

"I think so. Breathe, Anna."

"I am breathing, but I want to settle this so we can get back to where we were before and focus on—"

"I'm not sure that's going to happen." He stepped into her.

Anna stilled and closed her eyes. "You don't understand."

"I think I do. Do you know what I'm saying about the bar? Do you understand that I'm not thinking about anyone but you, Anna?"

She nodded.

"That I need you. Want to touch you every chance I get. I know there are limits to what I can give you."

She opened her eyes. "What does that mean?"

Dane laughed. "Now I have your attention. It means that I'm a little messed up when it comes to sharing or feeling. You share too much, feel too much. I tend to be the opposite. I gave up feeling a while ago."

"I don't think that's true. Look how you are with Trey, and you took me on that incredible date and sent me flowers. You seemed to be feeling when I showed up at your house. I think you are very good at feeling."

"Yeah?"

"Yes, don't sell yourself short."

Dane shook his head. "I'll try not to. Can we get back to me wanting to take you to bed now?"

"We weren't discussing that."

He could see her chest racing to keep up with her heart, all those feelings she warned him about. Dane took her in his arms and tried to help her hold on.

"Were you doing some moonlight gardening?" He wiped her cheek.

Anna blew her hair out of her face. "I'm a mess. This whole thing is a mess. It's fine that you were at the bar. After all, I said you were a one and done... I'm not interested in"—he tilted his head to catch her eyes—"you," she finished on a whisper.

He loved that she was lying, so he kissed her and took her to bed.

Chapter Twenty-One

"Stay," she said barely above a whisper some time later. He kissed the back of her neck and pulled her close. She fit perfectly into his body, and Dane was sure someone would call that fate too. He was beginning to think he was losing control of all the feelings. He should probably figure some things out, but right now they were naked and his mind could only process so many things. The rest would keep, he told himself, and once again Anna proved him wrong.

"I knew this was going to happen," she whispered into the darkness of her room.

Dane nuzzled into her hair, ran his hand along the silk curve of her, trying to stay in the physical.

"I told you. It was actually more like I warned you."

Dane kissed her neck. "This sounds ominous."

"It's the way I'm made. Try to remember that. I'm not good at casual, if that's what this is. My heart is rarely wrong. Crazy, but rarely wrong."

She rolled over until she was facing him. Dane saw the sparkle in her eyes even through the darkness. He knew what she was going to say as her well-loved body took in a deep breath and his heart began to hammer against his ribs.

"I lov—"

Dane kissed her. Swallowed feelings he knew neither of them were ready to deal with, not really. Anna only thought she loved him because she felt everything too deeply. She'd said it herself, and he saw it every time her eyes lit with something he wasn't sure he'd ever be able to live up to.

The kiss was weak. A cheap shot, he knew, but the honest truth was that he wasn't ready. There was no denying the feeling racing through both of them as he pulled her body under him. She looked up, their bodies straining for more, and Dane almost fell apart.

When the sun rose he would tell himself it was physical, that he was attracted to her, drawn to her because she was a challenge. That would probably get him through lunchtime, and then his heart would bust in two and beg him to let her in, keep her close. As the heat between them rose, his mind was still searching for order, figuring out a way to share who he was with every touch and sigh of his name.

Anna had been an out-of-nowhere surprise and now, despite slipping into her warmth one more time in an effort to keep things just as they were, Dane knew he loved her. But he had no idea how to get to a place where that made real world sense, so he held on, covered her, touched her. He was filled with an insatiable need to show her how he felt without words. Because the words, the thought that went behind what was happening to them was too much. He would eventually have to give her everything. Anna was an all-or-nothing woman. She would want, and deserved, all of him. Both hands off the wheel, a complete free dive.

His chest was racing by the time her name fell from his lips. Anna collapsed on his chest, her hands still as her mouth touched his neck and she drifted off to sleep.

Dane had managed to slow things down. Nothing had been said, but that didn't mean it wasn't there. There was a term in football called "hearing footsteps." When a receiver knows it's only a matter of time before he'll be brought to the ground, before the wind will be knocked out of him and he'll have to hang on to that ball for dear life. No player ever wants to "hear footsteps." It psyches him out and all but guarantees mistakes. It's the death knell to a guy's confidence. Dane breathed in, let it out slowly, wrapped his arms around her, and tried like hell to ignore the footsteps.

Anna opened her eyes sometime around two thirty in the morning with one thought, which was a rarity for her. The only explanation she had was that the thought was so huge, so ridiculous, there simply wasn't room for anything else.

She carefully slid out from under his arm and walked out to her living room. The books were all put away now and there was still popcorn on her coffee table. Anna ran her finger along the bowl, the thought still rolling around in her head.

Once again, she'd had sex with a beautiful man last night. What happened in her bed would put most fantasies to shame. She should feel desired and happy. Didn't all those women in the movies she loved walk into the kitchen with their hair messed up in the guy's shirt or something and make pancakes, only to have him drag her back to bed and tell her how gorgeous she was all over again? That's how most of them played out, wasn't it? Anna touched her lips, still felt him there, and allowed the one thought to wash over her.

He'd kissed her to keep her from telling him she loved him. It wasn't that he needed to touch her, she saw it in his eyes right before his mouth closed over hers. He knew what she was going to say. Before Anna could feel foolish, he'd followed the kiss by doing amazing things to her body until all thought was gone. But it was back now, that instant before, the look on his face that said everything.

What am I doing?

How had she gone from seeing him in a bar the night before with Tiny Skirt to relaxing into the warmth of him and almost spilling her heart all over the place? See, this was why she didn't do feelings. She told him that she felt too much, and it was the truth. Anna had what her father termed a "romantic heart"—it leaped before her overactive mind had a chance to think things through. That's why she kept that thing clamped down, allowed it out in fantasy, but never in the real world. Hearts got broken in reality, and Anna didn't ever want to feel broken. That was why she stayed on the sidelines, why she didn't let people like Dane Sivac into her world, let alone her bed.

Can't you just bask in the glow of more great sex, sis?

"Not now, Meg," Anna whispered quietly while she opened the shutters on the back window and the sprinklers went on to water her tiny patch of grass. She loved this house. Loved her life. Why wasn't that enough for her stupid heart? She had her family, Cynda, she even loved the guys she bowled with to varying degrees. That should be enough. So why was her dumb—definitely not as educated as the rest of her—heart pleading with her that this was different, that he was a grand kind of love to beat all others? Why did it insist that she needed to tell him, to share that she wanted him more than anything else like some kind of silly girl?

"Let's not get crazy," Anna whispered as she took the blanket off the back of her couch and wrapped it around her shoulders before she grabbed her remote and curled up on the couch. She didn't love him more than anything else. That was impossible. Her life was not dependent on anyone, let alone a man who wouldn't, possibly couldn't, listen to her.

Darn it, was he a listener or not?

Anna needed to put things in perspective. She squinted as her eyes grew accustomed to the television's glow. Scrolling through her collection, she selected *The Notebook*. It always made her cry, which she knew was a cliché, but she'd given up apologizing for her cheesiness a long time ago. She would stop it before the end because that part was simply too much. Tucking one of the couch cushions under her head, she settled in to be swept away. She hadn't told him she loved him. It's not as though they'd had that awkward moment where he said something like, "I... really care about you too." That had not happened. Instead, he'd beat her to it, "cut her off at the pass," as her Uncle Mitch liked to say. Another football fan, her uncle. They were everywhere, she thought.

"Cut her off at the pass." Yes, that's exactly what he'd done. She should be grateful, but instead she felt like she had something lodged in her heart, something that wanted to float freely around her in the early dawn as he slept almost silently in the other room. Something she should be telling him instead of feeling like they were on completely different pages, starring in different movies.

Anna, give the movies a rest. And what are you doing out on the couch when all of that man is in your bed? Meg again.

Anna knew the reason she was on the couch, why she'd slipped away. She needed space, she needed to regroup because when she loved, her whole heart jumped up and down. A half hour, maybe an hour was all it would take to calm that down. Then she would be ready to look him in the eyes and pretend she didn't want to be with him so completely.

By the time Ryan Gosling was on the roof of the old house, Anna heard her bedroom door open and seconds later she felt Dane's body sink onto the couch. He pulled her feet into his lap. Her heart woke up, and it had nothing to do with Rachel McAdams getting out of the car in that gorgeous burgundy hat and those gloves. Anna coveted those gloves every time.

"Is this?" Dane's voice was raspy with sleep.

"*The Notebook*," she whispered, trying to sound casual, if that was even possible under normal circumstances, let alone when she was naked under a blanket and he was sitting next to her in nothing but boxer briefs. She'd always found those less flattering on men than regular boxers. Her opinion was officially changed. Boxer briefs were now her favorite.

"I've never seen this."

Anna leaned up on her arm and caught his eyes. They were more purple, more van Gogh in the filtered light of almost morning.

"I know, I know." He shook his head. "How can that possibly be? Well, it's the truth. But you've never seen *Rudy*, so hush." He kissed her knee and grabbed a handful of the now-stale popcorn still on the table.

"It's a classic."

"So is *Rudy*." He crunched. "So what's up with these two? She's pissed that she's all dressed up and he's still working on the house? Or is she mad about that beard?"

Anna smiled into the pillow and kicked him just a little. There went her heart again. This was what fun felt like, she told herself as they lay there finishing the movie. Everything didn't have to be so deep, so emotional, or even permanent. They were having fun and nothing more, she tried to convince herself. But then she remembered she didn't do fun.

By the time Dane walked her back to bed, she had never been more confused in her life. The scene where she tells him she loves him and he takes her in his arms and does the same was missing from their story. There wasn't even the scene where she says she loves him and he breaks her heart by saying something like, "I'm not that kind of guy," or "I don't do love." Their scene was simply not there, cut from the story. Anna didn't know how to proceed or how to move forward with all her feelings and things left unsaid. She lay awake in bed, listening to the steady rhythm of their breathing, and had a feeling she'd never seen this particular tale played out on screen or in the theater. She wasn't even sure Will had covered the story of two people simply not saying anything. Maybe if one character were dressed like a man, or some other farce, but... Oh wow. Is that what this was? A farce?

While Anna had always loved a good comedy and Will was a genius at weaving misunderstandings, she certainly didn't want to live one in real life. It seemed she and Dane were in a strange limbo and as she tried to sleep, she once again wished for someone to throw her a line or at least give her some clue how this was going to end. Because it was certainly going to end, wasn't it?

Chapter Twenty-Two

The Thanksgiving Day parade was already on the television when Anna came down the stairs of her parents' house to the smell of cinnamon and bacon. It was a little after nine, and she was still in her pajama bottoms and her faded-to-almost-transparent Cal T-shirt. It didn't matter if they'd lost to Stanford. Hollis was outnumbered. Every time Anna wore their alma mater, her dad growled like a Golden State Bear and held up his hands as if they were paws. It still made her smile like a kid. The man had no shame when it came to showing the love for his Bears.

Anna grabbed coffee and some of the breakfast that had been laid out on the kitchen table. Despite feeling a bit restless, she kissed her mother and assumed her designated spot on the floor pillow by the staircase to watch the parade.

"Wayne Rogers was an old country singer when we were kids. How does he still look like he's not a day over forty?" Sage asked, sitting cross-legged and leaning up against the couch next to her husband, Garrett. He held a cup of coffee in one hand and had placed a baby monitor on the table in front of him. Neither of them looked rested. Anna supposed that was the only downside to her adorable niece. Olive was almost eight months old and had been sleeping through the night, but according to Sage, she was going through a "rough patch" lately.

"I'll bet Wayne does yoga," Sage added as the man in the bright blue suit with embroidery finished singing on the television. His cornucopia float with dancing squash moved down Central Park West, giving way to another marching band. Anna chomped into her cinnamon roll and washed it down with a sip of coffee.

"He puts foreskin on his face," Hollis said, eyes on the television as if she'd just revealed the most ordinary information. Garrett almost spit his coffee across the living room and Anna's mother, in the kitchen peeling potatoes, shook her head.

"Hollis Marie."

"What? I read it in a magazine at the OB's office last week. I'm pretty sure he was on some list of celebrities who use this face cream. It's made from foreskin. I kid you not. Thinking of giving it a try myself."

Hollis, who they now knew was just over three months pregnant, walked into the kitchen barely showing as the rest of the Jeffries laughed. Her husband Matt chuckled and took Annabelle's now-empty plate with a wink as he followed close behind.

"How many foreskins does it take to make the cream? Where are they getting these, like from kids being circumcised?" Meg asked. Recognizing Anna had joined them, Meg plopped her pillow down next to Anna and after blowing kisses at her, took Anna's coffee cup and drank the last bit.

"All right," their mother finally said. Anna was surprised it had taken so long. "That's enough. I highly doubt anyone is putting genitalia on their face, let alone Wayne Rogers. He's a legend."

"It's not the whole penis, Mother, just the foreskin."

"Thank you for clarifying, Hollis. Now let's get back to the parade."

Their oldest sister shrugged, grabbed another cinnamon roll, kissed her husband, and returned to the couch.

When Anna stood to get more coffee, the largest group of dancers she'd ever seen filled the television screen. Her father caught her eye from his chair in the corner of the room and growled, paws up. She laughed and fell into the rhythm of her crazy family. Somehow in the swirl of them all she'd managed to forget about Dane, forget about her life altogether. Being home had a way of doing that to her. Even though they were all grown up now, when they were home, their roles remained the same. Holidays were wonderful like that, Anna thought as she gave in to the joy around her and grabbed some more coffee, rejoining her youngest sister. They were the last two, the last single Jeffries sisters, which sounded about right. Meg had always made it clear she had no intention of getting married and Anna had... well, she had never said one way or the other. It must have been assumed, she thought.

Several hours later, Anna was changing out of her jeans and back into her beloved pajama bottoms. Dinner had been delicious. Her father was actually the cook in the family, but there was no way she was sharing that with Dane the night they went to Twin Peaks.

Dane. As the sun seemed to dip into the bay through the front windows of her parents' home, Anna felt the winding down of the holiday, and she thought of him. Every time she brought up his childhood or wanted to know that part of him, it seemed like a dark cloud rolled in. She wasn't sure how he'd gone so long without reconciling his loss. Of course Anna had never lost anyone. They were all gathered around the table sharing stories about their lives and jobs. She listened attentively as she always did. After stealing a snuggle with Olive and holding her hand to Hollis's stomach while she insisted that she was totally showing, Anna volunteered to do the dishes.

By the time it was dark, they had the dry-erase board propped up on the window seat cushion and the markers ready. Anna finished drying the roasting pan and slid it into the cabinet under the stove. Apple pie was warming in the oven and the whipped cream canister sat ready on the counter next to the two pumpkin pies her mother had made the day before. The same plates with the thin gold stripe border, the same gravy boat, and the same three serving spoons every year. One with an apple on the handle, one with grapes, and the last one, the largest of the three, had a cob of corn.

Anna noticed it all this year, each detail that somehow years before had whirled by in a blur. She imagined it was like being in the "nosebleed" seats as she'd heard Trey say once in reference to the seats farthest away from the playing field or basketball court. Anna was pretty sure they were interchangeable, but maybe he was only referring to basketball. It didn't matter. That's how she felt—as if up until this moment she'd been in the farthest seats. She'd finally been invited to sit closer and yet somehow still felt removed. Had she been invited, or were those seats always available and she simply didn't feel ready to take her place?

Even more startling was that Anna found herself looking at each tradition, each consistent Thanksgiving norm, and wanting it for herself one day. She'd started picturing a platter on her table, her family gathering in her tiny space. What did that mean?

"I'm in love with a man and we've had sex," she said without warning as she walked into the lively noise of their living room, carrying the forks and plates for pie.

In the split second it took for the room to go completely silent, Anna felt foolish. She'd blabbed her private life to a room full of... her family. That was okay, wasn't it? As her eyes traveled toward the off-white Berber carpet, they met her oldest sister. The one who had reveled in pushing her, teasing her, and also punching Robbie Martin in sixth grade and always making sure she got extra cherries when they made ice cream sundaes. Cherries were Annabelle's favorite, and Hollis knew that. Anna's eyes pleaded, knowing if anyone was going to break through the tension Anna had thrust them into, it would be Hollis.

"Well, gather round the circle, kids. Anna has something she's brought for show-and-tell. Let's start with the sex. Was it any good?"

"Hollis," their mother said, smacking her on the arm, and the whole room broke out in laughter. Hollis winked at her.

"Yes. It was amazing and I love him and he loves me, but..."

"Oh Middle Two, there's no but about that. Amazing is not a word you throw around a lot."

Anna smirked. "True, but there is a 'but.'"

"What's the 'but,'" Sage asked, gently patting baby Olive's back.

"We shouldn't be discussing this in front of the baby," their mother added.

Hollis rolled her eyes. "Yeah, maybe we should whisper."

"Hollis Marie, I swear to God you will change your smartass tune once my second, perfect grandchild arrives. I hope it's a long labor."

"Please don't wish that on me," Matt said, taking Hollis's hand.

"As entertaining as this is, I'd like to hear Anna's 'but,'" Meg said, propping her socked feet up on the coffee table. "Gare, cover Olive's innocent ears if you must."

Garrett laughed and under the glare of his mother-in-law's gaze, he gently pulled up the blanket over Olive's back. "She's asleep," he said quietly like a man who'd had plenty of practice dealing with cranky women.

"Anna, it's taken us a while, but the floor is yours, what's the 'but.'"

"It's stupid. I'm being weird. I wanted to tell him I loved him, but he kissed me before I could say it. I think he knew what I was going to say. That's weird, right?"

"Well, did you say it after the kiss?" Meg asked.

"No."

"Why not?"

"It was a long kiss."

More laughter.

"Is there a way you ladies could discuss this later? Banana, as much as I want to see you happy, I'm not sure I can take the details. Besides, we've already covered foreskin today," her father said.

"Covered foreskin, good one, Dad." Meg snorted.

"Sorry, Dad. I don't know what came over me," Anna said.

"I do." Meg stood up. "You wanted to say something about your life. What's happening with you instead of watching everyone else." Meg stood and walked into the kitchen.

"What's that supposed to mean?" their mother asked.

Meg turned the whipped cream canister upside down, stuck out her tongue, and right as their mother gasped, she filled her mouth with frothy cream. "I think it's pretty obvious," she mumbled.

"Anna's always behind the scenes. She's practically wallpaper sometimes."

"That's not true," her father said and looked around for confirmation from his girls.

Hollis shrugged and nodded, followed by Sage. Meg filled her mouth again.

"See," she continued mumbling, and their mother marched across the kitchen and took the canister from her hand, slamming it down on the kitchen counter.

"Stop that."

"What?"

"All of it. Other people are going to use that cream, and no one wants your germs. And Annabelle is not wallpaper. She's quiet. Do you feel like wallpaper, Anna?"

She was going to shake her head, but being presented with the question for the first time in her life, she wasn't sure. *Maybe*. Was that a proper answer?

Dane helped his sister tuck his nieces into the guest room while The Saint and their mother "chatted over coffee." *Uncle Buck* had been over for a couple of hours now, and Dane was struck by how emotional he felt this year. It had to be Anna, he thought as his sister closed the door. The room was quiet. His nieces had conked out, one on each of his shoulders, after the sugar rush of pie had plummeted. There was no way they were waking up until morning, but Jess insisted they wait in the hall for a minute. His sister had been on her best behavior all through dinner, hadn't asked about his personal life once, which was some kind of record especially when he knew his mother had been pushing her for answers.

This was her moment, he thought. She was operating under the guise of listening for whatever sounds concerned mothers listened for, but as they stood shoulder to shoulder in the dark hallway, Dane knew it was coming. She had him alone and before he could get one word out, his older sister—and friend now that they'd grown up and he'd stopped acting like an ass—pounced.

"Do you love her?"

"Mom. Yeah, she's kind of annoying with your perfect husband, but I still love her."

"Cut it out," she said just above a whisper. "Stop doing that. I'm serious. The professor, the one Mom told me about. You love her, don't you? I can tell."

"We just stuffed ourselves, watched John Candy, and your little angels started drooling on my shoulders. How can you tell something like that?"

"I don't know, I just can. You look happy, a little dopey maybe."

"I am not dopey."

"You kind of are." She bumped him. "So do you?"

Dane hesitated, but somehow emboldened by the dark and being home with his family, he nodded. "I do."

Her expression was at first soft, as if she were expecting the look on his face to convey the best part of a romantic movie. He must not have given her the right response because her all-assessing eyes combed over him in that way that got him in trouble every time in high school, and she slapped his shoulder.

"You haven't told her, have you? Oh God, did she say it first and you gave some lame-ass 'I care about you too' response? Men can be such assholes."

Dane held his finger to his mouth and tried not to laugh. "Aren't we supposed to be quiet?" He opened the door to see his nieces snuggled into their pillows and there it was again, that warmth, those feelings of wanting a future. For the first time in a while, Dane longed for what was ahead of him rather than missing what had passed. How was it possible one small glittery woman could be responsible for so much want?

"Nice try. They're asleep and not going to hear us," she whispered, closing the door. They stayed in the hallway.

"I kissed her before she could finish saying it," Dane said matter-of-factly, as if he were being interviewed during postgame and wanted to make it clear that was the extent of his answer.

"What does that mean, you kissed her? Like midsentence? You interrupted an I love you?"

Dane nodded, not all that proud of himself.

His sister raised her eyebrows. "Huh, well played."

"Yeah?" He looked at her.

"Yeah. I mean it's not the worst response. Hopefully you brought her back to bed and—"

"Okay, sharing time is over." Dane started down the hall.

Jess laughed and grabbed him before he got too far.

"Was she upset that you didn't let her finish? Do you think she knew what you were doing?"

"She knew. Knows, she knows I stopped her. I can see it when she looks at me now."

"So fix it."

"Okay. Excellent advice. Such detail. Thanks for that."

"This is simple. Make it up to her. Something romantic and big so she'll have to forgive you. Like you know when those guys on YouTube do those flash mob proposals?"

"I do not."

"Well, these people dance and sing and then the guy drops to his knee. Some of them are pretty cute, but I always feel a little awkward for the woman. Like she's going to say 'no' after all of that spectacle."

"What is the point of this little story?"

"I don't know. I'm tired and there are still dishes in that kitchen. My point is, are you sure she loves you?"

Dane nodded. He was sure—as sure as he was about his own feelings. That was another great thing about Anna: there was little, if anything fake about her.

"Okay good, then make the gesture. Step out of your comfort zone and show her what she means to you."

"Did you get that from Crazy Eyes?"

"Who's Crazy Eyes?"

"Long story."

"Well, that's my advice. Make up for acting like a moron and get on with it."

With that, she punched him in the shoulder and ran down the stairs. Before Dane made it into the kitchen, he could hear her singing "Dane and Annabelle sitting in a tree."

How was it this woman was a ruthless prosecutor? he thought as he turned right back around and sat on the couch. No way he was walking into a kitchen with both his sister and his mother singing and laughing. Even The Saint couldn't save him in there.

Chapter Twenty-Three

*A*nna drove back to campus for the last game of the season, scheduled for the Saturday after Thanksgiving, against UCLA. Dane had been to her class and had taken her to the movies, so it was her turn. Although they'd talked about what he did for a living, his passion, Anna had never been to a single game. It wasn't fair and besides, Trey wore glitter like a man in her class and she owed it to him, too. Cynda assured her it would be fun and Anna had a hard time arguing because in spite of their current "say nothing" period, she wanted to be near him, around something he did love.

Walking into Memorial Stadium, Anna was struck by the spectacle. It was overwhelming. So many people scattered among long gold benches. Men and women, young and old, dressed in blue and gold, bodies and faces painted. Excitement and pure joy, that's what Anna saw, and it about knocked her down. Families carried signs that read *Go Bears* as they made their way to their seats around the massive green of the field. The band was playing something Anna didn't recognize, but her body responded to the thrumming of the drums and the rhythmic cadence of the brass instruments as they managed to further energize an already electric crowd.

Trey was number nineteen, Anna knew that much, and searched the field for his jersey, but the only players on the field were on the other side. Cynda pulled her arm toward their seats, which were only four rows up from the field. She set down cushions with bear paws and gestured for an awestruck Anna to sit.

"Where are our players?" Anna asked.

"They're not out yet, still in the locker room. I thought we should get here early and give you a chance to... adjust." Cynda took a blanket from her bag. "You okay?"

Anna was mesmerized by the number of lights and the buzz of the crowd. The stadium reminded her a bit of a Greek theater, or The Globe even. She was struck by the similarities: the anxious crowd waiting to engage, to be entertained. It was so much like what she imagined things would have been like in Shakespeare's time. Perhaps if Will were still around, he would have been a football fan too.

"I... yes, I'm great. This is incredible."

"Really?"

Anna nodded, still looking up at the night sky as it contrasted with the glow of the stadium lights. Cynda patted her arm.

"What?"

"Nothing. You're special."

"How so?"

"No matter what defenses you put up, you're not a snob at all. You may be a product of your isolation, self-inflicted I might add, but you drink things in. I'm glad you're my friend."

Anna felt something fill her chest as her mind skipped over the idea of self-imposed isolation. Did she do that? Deciding to ponder that later, she took the jersey Trey had given her out of her bag.

"I wasn't sure if this was appropriate at an actual game, but it seems like they are everywhere so I might as well join in."

"Nice! Did you want me to help you out with that?"

"Not if it involves cutting it up like yours or showing my stomach. That is not going to happen, my dear friend."

"I would never cut a jersey." Cynda put her hand to her chest as if truly offended by the idea of harming a sacred jersey. "This is a T-shirt and I'm totally rocking it, if you must know. See the student section?" She pointed to a sea of blue several sections away—it was hard to tell one person from the next. "I'm on trend, per usual."

Anna laughed and pulled her jersey past her ponytail. Her eyes fell on the giant television screen currently showcasing the student section. Shirtless guys with letters painted on their chests, some with bear hats and others holding signs and yelling as if it was the most natural thing. There were young girls in some of the tiniest shorts Anna had ever seen, their hair painted blue and gold. They were singing and laughing. It was fun and freedom on a level Anna had never experienced even at that age. There they all were on the sidelines. Anna was used to that part, but all around her people were participating, partying, and enjoying themselves. Her heart was pounding in her chest as if it was the first time it had been allowed out. She looked closer and beamed, noticing the glitter everywhere. Glitter and sequins, a sports-infused fairyland that had Anna on her feet straining to take it all in.

"I'll go get us food," Cynda announced right as Anna began wondering who the students were in the blue-and-gold-striped rugby shirts waving enormous Cal flags. Were they part of the cheer squad, or was that a separate thing?

"I'm not even asking you what you want because you are football-game challenged. I'll surprise you."

"Get a lot of food."

Cynda looked surprised, and Anna found that shocking her was fun. "What? I'm hungry and this is so fun."

"What have you done with my friend?"

Anna laughed, and it felt so incredible she wondered if somehow she would be punished for this in the morning, kind of like a hangover after an excellent party. Not that Anna had much of a reference for that either, save maybe a few nights she went out in Oxford, but that was tame compared to what was playing out in front of her now.

"Lots of food coming up. You can get started on our sign. The markers are in my bag."

"I'm not sure, I've never..." Anna instinctively looked around at other signs.

"Don't do that. We don't want to copy someone else's. Make us something original, Professor. You can do it." Cynda turned and walked away, the embroidered red bear paws on her jeans pockets waving with each wiggle.

Anna shook her head, unrolled the blank poster board, and tried to think of something clever. She knew nothing about football or their phrases or sayings. According to Cynda, the goal was to be unique. Anna wasn't sure she had anything unique to offer until she realized exactly who she was. Of course she had a different perspective. She taught Shakespeare and she had Trey to keep her somewhat cool. Anna got to work on their sign.

Cynda returned with hot dogs, waffle fries with cheese, and two beers that she barely managed to keep from spilling all over herself as she sat down.

"Did you finish our sign?"

"I did, but I'm not sure you're going to like it. Trey will get it, if he even sees it, but maybe it's too weird for this crowd."

Cynda put a fry in her mouth, wiped her hand on a napkin, and unrolled the sign.

She laughed, and Anna felt like a child longing for acceptance. It was ridiculous, and she wondered if what was coursing through her right now was the reason she stayed away from things.

"It's perfect. You are definitely with the right crowd when it comes to screwing. I'll bet we make it on the Jumbotron."

"What does that mean?" Anna asked as ominous, loud music thundered around them. Up on the screen were images of smashing helmets and flying dirt. What looked like the doors to the locker room opened and the screen filled with Cal football players. It was so loud it sounded like a rock concert as the mini-movie ended with words *This is Bear territory* across the big screen that Anna now realized was right under a Bank of the West sign. Her mortgage was through Bank of the West. Huh?

An announcer who sounded a bit like a fictional God said, "Please welcome to Kabam Field, your Golden State Bears!"

The crowd went crazy. Smoke and sparks hit the air as giant guys in blue and gold with massive pads and helmets ran onto the field. As Anna stood, she wondered. First, which one of those padded guys was Trey, second, where was Dane in all of this, and third, why was the field called Kabam Field? Wasn't that a gaming company? Anna was pretty sure they were one of Hollis's clients. Wow, everyone really did love football. Where have I been, Anna thought as they clapped and sat back down.

Biting into her hot dog, Anna closed her eyes because she was unable to remember if she'd ever had a better one. It had to be the environment, all the fresh air. Hot dogs were usually gross, but this one was incredible.

Cynda laughed, and Anna realized she had mustard on her nose and wiped her face.

"Good?"

Anna nodded. "You go to every game?"

"Pretty much. It's free for us, so why not. Plus, it's fun." Cynda stood and looked down toward the field. "Your man will be some-where down there."

Anna would normally flinch at the idea of "her man," especially since she had no idea if he was her man or not, but something sort of primal stirred in her and she found she wanted someone to be her man, so long as it was Dane. She shook her head and took a sip of beer. It had to be the beer. She'd probably be beating her chest and dragging Dane back to the cave by the time the game was over. Oh wait, that was his job, wasn't it? No way in hell was she going to be dragged—he'd just have to live with that.

She laughed and then remembered there wasn't any man. Dane had stopped her from moving them in any direction. They were stalled, and the thought of that almost ruined her fun. Anna was holding their sign when all of a sudden, Cynda jumped to her feet, grabbed the sign, and started to yell. Something must have happened on the field. When Anna peered down, she saw what looked like a swarm of players, Cal's blue and gold mixed with UCLA's blue and gold, which Dane said was a variation. To Anna, they all looked the same. It didn't matter now, though. The energy was charged.

She took another sip of beer and joined her friend as they danced and cheered.

Dane's headset was cutting in and out. Frustrated, he pulled it around his neck and was looking for one of those tech guys who seemed to be up his ass like a Best Buy salesman: always there until the moment he actually needed one. With three minutes left in the first half and nothing more than the high-pitched sound ringing in his headset, he looked away for a moment. UCLA was up by four and Dane was anxious, aggravated in a way he wasn't sure had anything to do with football. Ever since Thanksgiving, he'd been thinking about that grand gesture his sister had mentioned. How the hell was he supposed to pull something like that off? What, like roses and a suit? He wasn't proposing for Christ's sake. He just wanted her to know that he loved her with pure 100 percent certainty. He wanted to watch her eyes go all soft like they had when she had invited him into her bed. Wanted to hear her say it, all of it this time. If that took some overpriced limo or a white horse, then he supposed he'd have to look into it because he needed her. Now.

All that would have to wait. The roar of the home crowd in his ears usually meant one thing. Dane's eyes flew to the field right as he saw Trey's feet leave the ground and the announcer bellow, "Open for Duncan and..." Dane held his breath as Trey flew through the air with a grown-man-size portion of the confidence he'd been waiting forever to see. There was no way the kid was missing this ball. It was his, Dane thought as Trey reached up for as perfect a play as this field had ever seen.

"Touchdown, Bears!"

Dane almost cried, not because they'd scored a touchdown, although that did tie up the game before halftime and made his life a whole hell of a lot easier, but because Trey was strutting, ball still in his hand, as he jumped and threw his chest into Birch, who was right there in the zone to congratulate him. Damn, that kid got to him.

Dane quickly wiped a tear away. The head struggle was real for any athlete, especially one who lost his dad. Dane should know. But somehow, little by little things had gotten through and Dane knew this wasn't just one touchdown, this was a breakthrough. Trey was going to be just fine. Even Coach Hall, who was normally pretty stoic during games, had a stupid grin on his face as he looked back at Dane.

Trey did it once more, this time with a running pass from Birch, before halftime.

"Thirty, thirty-five, forty..." The announcer counted down as Trey ran in another touchdown and moved them up one with forty seconds until halftime. The look on his face as he came to the sidelines was priceless. Dane shook his head.

"Look who decided to show up, man! Well done."

"Yeah." He was still breathing heavy. "Did you see her, did you see the sign?"

Dane was confused, thinking he must be talking about some girl he was dating. Was that all it took? Hell, he would have found Trey a girlfriend a long time ago if this was the payoff. "So what did it? Did something just click? Some of my great coaching finally sink in there?"

"I just screwed it, Coach."

"Sorry?"

"My courage, just like batshit crazy says. I screwed my courage to the sticking place and went for it. I trusted myself. I guess that part was you, but mostly it was knowing that things couldn't be any worse than they turned out for poor Macbeth."

Dane must have looked dumbfounded because Trey shook his head and turned his coach around to face the crowd. He pointed into the stands and there, no more than four rows behind him this whole time, was Anna. Cynda was holding a sign that read *Screw Your Courage, #19. We love you!* Anna was clapping, and it looked like she might be crying. Trey patted Dane on the back and in that moment, watching Anna in her jersey jumping up and down, Dane found his gesture.

The band started up as the team went back to the locker room. Dane should have followed, that was his job, but Trey had scored two touchdowns in less than six minutes. They could both take a break for a minute. Dane set his headset down on the chair. He took as big of a breath as he could manage with his heart taking up most of his chest and climbed the stairs into the stands. After that, everything went a little fuzzy for a while. He could hear his feet on the hollow metal of the stands, feel the cold railing in his hand as he climbed up toward the crowd.

She wasn't that far away, and everything came into focus once he saw Cynda pointing and Anna met his eyes. Her cheeks were red, her hair was struggling to free itself from her ponytail, and Dane wished for a moment she could see herself the way he saw her. She looked so incredibly happy and free. It made no sense; she was all about books, all about walls, but this Anna was different. Maybe he'd had something to do with it. Maybe that's why she loved him... because he'd taken her hand and brought her out into the fresh air. If even half of what his stupid heart was saying was true, he was good.

Love hard, son. Dane heard the same voice in his head, but now he knew who it was. When Dane used to come home from practice in high school, usually after he got his ass handed to him, and his father would be waiting for him in their living room. After Dane showered, his dad listened to anything Dane needed to get off his chest before throwing his aching body into bed.

"Sleep hard," his father used to say. "Tomorrow will probably knock you back down, so get your rest."

Dane swallowed the memory, grateful that he was now hearing his father's voice again, and hoped like hell his gesture of love wasn't too late.

Anna couldn't breathe. He was almost in front of her, and she'd just wiped her eyes and gotten over watching Trey finally reach his potential. This was too much. Emotion flooded her and while her mind wondered what Dane was doing up here and if he was going to get in trouble, her heart reached out and tried to pull him closer, faster. At some point, her mind won out and she noticed people turning to watch his approach.

"Cynda," Dane said when he reached them.

"Dane." Cynda stepped out of the way and he stood in their row, in front of Anna.

"I'm sorry. I screwed it up the last time."

Anna stood, still a little lost. Dane stepped into her and touched her face. She tried to relax, but she wasn't used to being the center of anyone's attention, and there were definitely more heads turned in their direction now.

"I guess I wasn't ready. I mean, I was but I didn't know. Aww, hell, your mind is rubbing off on me." He smiled, his eyes making those little crescents again, as if they were the only two people in the stadium. How did he do that? How could he be so comfortable with this many eyes on him, but when it was just the two of them there were places he kept closed off?

"Dane." Anna looked around, unable to calm her nerves or the feeling she was in the center of some storm she hadn't seen coming. "What are you talking about?"

"I'm making up for being a typical moron. I think that's what my sister called me."

Anna laughed and put her hand to her mouth. "Why?"

"Because I kissed you before you had a chance to tell me something."

"I don't know what—" She lost her words.

He didn't seem to be joking, and she wasn't sure what to do next. So many people.

"Anna, try to ignore all of these people."

"And the other thousands out there and probably a few million watching at—"

Dane glanced at Cynda and she stopped talking.

"Seriously? That many people watch college football? I knew pro football had a big following, but my God. This isn't even a big game, is it?"

"Anna."

"What?"

"Can you focus, please? I need to get back down there before those cheerleaders stop dancing, before anyone notices I'm gone."

Cynda snorted. "Too late for that, Romeo."

Why did she have to choose Romeo? Why did people always default to the dead lovers?

"Well sure, if you have millions of people watching you. I had no idea. Go." She kissed him.

"Unbelievable." Dane ran his hand across his face. He looked tired, but in that flushed, stayed-up-all-night-excited way.

Just as Anna was about to sit back down, Dane took her face in his hands, fingers playing with the back of her neck. She loved that he always did that. There were still mumblings that must have come from the people who found her personal moment more entertaining than the half-time show.

"I came up here because I want to tell you something."

"What?" Anna saw cameras flash and went to turn but he held her face.

"Ignore it, please. What were you going to tell me that night? The night after we made love."

"Dane! Do you have a microphone on?" She looked down at his chest, buying time. There was no way he expected her to blurt out her feelings in front of all of these people, did he? That stuff only happened in movies, and Anna was not equipped for Hollywood-size gestures.

"Left it down there," Dane said, smiling. Bigger and sexier this time.

"Thank God. I think this can wait."

"No. It can't. What were you going to say?" He bumped the guy who was now kneeling up with his iPhone in the seat below them. "Excuse me." Dane turned his back, eyes still on Anna.

"No problem. You get your girl, man."

"Anna, what were you going to say that night, the night I kissed you?"

His eyes held hers in anticipation. Anna felt like she was going to go up in flames like one of those ants under a magnifying glass the boys in her neighborhood used to torture in the blazing sun of summer. He was asking her to repeat in front of all of these people something she'd barely managed to say in the darkness of her bedroom. This wasn't how she did things, but then she caught his eyes, those beautiful van Gogh eyes that started out teasing her and were now looking at her as if she were something she'd never imagined herself to be—more than enough. The idea of it washed over her, wiping clear any distractions and petty insecurities. Anna kissed him, her cheeks burning, and said, "I love you."

It sounded simple to her own ears. Almost a paltry reward for his grand gesture, but that little crease between his eyebrows softened and his face eased into a comfort, a warmth that felt private and only meant for her. He reminded her that love, while squeezed into three little words, was everything.

"I love you too." He kissed her, deep and long despite the now-increased volume of the "oohs" and "awws."

When he pulled back, she smiled up at him and shook her head. He was now looking around and laughing as if he'd just woken up and realized what he'd done. It reminded her of *A Midsummer Night's Dream*. The folly of love, she thought, right as Cynda tapped her on the shoulder.

"I told you we'd make the big screen. Of course I thought it would be your sign, but this is much better."

Anna looked in the direction she was pointing and saw Dane climbing into the stands and their kiss. It was right there, larger than life under the Bank of the West sign. Anna stiffened and looked around as people began clapping. It felt like one of those dreams people have where they find themselves in mundane situations like work or the grocery store and realize they don't have any clothes on. She'd never had one of those dreams, but she felt naked all the same. Dane was still looking at her, his eyes surveying her face as if he already knew she was uncomfortable. Most women would relish the attention, the spectacle, but she was not one of those women. He kissed her gently again and ran back down to the stairs to his job.

She tried to stay focused on the romance, the love in his eyes, and the complete abandon with which he came to her. It was the stuff of movies, it was wonderful, and she should be floating around on a cloud. The problem was, as Anna watched her life played out on the big screen one more time, she had a feeling the cloud she was supposed to be floating on held a storm. Rain always ruined a football game, didn't it?

Chapter Twenty-Four

By Monday morning, their picture was on the front page of the school newspaper and the local paper. Must have been a slow news day. They were also kissing and smiling on the Berkeley website, and her students were whispering in class and grinning at her. By the time Sather Tower rang at noon, Anna was sitting across from the tenure committee.

"Miss Jeffries, what are your personal plans in the coming years?"

"I'm sorry?"

"Well, it has come to this committee's attention, actually the entire school's attention, that you were on the... What's it called again?" He turned to the man next to him.

"Jumbotron."

"Yes. That. It has come to our attention that you were recently seen at a football game with a poster quoting Macbeth out of context."

"I can explain. That was a—"

"Surely at this stage of your... career, I don't need to expound on the fact that the works of William Shakespeare are iconic, timeless, and certainly never fodder for a... football game?"

Anna said nothing. There was no point. Her mind and her heart briefly returned to that night, the glow of the lights and the silliness she and Cynda shared. Her heart danced around in her chest at the memory of Dane climbing into the stands to declare that he loved her. He loved her, just as she was. Annabelle Jeffries for once was the romantic lead. It was at that childish thought that the mean little voice took over.

And this is where all that nonsense got you. When are you going to get it, Anna? You are the wallpaper. Not the gorgeous dresser sitting center stage or the massive window with an ocean view. Wallpaper. What the hell was that voice, Anna thought. These weren't the funny or guiding voices of her bold, outspoken sisters. These thoughts definitely came from inside.

She swallowed. Her palms were sweating as she wiped them on her skirt, and she pushed them into her legs. She willed herself not to cry. Focus would restore any minute now, she simply needed to calm down.

"In addition, it seems you are now linked to one of this institution's football coaches. Is that possible?"

"I'm... I don't understand how this pertains to my track toward tenure."

They looked at one another and had Anna not found so much of herself, her worth, in becoming a full professor, she would have pushed back from the table and told them, in the words of Hollis Jeffries, to "Go fuck yourselves, sideways."

But Annabelle wasn't Hollis. She was wallpaper. Everyone knew that distracting wallpaper was removed. Steamed off the wall, scraped to the floor, and swept away in a dustpan. If she told these men where to go, that she loved Dane and it was none of their business, she could lose everything. Once whatever movie she was currently in with Dane was over, where would she be?

People are only given so much happiness in one life, Anna. You can't have everything. She took a deep breath, and all she knew in that moment was she was happy in her classroom, happy in her office. She couldn't lose those things. Life was all about choices and despite the now painful knot in her stomach, Anna made hers.

"We are friends. It was a bit of a joke, a skit if you will." Anna swallowed back her self-loathing in the name of preservation. It turned out she did love something more than Dane Sivac after all: the cold walls of this institution, whether they accepted her or not. She was nothing without her classroom, her books, and Will.

"Ah, okay. We are glad to hear that because I'm sure you can appreciate that this department has a particular... focus."

"Absolutely," Anna said in her best professorial tone. There was no longer a point in being stunned or embarrassed. She was going to be sick and needed to leave right now. Anna stood with the single thought that none of this would have been going on if she were a man. No way this would happen to any of the men currently looking down their noses at her.

God, what did it say about her that she sat there? She wasn't even wallpaper because if she was, that stuff would stick like crazy, just like it did when her parents remodeled their dining room. She had peeled off without so much as a fight. Anna politely excused herself, quickly made her way to the bathroom, and threw up.

The season was over and while they weren't going to a bowl game, they'd finished strong. Looking back on his first encounter with Crazy Eyes, Dane was happy Trey was finally on track. The game had ended at 27 to 10, and they'd sent UCLA packing. He woke up Sunday morning with Anna in his arms, and they'd hung out until she had to go home and prep for the last two weeks of classes. Life was good until Dane realized he didn't want her to leave, ever. Which scared the crap out of him because in the rush of the game, Trey's success, and Dane's own declaration of love, he'd forgotten that shortly after that kind of love comes the neck-gripping fear that it could all go away.

He hadn't planned on that part, had stayed stupid all day Sunday while he finally painted his bedroom and fixed two of the cabinets in the kitchen. But now it was Monday night and he could feel the grip of fear. Something was wrong. Two voicemails, four text messages. He hadn't heard from her. No return call, nothing. Dane folded the newspaper in his hands, the one with their picture on the front page under the heading "Coach Gets the Girl," and slapped it on his coffee table. Stupid title that had surely pissed Anna off, but that wasn't his fault. Maybe she hadn't seen it yet. Not likely, he thought.

This was not how things went after the big gesture. Hell, even the guy with the bad beard in that movie they'd watched on her couch had his woman's legs wrapped around him in the rain. About an hour ago he'd tried one more time and asked if she wanted to grab some dinner. No response, but now, as he was slouched back on his couch, Dane's phone vibrated.

Sorry. Busy day. I'll talk to you tomorrow.

Dane replayed every step as if he were searching for answers, but he already knew what was wrong. He didn't like it, but there was nothing to analyze. He knew. His gesture, while grand and pretty romantic, was just that: his. She was on his turf, probably already uncomfortable to some extent, although she seemed to be having a blast. He'd acted before he thought it through, went with his heart, and therein lay the problem.

Anna was used to being a whisper. He'd known it from the first moment her lips touched his. Maybe it was all that time in the library, or maybe she gave all her fun and energy to her students. Whatever it was, Anna was soft, unassuming, and private. She'd told him that the second or third time they'd met and he had agreed, told her he was too. *Shit.*

What had he been thinking? Wait a minute, he wasn't thinking, he was feeling. That was supposed to be a good thing. He leaped and declared his love. Wasn't that what all these other guys with flowy shirts and fancy words were doing? Women loved that stuff, didn't they? He was not going to apologize for loving her, for telling her in front of the whole world if he wanted to, or for some stupid school newspaper headline. If they were ever going to have a future together, they needed to get comfortable in each other's worlds, didn't they? He told her he loved her, that's what mattered, so why the hell did it seem like he'd royally screwed up?

Dane suddenly felt the same instinct he had anytime the ball was passed to him on a football field. He felt like running. Rewinding what he'd said, taking it back, and just running.

There was one small problem with that game plan. He loved her. He hadn't been paying attention, and it was desperate now. He needed her in his life. She wasn't someone he could put back, pretend it never happened. He'd been doing that with every relationship he'd had since his dad left. Left. Was that how he saw it? His dad died; it's not like he had a choice. Maybe he blamed him?

That was too screwed up to be possible. Dane let out a deep breath. If he wasn't careful, he'd be on Crazy Eye's couch. The rice maker dinged with his dinner and he decided he'd give Anna until tomorrow. At that point, she'd need to at least talk to him. In the meantime, he was going to sit in his home alone and watch *The Notebook*. Yup, it had come to this.

Chapter Twenty-Five

"That was great. Thank you. See what I mean about Bottom? Even with the ass's head, even though he's a bit of a clueless oaf, his lines are rich with truth. You'll see this a lot with Shakespeare. His seemingly small characters often have some of the most weighted or truth-laden lines. He says to Titania, 'Methinks, mistress, you should have little reason for that. And yet, to say the truth, reason and love keep little company together nowadays.' Do you think there's truth there? Love and reason are opposing. Who agrees?"

"I think Bottom is annoying," Maria said in the passionate discussion Anna had cultivated and encouraged all semester. "I don't like how he says things that are important, but he says them in a way that seems like he doesn't get how important they are."

Anna smiled. "Good point. He is an ass after all. So, why does Shakespeare do this? Why not give the important lines to characters worthy of such statements?"

"It's how he gets people to drop their defenses," Trey said. "No one is intimidated by a guy they've counted out and then—bam! He's hitting them with something deep. I like it."

Anna and the rest of the class laughed. She knew Trey's football game was back on track and she was happy for him, but his comfort in class, his ability to discuss and enjoy Will was so rewarding. Her heart swelled. This was what she was meant to do. There would be more Treys. Well, maybe not exactly Trey, but other students like him. They would need her to help them navigate the language. Nowhere else had she ever felt more needed.

"Jimmy, would you please read Puck's last few lines?"

Even the difficult students, even the ones who made her question what she was doing somehow managed to come around. Anna braced herself for one of her favorite parts in any Shakespeare play.

Jimmy stood. "If we shadows have offended, Think but this, and all is mended, That you have but slumber'd here While these visions did appear."

The class clapped and Anna felt her heart again. It was the last day of class. She might bump into these students again around campus, but their few short months together were over. It seemed fitting that Puck was saying farewell too. Art and life, Anna thought. Taking a deep breath, she began her last discussion of the semester.

"That was beautiful, Jimmy, well done." She nodded and when he gave her a hesitant smile in return, Anna realized some kids were a product of their parents, their upbringing. Jimmy Swift wasn't a bad kid. Maybe, as Dane had once said, there was a lot of pressure being at that level. The oldest son of wealth was surely its own kind of game. "So what is happening here?"

"Puck is saying that if you don't like the way things went in the play, you can pretend they were a dream," George said, still holding onto his girlfriend.

"Yes." Anna nodded. "Is that possible? In life if things are not as we wish, can we somehow pretend or dream them differently?"

"No," Trey said. "Things either happened or they didn't. You can't go back and pretend something didn't happen."

"Why not?"

"Because life doesn't work that way," Maria added.

Anna looked up and saw Dane sitting at the back of the room. The bell rang and she reminded everyone of the finals schedule as they filed out. Turning off her Smart Board, she swallowed back so much she was surprised she wasn't choking.

"I'm going to miss this class," Trey said, throwing his backpack on his shoulder.

"There's another upper-division Shakespeare class. There's no reason you shouldn't continue learning. He has so many other—"

"Actually, that's not what I meant to say. I'm going to miss you, Professor Jeffries. You've taught me a lot."

Anna's eyes began to water and as much as she didn't want to cry in front of him, his words were so comforting she couldn't help it. She quickly wiped her tears away.

"I'm sure we will see each other around. You have three and a half more years here. Maybe you could get your coach to redshirt you and we'll have four and a half."

Trey laughed and put up his fist. Anna fist-bumped him, her eyes crinkling. Such an incredible young man. Turning to collect her things, she heard Trey talking with Dane. She allowed herself a minute. Her heart jumped and everything she'd thought of saying to him, every word practiced through tears last night vanished.

You can't have everything, Anna. It's as simple as that. She grabbed her bag. When she spun around, Dane was in the aisle, arms folded, leaning against one of the chairs.

"Can I take you to dinner?"

It was a simple question. She'd been ignoring him. He knew. She saw it in his face and yet he was inviting her to dinner. God, this would be so much easier if he could just be the man she first thought he was. Why did he have to be such a surprise? Why did who she was with him have to feel so right? She didn't have the strength for anything more than honesty.

"I applied for tenure a little over six months ago."

"I know," he said. It was as if he knew this conversation was coming.

"They have a problem with my class structure. They have a problem with me and now, after the poster I made for Trey and your very romantic, but very un-sweater-vest declaration, they have a problem with you and me."

"Okay. Is that legal?"

"Probably not." She walked toward him and although she wanted him to wrap her in his arms, that wasn't fair because she was going to break his heart right along with her own.

"The thing is, I'm comfortable being the wallpaper."

"I'm sorry?"

"She cast one more lingering, half-fainting glance at the prince, and then threw herself from the ship into the sea."

"Will?"

She shook her head as if in a daze that could somehow save her, save both of them. "*Little Mermaid*. Hans Christian Andersen. Did you know he wrote that?"

"Is she your favorite princess?" Dane's voice was soft.

Anna was reminded of their first conversations. It wasn't that long ago they were firmly in their respective corners, sparring. She should never have let him inside because now, looking at him, she was pretty sure when she let him go he would take her heart with him. It was a beautiful metaphor, but at the moment Anna felt the literal pain. She took a deep breath and tried again.

"I'm comfortable being wallpaper. This has been great, but I'm not the woman you think I am."

"Okay. I'm not sure if that's a movie quote or a play reference. Help me out here."

"It's neither. It's my life. I'm the quiet one. I'm not that woman in the stands. Wind blowing in my hair, holding up a sign at a football game. I am not who you climbed into the stands for. I'm the woman you met months ago when you had questions about one of your players. I'm the sweater, the lunch box."

"I love that lunch box and the sweater too."

"I'm not what you want."

"Yes, you are. You are everything I want, mixed with all the things I never knew were possible."

Anna shook her head.

"I've messed this whole thing up. I should have stayed put and been happy with what was given to me. I pushed for too much and now they're going to take my job. If they take this away from me, if I can't—" She started to cry and when Dane moved to comfort her, she held up her hands.

"I need you to listen to me. I can't be with you. I can't have both, and I'm choosing this." She extended her hands as if the empty classroom could somehow comfort her. It was just a room, she knew that, but she needed the walls. Dane's breathing grew shallow at her words. She didn't want to cause him pain, but there was no way she was getting out of this without casualties.

"Anna, I'm taking you home with me. We are going to get a pizza and sort this out."

"I can't."

"Yeah, you can." He took her hand and somewhere in the center of her heart, Anna hoped he had some magical answer, some way for all of this to work out. A pizza, and Dane would make it possible for them to walk off into the sunset. But he wouldn't have that answer because the truth was simple. All this time she'd been wanting him to open up or she'd wanted to help Trey or reach her students. All this time everyone had looked to her, and the joke was on them because she was probably the most broken, the most hidden of them all. Just ask the darn committee.

Dane ordered a pizza. He'd finally managed to patch up some walls and paint the last room in his house. His outside was as close to paradise as his tiny yard would allow. About a week before Thanksgiving, he'd started working on the inside. There was still a lot of work to be done on the interior of his home, but the season was over and he was motivated. Even though it still smelled like paint, he led Anna into the living room and put the pizza on the coffee table.

She walked to the shelves that ran the length of the wall behind his couch. They were a bitch to hang straight, but as he stood back now, they looked good.

"This is all new. I didn't..." She looked over her shoulder at him.

"They weren't unpacked the last time you were here."

Anna nodded and turned back to the shelves. She touched the round silver frame in front.

"Are these your nieces?"

"Yeah." Dane came to stand beside her. He felt uncomfortable as if he was once again exposing his underbelly. He should be pulling back, but he didn't know how to do that anymore. It was like the floodgates opened when he finally let it out, finally told her he loved her, and now if it meant keeping her, nothing was off-limits. "They were two there."

Anna touched a square wood frame in the back that The Saint had given him for Christmas last year. "Your sister?"

"Yes." It was a fantastic shot. Black and white.

"These are incredible. Is this?"

Dane felt his eyes burn. He was nineteen in the picture with his arm around his dad. He couldn't speak. It was all the way in the back of the shelf, as if putting it there would somehow dull the pain. Hell, any shrink would be "proud" of him for having it out. It had been over ten years since he'd had a picture of his father anywhere other than his wallet. His mother had several in her home, but Dane found it too painful until recently. He'd come to learn the ache was grounding now. It sort of reminded him he was still alive and those left behind had a responsibility.

"My dad."

Anna's eyes teared, as if she were meeting a long-lost friend. Dane imagined there were a lot of tears inside her. A few of them may be for his loss, but he suspected most of them were for her own pain.

"He looks, I mean you look so much like him." She wiped her eyes and seemed to gulp a breath of air. "Oh wow. I'm sorry. These pictures are great. Your home is looking like, well, a home."

"Thanks. Let's eat. I only like cold pizza for breakfast." Dane tried to lighten things up, but he had a feeling things were going to get much heavier before the night was over.

He was losing her. He could see it in her eyes, and he had a feeling it had very little to do with the grand gesture. Sure, she would blame it on that or on these assholes giving her a hard time about her tenure. She would find something or someone to blame, but he recognized the fog in her gaze. He recognized it because he'd done it himself. She was retreating back to what she knew, what was safe, and he had no idea how to convince her to stay and fight for what they were, what she was when they were together.

"I don't want to be a girlfriend sitting on the sidelines. I've never wanted that, but then we met and..."

So that's what she was going to start with. Okay, he could field this one.

"Aren't we both on the sidelines now? I work on the sidelines and you teach. We have that in common. I'm not asking you to be anything other than who you are, what you want to be."

"Maybe not now, but later you will. No one can have everything, Dane. In the real world, I have to choose. Don't you see?"

He shook his head.

"Let's pretend you and I make this work. Sure, it's fine in the beginning, interesting even. After all, I'm an associate professor, and isn't that different that I'm dating a football coach? It's a perfect movie and we overcome everything. But in reality, a year in I cut back to one class or I lose my job altogether. Then before I know it, I'm putting off research so we can go on vacation or because I miss you and want to spend more time together."

"Anna."

"Then we have a baby."

He raised an eyebrow. Already on to babies. Okay.

"We do, and eventually I'm making breakfast and I'm so exhausted that I don't even have the strength to read a magazine, let alone put together prevailing themes in something worth reading."

"Holy crap, Anna. You've managed to make most people's lives seem like failures. What you are talking about is making a life, and it doesn't have to be that way."

"I'm not most people. I'm not simple. All of my sisters have something. They are incredible, and you have no idea the expectations I grew up with. I have to work harder than all of them. Teaching is the only thing I'm good at. I don't have time to eat hot dogs and play cheerleader."

"First of all, you liked those hot dogs and you enjoyed being a cheerleader for Trey. Don't minimize that because these assholes have scared you. If you want to kiss their asses, that's fine, but there has to be a line. Some point when you take what you want."

"That's what I'm trying to tell you. I want my life, the choices I made before I met you. I can't do this."

"Can't do what?"

"I can't love you. It won't work. Everything is telling me, showing me that it won't, that in the end, I'll lose. Can't you see that?"

"No. That's not what I see. I'm not sure what you want me to say to all of this. I mean, why do you watch romantic movies then if it means nothing once the lights come on? Hell, don't the women in your plays find love?"

"Yes, and it destroys most of them."

"Okay, so bad example. Aren't your sisters married? Don't they have children?"

"Yes. But they are not me. They are kind of brilliant and special."

"And you're not? Oh, come on, Anna."

"I am not like them. I... I'm scared."

"What are you afraid of?" Christ, he didn't know how to help her.

"I'm afraid I'll lose."

"What? Your job?"

"My job, you, myself. I'm scared I can't do it all. I remember this one summer we went to this fair. I think we were in LA maybe. I was young. But we were at a fair, a carnival thing, and this guy in a rain-bow-striped vest, I'll never forget him because he was quite a character. He taught the four of us how to juggle."

"Sounds fun." Her face seemed a little lighter, but her eyes were still glassy. Dane hoped like hell this was going somewhere good.

"It was. Hollis learned quickly, Meg did too, and she was the youngest. Sage was a natural."

So much for good, he thought as she started to cry.

"I know I sound ridiculous. I know, but I... no matter how hard I tried, I just couldn't do it."

Dane took her in his arms and said nothing. He let her cry and somehow even to his less-than-excited-about-English mind, he recognized the symbolism. She was going to kill him, kill them with a story. He held her a little tighter because there they were again, the footsteps.

"This is my fault." She pulled back. "You snuck up on me, and I know better. I have a routine and I know what works for me. I don't know how to make this work and hold on to my life. I know that's selfish, but this is who I am. It's kept me sane all these years, and I need it. You can't ask me to let go and fall into you."

"I'm not asking you to let go of anything, but you're wrong."

Anna wiped her eyes, looked at him, and began moving toward the door. The pizza was cold.

"You are so much more than those four walls, Anna. You've trapped yourself in there, and now all these guys need to do is threaten to take it away and you're paralyzed. Teaching is a part of you, one part. Maybe loving me, having me love you is another part. No juggling. Side by side. Another part of you loves Will and bowling. This is all who you are, but the sweater-vests are telling you that you're only allowed to be one thing. Screw them. You need to call their bluff. Like in your classroom, show them it can be another way."

"I'm sorry. That's not how I work."

"You can change that. I... hell, I'm all about feelings these days. I've shared everything with you." Dane had gotten good at assessing situations, plays, and strategies. He also knew a healthy amount about fear. Things weren't looking good. "You know what? That's not true. I haven't shown you who I am. Climbing into the stands isn't who I am either, Anna."

He was losing her and to his heart, that was inconceivable, so Dane gave the very last piece he had in the hope he could save them both.

"Please sit."

Anna seemed hesitant, as if she had almost escaped the pain and he was pulling her back in. Yeah, well, that was too bad because if she walked out that door, the two of them were going to be in a hell of a lot more pain. Dane sat next to her on the couch.

"I have a tendency to close up. According to my mother and at least one of the shrinks she paid for."

"Shrink? You've been to a psychologist, like Trey?"

Dane laughed, a little. "That word always seems to get people's attention. I wonder if shrinks know we think they're creepy."

"It's not something to be ashamed of. I mean, of course you're not ashamed. I meant—"

He put his hand over hers. If he didn't, she might wring a hole in her sweater. Nerves, he knew that now. Knew her. Now, if he could somehow find a way to let her see him.

"I'm not ashamed. Not anymore. I didn't see a sports shrink like Trey. Mine were all regular shrinks over a few years after my dad died. Let's say I didn't handle that little life event well."

"See, how do you do that? How do you take something so big and make it feel so small?"

He could see the struggle to understand him in her eyes and wondered if somewhere in her words she was telling him he made her feel small or her concerns feel small. Dane took a deep breath.

Swallowing back what felt like years of pent-up feelings, he decided if he wanted her to put it all on the line for him, he needed to go first. Just like Crazy Eyes said, "Stepping out of one's comfort zone can open the window to a life they never imagined or were too fearful to want."

Here goes nothing, he thought.

"I went to USC my freshman year. Football scholarship, but my grades were pretty good too."

Anna looked at him.

"I got the call after Chemistry, second semester. It was a Tuesday, five minutes before eleven. It was February and overcast. Colder than normal for San Diego. I remember every detail, still, like it was yesterday."

"Dane." She put her hand over his and where he would normally warm her, this time he felt the chill in his bones. What did that mean? Maybe this was stupid. Maybe she was going to leave him anyway. He didn't care. He would never forgive himself if he didn't fight with everything he had.

"His chief called me. Did you know my dad was a firefighter?" Anna shook her head.

"Sorry. I should have shared that. He was the most important person in my life. At that age I could barely separate my life from his, you know. I was young and sort of on this wobbly boundary into adulthood, but he was larger than life for me. He was"—Dane felt his eyes burn—"a great dad. My best friend, and I know that sounds stupid, but he was. And just like that, one phone call, one plane ride, and he was gone." He quickly wiped away a tear.

"I didn't know how to deal with it. My mom and my sister had each other and I know I had them, but at the time, it didn't seem like that. We were always the brawn and they were the brains. It was a family joke. God, my whole fucking life fell apart. It was like everything he taught me went out the window after he was gone. I could never get my head around the idea that I was never going to see him again. There are times, almost fifteen years later, I still can't. Sometimes I'll wake up and wonder if it was all some big joke."

"What was he like?" Anna asked through her own tears.

Dane shook his head, looked up at the ceiling as if that would help him, and smiled. "My mom used to say he was made to be a father. He was always so happy to be around us, you know? Even if we were hanging on him. He did everything with me. We fished and hunted. He went to all of my games unless he was on shift."

"Sounds pretty amazing," Anna whispered.

Dane nodded, feeling foolish and somehow relieved at the same time. It's not like his father's death was a secret, but it was something he'd put away a long time ago because it was too much. Painful in a way he was not equipped to handle when he was a teenager and more than he'd ever experienced since.

"I tried everything to help the pain, 'fill the loss' as my mom said." He took a deep breath and figured he was this far, he might as well finish up. "I wasn't as gracious as my mother or as healthy as my sister. Even at twenty-one, she said things like, 'At least we had him for the time we did,' or she'd ask me if I could still feel him with me." Dane wiped his eye.

"I didn't feel him, and I wondered why. So I jumped off things, drove too fast, and tried everything that promised to numb me, fade the memories. I was desperate for a while. Lost, I guess."

"Is that when you found someone to talk to?"

"No, that's what I did while those people were trying to talk to me." He decided she didn't need to know the extent of his stupidity. It wasn't a time he would ever be proud of.

Anna kissed him, soft and so pure it was like slipping into fresh cotton sheets after a rough game. She affected him that way from the first touch. The woman was everything: able to get Trey to wear glitter, awkward, funny, soft, and sexy. She was it for him, the whole package, and now he'd told her everything, shown himself in a way he'd never imagined possible. Things should be great. This was where the great part started, cue the soundtrack, Dane thought as Anna pulled him onto the couch and with a playful grin masking the trouble still behind her eyes, finally agreed to watch the best movie of all time—*Rudy*. Dane knew it was a pity play, that he'd spilled his sad guts and in return he would have her in his arms, but he didn't care. Relationships were work, right? That's what they were doing, working things out. This committee would back off eventually and Anna would see she could have anything she wanted. There were no limits. She'd see that.

About halfway through the movie, she'd fallen asleep. Dane gently pushed her hair off her face, kissed her, and despite every positive thought he was force-feeding his brain, his heart began to ache because while he'd spent most of his life creating a plan to win, he realized the next few plays were Anna's. If they were going to work, she needed to find room for them, go all in. Dane loved her, was certain there was nothing she couldn't do, but he had a feeling Anna was her own worst enemy. He hoped like hell she had a good defense or there was no way they were going to make it.

Chapter Twenty-Six

They walked into Philz the next morning for coffee and bagels before Anna needed to get to work. Dane was now off-season and while he still had meetings and cleanup before the new year, he had more time and Anna saw yet another side of him. As they stood in line, she was reminded of the night she texted him for the first time and he asked if she wanted to get coffee. That had only been a few months ago, but as he stood behind her now, arms around her waist, she felt so loved and familiar. It should have been wonderful, and she should have felt so grateful for the warmth in her life. Why wasn't she working that way? What was wrong with her? Anna took in a breath and let it out slowly. She wanted to believe she could have everything, that her cup could runneth over as Meg had quoted, but it all still felt temporary. She wrapped his arms around her tighter as if she were basking in the final seconds of a great movie or the last bite of birthday cake. She tried to relax.

"Cinnamon raisin?" Dane asked before ordering.

Anna nodded and grabbed the two coffees now sitting on the counter. She found them a table by the window while he paid.

"Look at us being normal." He took the seat across from her.

She touched his hand. He was wearing a baseball cap backward and a plain sweatshirt. No team, no logo, just Dane. Jeans and stubble, nothing to prove and no one to work on at the moment. It was a lovely side of him, and she relaxed into what a life together might look like.

"You don't have to be anywhere for over an hour, and I haven't been up since four thirty. This is progress, Professor. I think we might be good at this being normal business."

Anna flinched a little at the "professor" title. If he was going to be Just Dane, then she wanted to be Just Anna. The problem was, as she sipped her coffee, she wasn't sure who that was. Outside of her studies, her research, her life's work, she was what? A third-in-line daughter to professional and accomplished parents, a... homeowner. She had that. She was a friend and a sister. Her pulse quickened as she grasped for an identity, one she'd need if her season were ever over. She was on a bowling league, that was something, but chances are if she wasn't a professor, the novelty of that would wear off. Why would she even live in this area if she didn't teach?

Their bagels arrived, warm and wrapped in white paper. Anna glanced at her plate and looked up at Dane.

"Are you okay?"

She nodded.

You are thirty-two years old. There is a great deal to your life. Stand up straight and stop this right now! Anna could hear her mother demanding. Surely once a grown adult started hearing her mother talking to her like a child in her head, that was close to crazy, wasn't it?

Anna took Dane's hand.

"I like the stubble."

"Yeah? Maybe I'll go all mountain man through the winter."

She laughed. The food and warm coffee hit her bloodstream. She was going to be fine. Reaching across the table, she touched the side of his face. God, she loved this man. She had no idea she was capable of something so deep down in her bones. It was frightening and exhilarating at the same time. Wrapped up in her now-famous feelings, Anna forgot where they were, forgot who she was as she naively leaned across the table and kissed Dane. It was a simple kiss, sweet even. His face softened and stretched into a sexy smile that promised things she was no longer imagining. She had firsthand knowledge.

"What was that for, because I'd like to do it again."

"Just because I love you."

He grew serious. "I love you too."

Her eyes drifted to the line, which now extended out the door, and the air whooshed out of her lungs. There were two students doing an awful job of pretending to do something else while taking a picture of Anna and Dane having breakfast and... kissing. She didn't know the two girls and wasn't about to say anything. She finished half of her bagel and wrapped the other half to go. The line moved forward and there, shooting fire-and-brimstone daggers at her, was Professor Graston of the tenure committee, and next to him was Dean Bradley, her boss.

Anna nodded to both men and despite her immediate urge to remove her hands from Dane's, she stayed put. Dane must have noticed something in her face. He glanced over his shoulder and back at her.

"Please tell me those aren't the sweater-vests?"

She drank the last of her coffee and nodded.

"Unbelievable," he said, barely above a whisper. "These guys should be in Harry Potter with Crazy Eyes. What's that guy's name? The main one without the nose?"

"Voldemort."

"Yeah." He sensed her tension and cleared their table. "That's who they are," he whispered into her neck as he reached behind to throw out their trash.

Anna wanted to laugh, wanted walk right past them and mentally flip both men off, but that wasn't her way. Instead, she tried not to move away as Dane put his hand on her lower back. They left through the side entrance.

He knew it was over before they even reached the door to her office. It wasn't what he wanted, but if all it took was seeing a couple of uptight assholes during morning coffee, it needed to be over. They'd never work until Anna dealt with what was clearly shoved way under her own bed.

She closed the door behind them. With her back to him, she leaned on her desk.

"I'm sorry," she said so quietly he could scarcely hear her.

Two words were all it took and as hard as he tried, care and concern turned to survival, to his own pain. He stepped closer. "You're sorry? So that's it then. You're sorry and I'm just supposed to back away like some yard boy, head back to the grass?"

"That's not what I'm saying." She turned to him, still leaning on her desk, and Dane wondered if she needed it to prop her up.

"But it is what you're saying." He tried to keep from crowding her. "I love you, which by the way, I don't do. Ever. But I'm sticking with it. I see you in every corner of my life now and I've shown you who I am. All of it, Anna. Isn't that what this is all about? Handing over our stupid hearts?"

"I know, and I'm sorry."

"Stop saying that." He needed to calm down.

When he had first given her all of his feelings, let her in, he dreaded the idea that it would somehow soften him in her eyes. Or worse yet, that she would pity him. Closely behind that dread was the nagging fear of rejection. There was never pity in her eyes, only understanding, and he could have sworn she loved him more for giving her everything. He should have known it was always the small nagging feelings that hit the hardest. He braced himself for good-bye.

Anna kissed him one last time, held his face, and he watched the tears stream down her cheeks as her forehead rested on his.

"I will love you for the rest of my life," her voice stuttered. "You have given me so much more than I ever knew was possible. There is nothing in this world that I want to believe in more than us, but I'm damaged, Dane. I honestly didn't know how much until I met you."

He kissed her because the idea that he might not get to ever do it again strangled him with need. She stepped back, sobbing now. "I don't expect you to understand. I barely get it myself. I just know I can't."

Dane tried to clamp down on his own flood of emotions. There wasn't enough room for both of them at this point. There was nothing he could say, so he just stood there probably looking completely dumbstruck.

Anna wiped her eyes, leaned forward, and kissed him on the cheek. "Be happy, please be happy."

And then she opened her office door. She didn't walk him out. She knew him well enough not to try to handle him. Instead she let out a deep breath, walked toward the window, and stood with her back to him. Dane almost flinched in pain. She was still crying, but there was nothing he could do. He walked out, got into his truck, and buried his face in his hands.

Chapter Twenty-Seven

*A*nna spent the weekend updating grades in the system for all three of her classes. She started off sitting at her kitchen table and had to move when it occurred to her the first time she'd kissed Dane, it had been over her computer at that exact table. She tried the couch—no good—and she sure as hell wasn't going anywhere near her bed. He was everywhere and along with every memory, the pain she'd caused him.

"The wheel has come full circle," Anna said to her empty house as she took a seat at her dining room table. It was finally put back in place, and it seemed to be the only spot in her home that didn't hold a memory of Dane's laugh, his touch, that way he looked at her. God, what had she done? Why was she sitting alone in her house quoting *King Lear* of all plays? Actually the themes in Lear were spot-on. She'd brought this all on herself and if it was, in fact, all for the best, if she did what she needed to do to protect herself, why did she feel so awful? It was done. She broke it off with Dane. She had her life back, so why did she have this wretched feeling nothing was ever going to matter again?

It's the weekend, she told herself, curling her legs underneath her and focusing back on her laptop. She'd been sitting at home wallowing all weekend. Once she was back in the classroom, she'd be fine. She'd hit her stride and find her routine again. She'd stopped crying last night, iced her eyes, and hadn't cried once today. Granted it was barely eleven o'clock in the morning, but she was taking that as progress. Everything passed, this twisting in her chest would too. Anna had not returned any of Cynda's calls or texts since Thursday night when she left Dane's house. There was no way to explain what she'd done, what she'd thrown away. Cynda never did well with the silent treatment, so it came as no surprise when Anna heard the knock.

When she opened the door, Cynda was holding a box of tacos and beer.

"Haven't we done this before?"

"Don't try to be cute. Out of my way." She pushed past Anna and went straight to the dining room where she threw her purse on a chair and put the food and drink on the table.

"Please don't be pissed at me."

"I'm not, but you can't not answer. My mind goes crazy. I picture things, dumpsters, dark vans with no windows, things. You know?"

"I do."

Cynda pulled her into a hug, and Anna steeled herself to at least make it to noon in her current noncrying state.

"Did you two have a fight?"

Anna sat down, opened a beer, and put a taco on a napkin in front of her. She shook her head.

"Then what's up?"

"Nothing's up. It's over."

Her friend's face morphed into that WTF expression she'd perfected.

"I don't want to talk about it. I ended it because my work is important." Anna looked at her laptop screen as if that somehow gave her words more weight.

Cynda sat down and grabbed her own food. They crunched in silence.

"Okay, so it's over. I mean you're not the first woman to break up with a man. How do you feel?"

"Awful." Anna couldn't look at Cynda. Her eyes couldn't handle any more tears.

"Good."

Anna looked up. "What?"

"You heard me. Good, you should feel awful. You broke up with a perfectly wonderful, heart spilling all over a football stadium, flower sending, beautiful man. I mean that's just on the surface. I can't imagine what went on in the bedroom. Dear God, I'm feeling weak thinking about it. You broke it off because these little twits told you a Shakespeare professor needs to be some starched-up, frigid puritan? Shame on you, Anna Jeffries. I expected more from you, from my friend."

"Are you done?"

Cynda crunched. "Yeah," she said through a full mouth. "I think that about covers everything I thought of on the car ride over. You know, assuming you weren't dead when I got here."

They ate in silence. Anna's head spun while her heart throbbed in her chest. She was trying to be adult about this. She'd made a decision and now it was time to move on. Pick back up where her life was before Trey Duncan had trouble participating in class and before the first flippant insult fell from Dane Sivac's perfect mouth. It had been mere months. It shouldn't be this difficult to return to a life she'd spent years building, and yet she couldn't seem to get her act together. She was being productive, but she was existing.

Worst of all, she had somehow lost her ability to hide in her imagination. It was as if she was somehow thrown to the ground and forced to stay in reality. Brad delivered a box yesterday evening, and all Anna saw was her UPS man. No flutters, no "look how the sun lights up his thick hair," nothing. He was just a guy delivering her mail and this time when he handed over the package, she saw a ring. Brad was married. It turned out he'd recently tied the knot with his "soulmate." That's how he said it, and while the old Anna would have shimmered with romance and make-believe, the person she was left with simply nodded, closed her door, and went to bed early.

"My UPS guy is married." Anna leaned back in her chair and put her socked feet up on the dining room table. She felt almost drunk with self-disappointment.

"Brad?"

Anna nodded.

"When did this happen?"

Her friend was giving her enough room to share, hoping she would get some of the pain out on the table. Anna recognized the gesture, loved her friend for it, but was currently only capable of putting her feet on the table.

They spent the next hour in chatty surface conversation and when Anna walked Cynda to her door, she thanked her for the food.

"I'm sorry," Cynda said, abruptly turning from the door.

"For what?"

"For you, for the pain you are so obviously in. I'm sorry for that."

"I did it to myself."

"I know. I'm sorry for that too. I wish there was some way for me to show you what I see, all the vast possibilities for you. But that's not possible, and I'm sorry."

Anna felt her eyes burn, and she needed to get Cynda on her way before she collapsed on the floor. She knew friends were for these times in her life, but she wanted to be alone. After what she'd done to Dane, she deserved to be alone.

Anna said nothing, which she knew would make Cynda even more concerned, but there was nothing to say that didn't involve more tears.

Cynda hugged her quickly and left.

Anna walked, almost zombie-like to her bedroom, crawled under the covers fully clothed, and prayed for sleep.

Dane wasn't supposed to meet his family in North Lake Tahoe until the twenty-third because he'd wanted to spend time with Anna while she finished up classes and finals. There was no point in that now, so he drove up Friday night. He'd skied every day until the sun set so he would be nothing short of exhausted when his face hit the pillow. It occurred to him while he was familiar with loss on some level, it had never been like this. This drifting, slow loss was more painful. There was no way to compare it to losing his dad—that was in the past and painful to look back on—but this was as if someone had shown him a future and pulled it back the minute he committed to wanting it. He never claimed to be anything other than who he was and she'd loved him, a love that he never saw coming. He loved her back. She was the love of his life—he knew it with everything he had.

Why didn't he let her say it the first time she wanted to?

Would that have changed anything at this point? She left. He gave, and she climbed back behind her desk.

Dane lay on the couch, a bag of barbecue potato chips on his chest. The game was on, but it could have been Shakespeare for all he was paying attention.

He sat up and tossed the chips on the coffee table. His mom and sister were at the table playing cards while his nieces were curled up on the other couch around their laptop, playing something that had to do with checking crops and taking care of animals. He shook his head, walking past them.

"What the hell ever happened to getting outside?"

"It's dark," his sister had said last night when he'd made the same comment. "What do you want them to do, night ski?"

"There's such a thing."

"Really? Huh, I'll have to look into that for five-year-olds."

Her husband, The Saint, laughed.

When Dane finally got his mother alone in her study, he told her what was going on with Annabelle. He'd never asked for much in his life, but he needed her. Nothing was going to work if she was gone.

"Can't you do something about these assholes?"

His mother shook her head, and Dane felt the same irrational rage he used to when she told him he couldn't have the car for the night, except more adult and a whole lot more irrational.

"I don't have any say over other departments and even if I did, she wouldn't want that. Anna seems like a woman of her own making."

"What does that mean?"

"She's in her world, Dane. She's an academic, and sometimes that isn't simply a label. It suits her, and I'm not sure she's capable of coming out into the sunshine with you."

"That's not true. She's... Oh Christ, she's everything. Maybe I shouldn't have pushed, the grand gesture thing was a stupid idea. Yeah, thanks, Jess," he called out to the living room.

"Okay, sure. This is my fault. Makes sense," Jess said.

Dane tried to swallow the lump in his throat, and his mom stood from her desk and hugged him.

"Maybe she just needs time."

"Maybe," Dane said, pulling back before he started crying like a toddler.

Returning to the living room, he allowed his heart to pretend time was what Anna needed and threw himself onto the couch. Hawaii was holding their own against Tennessee in a bowl game, so anything was possible, Dane thought. It was Christmas Eve, after all.

Chapter Twenty-Eight

*A*nnabelle normally loved Christmas, but this year she drove to her parents' house on Christmas Eve and was back home by three o'clock the day after Christmas. The campus was deserted as she made her way to her office, which somehow made her more melancholy than she already was. She'd spent Christmas holding the precious newness of her baby nephew. Hollis gave birth to Ansel two weeks before Christmas, and he was the most precious thing Anna had ever seen, next to perfect Olive that is. Her family was growing and the love, the feelings that Annabelle normally had in her place as Middle Two in the Jeffries clan, were somehow shifting.

On Christmas morning, Anna found herself for the first time not simply watching, she caught herself needing, wanting some form of the love and sharing. It was startling, especially since she had recently given up on any chance she had at that type of life.

During the drive back home, she chalked everything up to the warm and fuzzy of the holidays. The upside was she had found her imagination again because she could almost see herself making a life, sharing a life. That little piece of fiction would have to tide her over. She'd made a choice, and now she would simply have to find perspective and move forward. Glancing at her watch, she noticed it was a quarter past six. No music from Sather Tower. She was taken aback for a moment but remembered the bells were silent when school was not in session.

Anna closed her laptop and decided to go home. As she walked to the parking garage, she noticed the silent tower, dimly lit and looming over the campus. Looking up at the night sky, she was struck by the beauty of the campus, the outside. She had always been caught up in her thoughts while walking to or preparing for class. Berkeley was a formidable campus. Not everyone was given the honor of being on campus each day, and those students and professors who were had a weighty responsibility. She had known all of this since the first day she toured the campus with her parents as a sophomore in high school. There'd been years of walking to class, prepared and purposeful, but she had never done what she was doing now. Never stood in the crisp night air and looked up at the breathtaking sky framed by massive trees and green.

She had barely noticed the tower, other than its music, and even when she did, it was to check the time and figure out where she needed to be. Anna was reminded of the faculty social when Dane had told her she always seemed like she was off somewhere. If that wasn't foreshadowing, she didn't know what was.

Her cheeks were cold as she walked through the darkness of the campus toward the tower entrance. She was almost certain it was closed but noticed a man with his back to her who appeared to be locking the door.

"Checkers?"

He turned, keys jingling. "Miss Anna. You almost gave me a fright. What are you doing back on campus so early?"

"I…" She was going to explain that she had work, that she was preparing for the new semester, but suddenly all of that sounded ridiculous in the beauty of the night air. "Can I go up in the tower?"

Checkers walked closer to her, the muted light of the flashlight pointed at their feet. "You ever been up there?"

Anna shook her head.

"Oh, well, that needs to be remedied right away. I'm not supposed to let anyone up there after five, but I'm in a rule-breaking mood. You, Miss Anna?"

She nodded and grinned, probably for the first time since she'd left her family.

"Let's do it." Checkers turned back and opened the door to Sather Tower. He flipped on a light switch and walked Anna to the elevator. "This will take you all the way up."

"You're not coming with me?"

"Nope. I'll stand guard down here. It's nice to spend a little time up there alone. Everyone should get to do that. Clears the mind." He pushed the button for her.

Getting on the elevator alone now, the idea that she'd never been to the top of the tower in all her years at Berkeley seemed even more unbelievable. She was sort of like those people she'd heard of who lived in San Diego and had never been to LA. She didn't understand how someone could be so close and not want to see more and yet, there she was, just like them.

What caused a person to avoid something so close, right in front of them? Anna had never been a fan of heights, so that would probably have been her excuse if anyone had asked before tonight. Now, though, as the elevator dinged and she stepped out onto the observation floor, it felt like more. Deeper. She was beginning to think the things spinning through her head weren't as simple, as whimsical, as she'd always let herself and other people believe. Her thoughts, the things she told herself, were often limiting and sometimes cruel. Why wasn't she allowed all the happiness her heart could stand? Why was she allowing limits from any committee, any group of men?

Anna walked toward the open air, and once again, Checkers was right. Her mind began to clear. The breeze whistled through the almost illuminated tendrils of the structure, and she gasped at the view like a child seeing something for the first time. The city lights, the magnificent glistening bay. The alluring mist of a winter evening and the rolling hills more green.

God, how did I miss all this green?

Looking out over the darkness of a campus she thought she knew so well, Anna realized she'd missed the whole point. Maybe it was because school wasn't in session and she was forced to stand alone in silence. She thought of Dane, the look on his face when she basically excused him from her life, closed the door behind him. A tear slipped down her cheek and she quickly wiped it away. There was no time left for tears. It turned out Anna had a lot to learn if she was ever going to be happy, let alone get the life she now envisioned for herself. She was no longer willing to accept the life held right in front of her like words on a page. What would Will have thought of such an absurd notion? Words were put on the page to be read and tossed aside in the name of bringing them to life. That's what Trey Duncan had done, and that was exactly what Anna intended to do.

Dane had stayed in Tahoe for as long as he could because he was having a hard time figuring out how to return without Anna. Being away from her, away from familiar places had been his only saving grace even if it wasn't much consolation. He'd managed to have a good Christmas with his family in spite of his own aching heart. His nieces had a way of pulling him out of himself every time. Children were special that way, he thought as he drove across the Bay Bridge. He loved being an uncle, being that guy in his nieces' lives who got to wind them up before bedtime and sneak them candy bars when they were supposed to be getting something for dinner. Recently he'd become the uncle who met them on the couch before their parents were awake to watch cartoons and eat dry cereal. He hadn't planned it. Like most of the best things in life, it simply happened. He woke up early the second morning he was there to find Sidney and Claire still in their pajamas, hair everywhere, on the couch with a box of cereal between them.

The pain of the memory had almost knocked him over as he stood watching them. But after a couple of minutes of their laughter, whispers, and crunching, he felt himself let go. He took in a deep breath, let it out, and somehow knew the best way he could honor his father's memory was to keep what made him so special alive in his granddaughters. On that simple thought, Dane joined them. Plopped himself down on the couch between them and grabbed a handful of cereal. They snuggled right up and just like that it became something new, something he shared with his nieces.

Dane wanted children of his own. He wasn't sure he'd ever allowed himself to think about it before he fell in love with Anna, but now it was as natural as saying he wanted to kick Stanford's ass next season. He wanted everything with her, and he wasn't sure how much time would need to pass before the desperate need dulled to something more manageable. His heart would never heal completely. She'd always have it, but maybe over time he could manage to reclaim some pieces for himself.

He was exhausted and had every intention of going home and collapsing on his couch. He wasn't sure he was ready to tackle his bed without her yet, but the couch sounded good. Maybe he'd make some rice. The plan was to go home, to keep his distance, but he found himself driving toward her house anyway. He'd been gone for two weeks. It was two days into the new year. He just wanted to drive by and see her lights on, wonder how her Christmas was and if she was doing a better job of getting on with her life. He knew it was pathetic, but it was late and he was alone. Honestly, he didn't care. He just wanted to be near her, even if it was for a moment.

Dane turned onto her street and tried not to feel like a weird ex-boyfriend stalker. The minute he saw her house up ahead, he didn't care what it looked like. Her lights were on. The first thing he noticed was that the hedges leading up to her front door had been thinned and shaped. They looked great. There were also potted plants near her front door and two bushes under her front window. He couldn't tell what kind they were in the dark, but her yard looked incredible. Tiny lights illuminated her walkway and as he finally passed her house, he glanced back and noticed rosebushes by her carport. His chest hurt. He wanted to plant those, help her with her yard, but if he loved her, that meant he was supposed to be happy she had them regardless of who planted them.

Yeah, that crap was probably part of the "emotional wholeness" package Crazy Eyes was selling. Dane didn't want to love Anna and let her go. He wanted her to choose him over all the rest of the mess in her life. But clearly, if Professor Jeffries was well enough to do yard work, Dane guessed that made him the fool. He picked up speed and didn't look back. His couch and his rice maker were waiting for him at home. Take that, Anna.

Chapter Twenty-Nine

*A*nna sat at her laptop for the first time in almost a week. She'd been busy getting a life.

Her new landscaper, Kenny, had helped her transform her front yard and gave her advice on the succulent garden she was now nurturing by her back patio. She also bought a chair and a small table for out back so she could read outside. The roses Kenny had planted near the carport were so fragrant she could smell them all the way on her back patio. It was turning into a magical sort of space, and she thought about hanging some lights to create a permanent *Midsummer Night's Dream* all year round.

The lights had been Cynda's idea after the two of them returned from the Oregon Shakespeare Festival. After her night at Sather Tower, Anna had gone home and bought tickets to *As You Like it*. Then she'd texted Cynda, who was always up for anything and probably happy Anna was finally coming back to life. They bought plane tickets and went. It was fun, spontaneous, and outdoors. Anna had forgotten the joy of Shakespeare under the stars and as she and her best friend sat on blankets and drank wine, she fell in love with Will all over again. She could practically feel herself healing from the inside out. Checking off things she knew needed to be done on her way toward the real life she now envisioned for herself.

The last step before she even dared to approach the huge piece of her heart that was missing was the reason she'd opened her laptop. Faculty meetings started tomorrow, and Anna had received an e-mail stating that the tenure and the curriculum committees would like to meet with her "prior to the new semester getting underway." They made it sound like a freaking garden party, she thought, reviewing the rest of her e-mails. Her eyes grew heavy and she wanted to practice what she and Hollis had gone over, to make sure she got every word right. The committee meeting was first thing in the morning, which was perfect—Anna wasn't sure she could wait much longer.

Once Anna had told Hollis her plan, she'd come over two afternoons last week to help her get everything in order. Even with a new baby, she was still her big sister and a master at the skills Anna had diligently practiced in front of the mirror. When she couldn't review her notes anymore, Anna climbed into bed and replayed the last couple of months. She hadn't been pushed around like this since Billy Meyer put his leg up on the bus to block her from sitting in the back four benches. She'd sat in front of his leg until they graduated from high school. Never said a word, just took it because she needed to get to school. Apparently Anna had started hiding at an early age. That stopped tomorrow morning. She clicked off her light, and as she had most nights, she thought of Dane, wondered what he was doing, and hoped on every book she had that when she was ready, she wouldn't be too late.

Anna woke before her alarm and decided to wear the new sweater Meg gave her for Christmas. Bright sky blue, with three-quarter-length sleeves, it was a little more formfitting than Anna was used to, but she wasn't in the mood for a cardigan. Not today. She grabbed a coffee on her way into the administration building. Sitting in one of the three chairs in front of Greta's desk, Anna looked at her watch. They were late. The meeting was scheduled for seven o'clock and it was almost a quarter past. In an effort to calm her nerves, Anna hummed, popped a chocolate-covered almond in her mouth as if candy in the morning was something she did all the time, and crossed her legs. According to Hollis, "heels are a woman's Scotch glass," so Anna had worn the highest heels she had. She laughed inwardly at the idea right as the office door opened. She was ushered inside like a petulant child summoned to the principal's office. *That garbage stops right now*, she heard Meg's voice in her head and knew with her oldest sister's words and her youngest sister's courage, there was no way Anna could lose.

"Professor Jeffries, please take a seat."

"Actually, I'm not staying." Anna took a shallow breath. "I've e-mailed my semester lesson plans to whoever among you makes up the curriculum committee. I've never been formally introduced to any of you, so I wouldn't know. Regardless, my requirement as an associate professor has been met. Please let me know if you have any questions or comments."

"Are you sure you would not like to take a seat and discuss this as civilized adults?" Bow Tie said. She always forgot his name, which must have been a mental block because his ties were silly enough to stand out in the name memory game.

"No. I do not want to sit, and it's a little late for civility. I'm withdrawing my application for full tenure. I no longer want to be a full professor at this university."

"May we ask why?" three of them said, almost in concert.

"Because of this tenure committee. If being a full professor means aligning myself with only 'certain types of people' and subjecting my students to some boring and, quite frankly, archaic form of teaching, I'm not interested."

"I see," Professor Roberts said in that tone that was meant to cause Anna doubt, shrink her back into place.

Sorry, gentlemen, not today.

"No. You'll never see, and that's part of the problem. I'm happy where I'm at and I'm thrilled doing what I do, the way I do it. It's enough for me. If the dean would like me to provide additional information, please have him contact me directly. As of last week, all application papers have been withdrawn, so gentlemen, we have no further business. Also, unless you provide a documented reason to be in my classroom again, please know none of you are welcome."

Anna turned to leave, her heart pounding in her chest. She wasn't sure she would be able to take in one more breath, but then realized she'd almost forgotten the most important part. She walked back to their table and leaned in, just as Hollis had instructed. "I almost forgot. I have contacted my attorney and was informed that I am well within my rights to tell you that it was a violation of my employment contract for you to insinuate yourselves into my personal private life. Make another comment about who I'm dating or what I do in my free time, and you and this university will have a lawsuit on your hands. Was that clear enough?"

Bow Tie cleared his throat. "Thank you, Ms.... my apologies, *Professor* Jeffries. We will make a note in your file."

"Good."

Anna left before another word could be spoken or she passed out right there on the floor in front of them. She nodded politely at Greta, who seemed surprised to see her leaving so soon. As the building door swooshed behind Anna, she first began to cry; but as the tower began to play the carillon, her heart filled with something close to happiness. It was seven fifty, but more importantly, the bells rang out and filled the air around her as if to say, "Well done, Annabelle Jeffries." For the first time in a while, it felt good to feel too much. Anna was more alive than she'd ever been and she'd "kicked ass," as Hollis had demanded.

Anna was in her office when Dean Rachael Sivac walked through her door. She wore a multicolored scarf around her neck as she opened the buttons of her jacket.

"Dean, it's a pleasure to have you—"

"No need, dear. I think you've kissed enough ass this year." She sat across from Anna and draped her coat over her lap.

"Can I get you some coffee?"

She shook her head. "Already had too much this morning. I heard a rumor you caused quite a stir in your department this morning."

"I suppose I did."

"Good for you. If you ever need that lawyer, let me know. I... know a few decent ones."

Anna laughed.

"I won't keep you long. You've already made your choices, but I think we have some things in common, Anna. I too love what I do and believe it is what makes me the woman I am. Don't ever lose that or allow yourself to get dragged under by any man's more important life. That being said, when I lost Dane's father, I never once thought about how important my teaching was or what my next step up the ladder was going to be. All I did was hold the towel he used after his shower that morning and collapse into a ball on the bathroom floor. When the rug was ripped out from under me, all I wanted was his smell, the sound of his voice, his grumpy face across the breakfast table. He was never a morning person." She smiled through a pain that still seemed so fresh Anna found it hard to believe it had been over fifteen years. She reached across the desk and put her hand over Anna's.

"Your life is certainly not mine, but I wanted you to know that although all of it seems equally important right now, and your career and your reading and loving my son are all crowded in your heart jockeying for space, at the end of the day, or on some odd Tuesday afternoon, the only thing that will matter for either of you is what you share when you're all alone. That's the root, Anna. The tree simply grows from there."

Anna couldn't speak. Dane's mother stood and wrapped Anna in her arms. She knew she had no right to be comforted by a woman who had been through so much, but in that moment she wasn't willing to be the wallpaper.

Chapter Thirty

*A*nna walked into her first class of the day. It was packed, which was an incredible feeling considering what she'd just done and said to the tenure committee only a week prior. She would admit to a bit of badass remorse when she woke up and prepared to greet a new class. While there hadn't been any fallout, she still wasn't Hollis. She still had the same insecurities, but after all these years, she'd finally learned to juggle. That didn't mean any of this was easy, but every time she started to doubt herself, she remembered where she was heading, focused on the... touchdown. Anna smiled at the thought and as if her memory of Trey had somehow conjured him up, there he was as she approached the front of the class. He bowed in Puck-like fashion and Anna bowed back, and they both laughed.

"Just couldn't stay away from us, could you?"

"Us?"

"Will and me."

Trey shook his head. "Yeah, that's what it is." Trey smacked the shoulder of a guy about his size sitting in the front row. He stood up and was joined by a second football player. Anna was amazed that the second young man almost made Trey look small.

"These guys heard me bragging about you and your class, so they signed up this semester."

"You weren't on that stupid website, were you?"

Both of them looked at Trey, who shook his head unconvincingly.

"Seriously?" Anna said.

"What? There are worse things than being easy to look at, ma'am."

"I suppose." Anna let the discomfort roll off her shoulders. She was getting good at this, but she still knew how to pull out Professor Snooty Pants.

"Well, gentlemen"—Anna extended her hand to both students— "welcome to my class. Please take your seats."

They exchanged handshakes, fist bumps, whatever it was guys did these days, and lowered into their seats. Anna followed Trey to the door.

"Any Shakespeare this semester?" she asked.

Trey shook his head. "Lord what fools these mortals be."

Anna beamed. She was so proud of him. "You realize I'm never going to be able to do that play in class again."

"Why's that?"

"A finer Puck I will never know."

Trey hugged her. "Winter conditioning and workshops start up tomorrow. You have two new players. You'll want to be supportive. Will I see you there?"

Anna raised a brow and wondered how much Trey knew. "You might, you just might."

"That's what I like to hear." Trey walked away without another word.

Anna felt her chest swell. Soon she was filled with the joy of a new class, new ideas, and completely new perspectives. She had two new football players in her class. If this kept up, she'd need to talk with...

There it was. She'd been thinking about a way forward for weeks, and Trey had walked both of them right through her door. Anna suddenly had her play and she could not wait to get back in the game. There was always the chance she'd lose, but she was willing to take the risk.

* * *

Dane welcomed the return to a schedule because after buying a new washer and dryer, he'd been up watching late-night television and was now the proud owner of a pressure cooker. Jeb had finally called him a lost cause when he'd called it a night last week after one beer. Dane was relieved to be back at work because he was going nuts. He'd given Jeb and his team the proposed training plans for all of his players, so there wasn't much to do, but at least he could start looking for new talent, anything to take his mind off Anna.

"Excuse me, I'm looking for Coach Sivac."

Christ, you're hearing her voice now too.

"He coaches football, poor guy."

Dane's head whipped toward the door. Now he was certain he wasn't hearing voices. Anna was standing in the center of the locker room. Never had it been more obvious that it was impossible to get over her than when his knees went weak like some young girl. One of the offense players, a freshman who was looking at Anna like he had a professor fantasy all his own, finally pointed her in Dane's direction. She walked toward him wearing a burgundy sweater and a sexy smile: a deadly combination. Clad in jeans, she looked incredible, lighter. While he should have been on guard, pissed that she'd come into his space, he wasn't. From day one, she had always managed to get right under his skin, and he was so happy to see her his heart nearly leaped out of his chest.

"Excuse me, are you Coach Sivac?"

Dane nodded and crossed his arms over his chest. Anna's face grew a little tense. She seemed nervous but different from the first time they'd had a similar conversation. He knew her now, but she knew him too. Anna smiled.

"You're a football coach?"

"I am."

"Huh. Well, I'm hoping you can help me."

"I doubt it." Dane realized he hadn't bantered with anyone in a while and missed her even more.

"I have two of your players in my class, and I'd like to get some commitment from their coach."

"Really? I thought professors and coaches didn't work well together."

Anna stepped into him. "Well, that's the thing. We are, that is, I am trying to change that dynamic."

"Could you... would you mind backing up?" Dane asked, trying to keep a straight face. Truth was she'd ripped his heart open and all but dismissed him from her office. He should be pissed, ready to show her he didn't give her even a second thought anymore. Problem was, he wasn't such a good actor, and something had changed. She was different. He was intrigued, and his stupid heart was hopeful again as if it had just awakened from a long winter nap.

"Sorry. Must be a Shakespeare thing. I'm usually... reading?"

They both laughed.

"Not as sexy from my side. I think your 'it's a sports thing' played better."

"Oh, I don't know. You had my attention. What's up, Anna? I know two guys are taking your class, but it's the first day. Not sure there's much to discuss."

"I'm not here because your players are suddenly wising up and loving Will."

"Then why are you here?"

Anna bit her lip, appearing nervous, but in an instant that all changed. Their eyes met and this time, she didn't look away, didn't flutter her eyes. She remained focused on him, seemed to almost sink into his gaze. Something was definitely up.

"I'm here because... You learn you can do your best even when it's hard, even when you're tired and maybe hurting a little. It feels good to show some courage."

The quote was definitely not new, but this one wasn't Will's. Dane thought he recognized it, but when she looked at him, all he could think about was wanting her more than he had the first time. His mind drew a blank.

"That's not Will."

Anna shook her head. "Joe Namath. Did you want to know his stats?"

"You know Broadway Joe's stats?"

"His name is Broadway Joe? I knew I liked him. He has some amazing quotes. Did you know he was a Super Bowl VIP?"

"MVP. Why are you quoting football players?"

"Because I love you."

There went Dane's heart, right out of his chest. Just about every player left in the locker room turned in their direction. He'd fantasized about this moment since the day she'd ended things. But contrary to Anna, Dane always found reality was so much better than anything he could conjure up.

"I'm trying to take an interest. I want to get to know what you're passionate about and I want to be supportive. I want life to be filled with tailgates and opera. I'm sorry that I hurt you."

Her eyes started to well up, and Dane wanted to touch her, take her somewhere private, but she wasn't done.

"I've missed you. But I have been working on myself. I have plants now and I went up inside the Sather Tower. Have you been up there?"

Dane nodded.

"It's incredible, and I want you. I am so sorry that I chose something else. There's nothing else, Dane. You found me, loved me, and now I can't just be the wallpaper anymore. I can't go back."

"People are looking at us, Professor Jeffries."

Anna looked over her shoulder, turned back, and smiled through her tears. "I don't care."

"That's new."

"I know. There are a lot of new things about me."

"Did you keep any of the old stuff? I'm still pretty in love with that woman."

"Really?"

"Yeah, I'm a sucker for those sweaters. I love you too, Anna." He stepped into her, crowded her, and she didn't seem to mind. Anna wrapped her arms around his neck and Dane instantly felt like life made sense again.

"I love you. I'm sorry it took me a while to get here, but I've always been a late bloomer. Speaking of blooms, I have a succulent garden in my yard now and when you—"

"Anna."

She stopped talking.

"I'm going to kiss you now. I'd love to hear about the plants a little later, but right now I'm going to kiss you in front of just about every football player in the school. Are you okay with that?"

Anna nodded and grabbed him first.

Epilogue

*A*nna packed up the rest of her desk and handed the box to Dane.

"Is that it?" he asked.

She nodded and took one last look around the tiny office that was no longer hers. Some other associate professor would inhabit her space and fill the bookshelves. Letting go, Anna was learning, got easier with practice.

"Are you all right? Nervous? You've barely said a word." Dane put the box in the back of his truck with the rest and climbed into the cab.

"Nervous, but also excited. I was there for four years. It was comfortable."

"And now you're in the big leagues." Dane parked on South Drive. "I get it. Butterflies, sweaty palms."

Anna laughed. "How is it you can make everything sound like football?"

"It's all a game."

They walked past Sather Tower and Anna looked up. She promised herself she would never take any of it for granted again. Shading her eyes with her hand, the sun glinted off her engagement ring and she was aware that her cup had runneth over multiple times in the past few months.

"Most important question, are you happy?" Dane propped the door of Wheeler Hall open with his foot and waited for her to go first.

"I'm ridiculously, silly happy." She moved her box to the side so she could kiss him. "Let's see, it's… June. In less than six months I will be marrying you." She kissed him again, now more deeply. She wanted him to know every day how much she loved him, how he had saved her from accepting less. "How could things be any better?"

They stood in the doorway, kissing one another as if they had nowhere to go and no one would dare to interrupt. "Better than any fantasy?"

"So much better," Anna said, her forehead resting on his.

"Better than Darcy?"

Anna pulled back and patted the side of his face. "Don't push it, Sivac." She walked through the door, leaving him laughing.

Trey and Cynda were waiting as they walked into the third office on the right. Anna ran her hand along the nameplate: *Professor Annabelle Jeffries*. She took a deep breath. Despite the politics and the mess, she had not sold her soul to get here, and that felt fantastic.

"Took you guys long enough." Trey grabbed the box from Anna and set it on her new desk.

The desk was larger than her other one, but she'd requested and was given the old red crushed-velvet chair from her previous office. The old and the new, Anna thought.

"Congratulations, Professor with tenure and benefits," Cynda joked as she popped open a bottle of champagne.

Shortly after the new year, Anna's students—past and present—had put together a petition for Dean Bradley. They'd collected signatures and rallied the support of their influential parents and their parents' even more influential money. Neither the dean nor the committee would ever admit to it, but Anna's students were the reason her application for tenure was reinstated and expedited. She was notified of her tenure the second week in May.

They all raised their plastic glasses, and Anna had never felt less like wallpaper in her entire life.

"Proud of you," Dane said, pulling her into him with the arm not holding champagne.

"Thank you. Me too, I think." She set her drink down and draped her arms around his neck. "I love you so much." She could almost feel Trey and Cynda rolling their eyes, but she didn't care.

"For she had eyes, and chose me," Dane said, touching the side of her face.

Trey coughed, and they both looked over in time to see him shake his head. "Fail, man. What's that you always say in practice? Ask. Should have asked."

Anna tried not to laugh, but she couldn't help it. He was adorable, not that she was going to tell him that because, well, few men wanted to be adorable.

"What? That's Will. It's beautiful, right?" Dane looked to all three of them for clarification.

Anna nodded, wide-eyed and not sure how to break the news that his one foray into Shakespeare was not as dark as *Macbeth*, but a far cry from romantic. "It is beautiful, on the surface, but it's *Othello*." She wasn't sure why she thought that hint would help, and she couldn't care less if he knew one line of Shakespeare.

"Comedy?" Dane wasn't letting it go.

"Tragedy."

"Aw, hell. I need a cheat sheet or something."

"Does that mean I have to learn the difference between the split and the tight ends?"

That made him smile, and Anna knew she would never get tired of that face.

"Easy, think of them as bookends on the offensive line, one on each end," Trey said. "And, I could have told you to steer clear of *Othello*, man. Amateur move." He patted Dane on the back.

"Thank you. How'd you like to run stairs, Mr. Double Threat Pain in the Ass?"

They all laughed.

"How can such a great line come from a tragedy? Is it really tragic, or just sort of sad?"

Dane wasn't going to let this go.

"Well, that's Othello telling Iago that his wife chose him with her eyes open. Essentially he's saying he's confident in her love for him. He's not jealous."

"Sounds good."

"By Act V, he kills his wife," Cynda said, pouring them all another round of champagne.

"Oh, wow. Not the right quote." Dane pulled her close again.

Anna put her hands on his chest and didn't care if the man ever spoke one word of Shakespeare. He was everything she never knew she wanted and more. She kissed him. Despite the grumbling from Trey and Cynda, Anna stayed in the kiss and was reminded of the first time her lips touched Dane's. This kiss was no longer hesitant—it was familiar, longing, and timeless, with maybe a bit of desperation. It could have been called a kiss of fiction, but this one was real and full of life. Will would have been proud.

Thank you for reading *Playbook – A Love Story*! I hope you enjoyed Annabelle and Dane's story as much as I enjoyed writing it. If you liked the book, please consider leaving a review at the book retailer of your choice, as well as Goodreads, to help other readers find this story.

Please make sure you're on my newsletter mailing list at: tracyewens.com to keep up with the latest news about my books.

Thank you, wonderful readers, for making this amazing journey possible. I appreciate each and every one of you! Keep reading for a look at *Exposure – A Love Story*, which is Meg and Westin's story.

All the best,
Tracy

Chapter One

M eg Jeffries wasn't wearing underwear. She wiggled a bit in the backseat of the taxi as if to confirm she was now fifteen minutes from her apartment and all but naked under the rainbow fabric of her favorite skirt. If she asked the driver to turn around now, she would be late, and that was not an option. Not today. As traffic on the Bay Bridge slowed, she thought about stopping somewhere along the way but realized she no longer knew the city where she'd grown up. Fashuation, the trendy boutique her older sisters adored when they were teenagers, was now a dry cleaner.

Meg leaned her forehead against the cold glass of the window. *Nothing is the same.* In more ways than just her underwear. Besides, she sat up, willing her insecurities away, she was not asking the balding driver who reminded her of a gruffer version of her grandfather if he knew of a place to pick up some panties.

If she'd started working out as she'd promised herself last week, there might have been something in the oversized bag she carried everywhere. Maybe some bike shorts or bathing suit bottoms. When she'd researched the gym up the street, she had noticed they offered water aerobics. There was even a coffee shop en route from her apartment. Normal people worked out and drank coffee, and Meg was giving normal a real concerted effort these days.

Searching the gym's website, she'd landed on the page that described four different membership packages when an e-mail came in from one of her colleagues. It included a link to an article and a rolling eyes emoticon. She'd read the Op-Ed piece it linked to arguing that climate change was "natural" and "simply something for the bleeding hearts to worry about." It had pissed her off enough to close her browser and fire off a two-paragraph e-mail to the paper responsible for the article. Not that she hadn't heard the same drivel hundreds of times before, but it still hit her anew every time. So, instead of picking a plan and joining a gym, she'd put Vivaldi's Concerto in G Minor for 2 Cellos on repeat and made zucchini muffins.

Two rent payments into her new place, and it turned out the only "normal" thing she could manage was baking. It was a bit of an obsession. Since her neighbors were gluten-free vegans, that left a lot of baked goods for late-night snacks. Another contributing factor to her present state of undress, she thought as the taxi took a sharp left and threw her into the door where a wad of dried chewing gum was squished into the miniature ashtray. Perhaps if she'd joined the gym instead of shoving carbs in her face and sending angry e-mails to people who simply didn't care, she would emerge a civilized adult. A woman with a schedule and flat abs. A professional with the basic reassurance of undergarments before she attempted to speak in front of an audience.

It was that damn green skirt. The one that was too tight now that she was in the middle of a love affair with her oven and had discovered the falafel joint around the corner from her apartment. Both were to blame. She'd had on perfectly respectable panties until the green skirt, combined with the panties, made her ass look like it was in four sections instead of two. So, she took off said panties, hoping for a smoother look, but after several more tugs and grunts decided she looked ridiculous in green corduroy and went with her favorite skirt instead. Not only did it have an elastic waist with a silky tie, it was every color of the sunset. That was why she'd bought it four assignments ago. The skirt billowed out and made her feel pretty. Last time she'd worn it was on the plane home from her last shoot in Canada after spending three weeks photographing the gray wolf.

God, what she wouldn't give to be back with the wolves, or anything on four legs for that matter, instead of pulling up in front of the Moscone Center naked as a jaybird, to use an Uncle Mitch expression. She certainly wasn't naked, but when the valet opened the door of the taxi, a breeze danced along Meg's skirt, and she sure felt a little exposed.

"No one knows," she said more to herself, but the valet with the gauges in his ears looked up.

"Sorry?" he asked as he patiently continued holding the door.

Meg grabbed her bag and her GoMacro protein bar. She'd decided to skip lunch after pinching her way into clothes that used to fit, but in the end decided she might need a little snack later. She wasn't sure what kind of food would be served at this event, so she brought her own.

"Nothing. I'm a little... nervous." Meg turned toward the valet as the cabbie rounded the front of the taxi for his money.

"Does this look okay?" She glanced down at herself and was certain no one could see the important piece of clothing she'd left behind.

"Yeah, I like the skirt."

"Thanks. I bought it in Morocco."

"Seriously?"

"They have spectacular bazaars there. Have you been?" Meg stepped aside, letting him close the taxi door while she fished through her bag for her wallet.

"To Morocco? Um... no. I'm still saving to get down to San Diego for my sister's wedding."

Meg caught herself again in that eternal state of jet lag. She'd been home three, almost four months now, but somehow she still felt disjointed, as if she was floating in an existence in which no one else could relate. There were times she'd run into other photographers on assignment, and it was standard to ask where they'd come from or which remote corner of the planet they were off to next.

Working for *National Geographic* had been the escape hatch from a boring life that Meg had shunned for as long as she could remember.

Now that she had changed directions, she was beginning to wonder if that hatch swung both ways.

"Right. My sister is getting married too. That's common ground." The guy nodded and watched as another car approached.

"Well, do you have a frequent flyer account? Sometimes you can catch huge deals." The cab driver was glaring at her now. Meg opened her wallet.

"I'll keep that in mind," he said. "Are you here for the climate thing?"

"Yes, I'm presenting... something." Meg handed cash to the taxi driver and looked down at her jumbled papers.

The valet reached over as the cabbie handed him something before speeding away. The next car in line pulled forward.

"You might want to put the other one on if you're going to be in front of people." He handed her an earring.

Meg instinctively touched one ear, found the dangling stone, and moved to the other one, which of course was bare. An earring was a simple thing, but she felt out of control. She had been up to her waist in rivers, tracked mountain lions, and dove into icy waters all for the perfect shot, but this looking presentable business was intense.

"Thank you." She slid on the earring.

"No problem." He rounded the next car to open the door for the driver. "Knock 'em dead. Try to... what's that they say? Oh, yeah. Picture them all naked." He handed a ticket to a slender balding man, climbed into the car, and was gone.

Was that a joke? Could he see through her skirt?

Meg shook herself free of her absurdity and stepped past the automatic doors into the beige and sparkly lobby of the convention center. Eighty percent solar, she remembered reading on their website. It was a beautiful building, made even more so because it was gentler to the earth than most massive venues. She liked gentle.

Taking a deep breath, she straightened and followed the signs pointing to the Symposium for Climate Wellness Initiative. Kind of a ludicrous name, Meg thought, but they'd invited her to talk about the shrinking habitats of polar bears. Their name didn't matter and neither did her panties, she reminded herself.

Underwear or no underwear, this cause was her "wheelhouse," as Amy, her new agent, had said, tossing her shiny hair and crossing her perfect legs while sitting behind her perfect desk.

Lord, I have an agent now.

Meg rounded the corner near a bronze statue of three dancing figures.

Are you nervous? Her sister Anna texted before Meg had a chance to take the picture. It somehow felt like she knew Meg was in a mini-state of panic. Meg began typing a response. *Not yet, but I don't have any under…*

What the hell was she doing? It's not like Anna could help her or bring an extra change of clothes the way their mom used to when one of them had an accident in preschool. This was the real world, and Meg was a grown-up for Christ's sake. Besides, as much as Meg loved her sister, Anna would not understand forgetting underwear. She was poised and orderly, and Meg was, well, not. That didn't mean she had to share every detail of her disarray.

Nope. I'm great, Meg texted back with a smiley face and tossed her phone into her bag. It would be so like her to get distracted right outside where she needed to be and miss the whole thing. Did lying through text message count? She had a feeling it did, which went against her "no lying" policy, but technically she was great. Great might be an overstatement, but she was at least good.

She kept reminding herself to focus. This was serious business. She needed to find a way to make a living, or she'd be stuck taking pictures of fruit for lifestyle magazines or cranky families at one of Murphy's Portrait Studio's ten locations.

Abstract images lined the hallway as Meg followed the sign pointing toward the main auditorium. She didn't recognize the photographer's name, but the images were manually processed. It had been awhile since Meg had been in a darkroom. She could experiment with some city images and work in paper now that she was back. Maybe she could teach.

Now you're losing it, some rational part of her brain muttered. It was right. She knew how to take photographs, which didn't mean she had any clue how to show someone else. Besides, she'd pissed off enough people in her photo workgroups at Berkeley. A classroom of Photography 101 kids didn't need some bitch crushing their dreams right out of the gate. Anna had a way of reaching students, seeing things through their prism. Meg only saw things through one lens — her own. That sounded harsh even to her own ears, but the truth was she'd spent most of her adult life arguing with only herself.

Everything had shifted now, admittedly her own doing. A few short months ago, she was washing her shirt each night in a river, and now she was about to stand in front of thousands of "activists" and share the scary truth about the bears she loved more than most people.

No wonder she forgot her underwear. There needed to be a reentry period for this kind of stuff. She'd planned on taking it easy, dipping into her savings if necessary, but then last month's *National Geographic* cover came out and Amy said she was "hot, hot, hot."

"If you ever want to make a living as a 'normal person,' you'd better seize the day," Amy had added.

Meg sure as hell never wanted to be normal growing up, but she did feel a pull toward something more. Random family breakfasts, a can opener that wasn't part of a multipurpose tool, full-size toothpaste. Meg returned home to put down roots, but as she pulled the doors open to whispers of backstage conversation, she wasn't so sure she was cut out to be among the humans.

Westin Drake rolled over in bed to escape the harsh light of morning. Through a haze of bite-sized memories from the night before, he first realized he was desperately thirsty. Reaching toward the nightstand for a bottle of water, he noticed the glossy photograph and demo his date had slipped him after she introduced herself at the Save Something fundraiser. She had pretended not to know who he was and did a damn good job of it, he had to admit. She'd taken the seat next to him, talked a lot about herself and how she'd come to be involved with the nonprofit, even sprinkled in a little bit about her family back home in Georgia. West bought it hook and line. He'd spent the evening dancing with her and eventually had Vince drive her home.

Outside her house, she'd said, "I don't usually do this, but you're incredible. What did you say you did again?" West had invited her back to his hotel and kissed her. She was gorgeous and at least played smart. Well, until she reached into her bag and handed over her promotional materials. He had no idea why he bought the bullshit. Maybe he foolishly thought things would be different now that he'd moved from LA to San Francisco, or he wasn't too bright, as his oldest brother would say shortly before smacking him on the back of the head when they were growing up.

Whatever the reason, West had found himself in the same situation he swore to avoid, but this time he made a few more cocktails and decided if she was going to use him, he was going to use her right back, right there on his hotel suite couch.

Yeah, that routine usually sounded better in his head, but the truth was he only played a badass womanizer on the big screen. In what little reality he had left, West wasn't wired to be an asshole. Which was why even though he'd taken April, the aspiring singer, to bed and even though she'd screamed out his character's name instead of his—twice—he'd still held her and agreed she could stay the night.

West closed his eyes, guzzled some water, and not for the first time in his life kicked himself in the mental balls. Why couldn't he be one of those guys who had rules? Boundaries when it came to his bed—who was allowed in it and for how long?

The answer, while he hated to admit it given his current situation, was simple. He'd had female friends growing up, and brothers who would kick his ass if he started acting like an idiot. Then there was his mother, who called him every Monday on her way home from her Jazzercise class even after he moved to LA. The truth was, he liked women, often with their clothes on.

The one asleep in the king-size bed of his hotel suite at the Fairmont San Francisco with "Free Samples" emblazoned across her ass in sequins had shared something with him last night. Sure, it was purely physical for both of them and opportunistic on her part, but she showed her true colors after he kissed her. He still unzipped her dress, so he was a willing participant. The universal rule was that nothing good ever starts with a lie, but West was weak and male, and he took her to bed anyway.

So, as mind numbing as he was sure the conversation over a room service breakfast would be, he would smile and offer her more coffee. They would eat and then he'd hand her off to the sainted concierge West called "Towner." She would ensure April was delivered safely and discreetly home. West knew no other way to treat people.

He had tried for aloof badass ever since women began throwing themselves at him solely based on his movies or an absurdly air-brushed picture of him in a car he'd never drive. West had wanted to be that guy at different points in his life. It looked much easier, especially during the years he spent climbing out from under the shadow cast by his brothers, but he had long accepted that a clear conscience was worth more than anything.

With all that swirling around in his still-dehydrated brain, he re-solved to order breakfast once again, sign anything that wasn't skin, and feign interest in her music career or her desire to start a celebrity event-planning business as a backup.

West quietly pulled back the covers and made his way to the shower.

Moments later, towel at his waist, he grabbed his phone vibrating in the jeans he'd thrown over one of the gold upholstered armchairs the night before. He should have left the phone right where it was, but instead, he swiped the screen.

"Where the hell are you?"

"Good morning, Hannah. Are we talking physically or mentally? I've been thinking about Malta. Have you ever been?"

His manager said nothing, but her breathing had become a lan-guage all its own. West was fluent.

He gave in. "I'm home, I mean at the hotel. Why? Where am I supposed to be?"

More breathing. "Symposium for Climate Wellness Initiative. Annual event. Ring any bells?"

West remembered because of the stupid name. He looked at the clock on his phone. Right as he realized it was already 11:30, April rolled over, stretched, and gave him the woman-waking-in-a-big-bed grin.

"Shit." He turned to face the bedroom door, willing April to get her bedazzled ass out of bed. There would be no luxuriant farewell today.

Hannah Leighton continued breathing through the phone. "Yeah shit is an understatement. You're introducing Megara Jeffries. It's a big deal, West. *National Geographic*. You said doing new vodka-flavor unveilings and night club openings were not considered community service, remember? 'I have a conscience. I need more,'" she mocked in a baby voice.

West closed his eyes. He had said that.

"Do you remember that?"

"Not quite in that voice, but yes."

"And since I'm your kick-ass agent, I reached out and showed these hiking-for-fun bleeding hearts that you would be a perfect spotlight for them." Her voice was much louder now. "She's been on the cover of *National Geographic* twice for crying out loud."

"Right." West tossed the red bra hanging from the doorknob and the piece of material pooled on the ground near it toward the bed. April's outfit had passed for a dress last night, but in the harsh light of almost afternoon and his agent's amplified breathing, it looked more like a Halloween costume. He kept that last observation to himself, glancing at April, who apparently had not met Hannah, or she wouldn't be crooking her finger in a gesture that invited West back to bed. He shook his head and pointed to his phone in an animated panic.

April's eyes grew wide as she blew her blond locks out of her face, scooted out of bed, and eagerly nodded as if she were privy to an important crisis. She held her finger to her mouth and tiptoed into the bathroom. Before the guilt in his stomach bloomed, Hannah was back in his ear.

"West?"

"I will... How much time do I have?"

"Thirty minutes."

"Where?"

"Moscone Convention Center."

"I'll be there."

"Tamara sent you clothes. Did you get them?"

West considered the living room and noticed the wardrobe bag hanging on the front closet door.

"Yes. I'll be there and in whatever is in that bag. Need to go."

West hung up before more breathing erupted into more yelling.

"Baby, are we late for a photo shoot or something?" the husky voice spilled from behind the bathroom door.

We? West ran a hand over his face, hoping to erase every choice he'd made since yesterday morning's Kinesis workout, but the sandpaper feel only reminded him that the clock was ticking. He called down to Towner.

Alice Towner was a saint. West already knew that, but he would now need to add wizard since less than fifteen minutes later, he climbed into a waiting car after kissing April on the cheek outside the service elevator and assuring her he would share her songs with some of "his people." Christ, he was a good actor.

Once again, he awkwardly offered Towner some folded bills.

"Thank you, but I brought my lunch today," she said in a voice that usually had West sitting up straighter.

"You should try that little deli next to the dry cleaner. It doesn't look like much, but they have scrumptious chopped liver," Towner said before closing West into the quiet of the black sedan. She offered some version of the lunch comment every time he tried to give her money in a voice that reminded him of his Aunt Margaret. Not the tone, but the wisdom behind it.

Twice a year, once the day before Easter and then again during the Christmas season, his mother's sister came up to Petaluma from "the big city." She giggled a little every time she used that label for San Francisco, as if she was the first person to think of it. The van from

Bayview Care Community pulled in at three o'clock sharp. She insisted on it so she and West would have plenty of time to be "seated and prepared" at the backyard picnic table for tea at exactly four. When West was little, he cringed at being forced to wear the bow tie she had given him at Christmas and having to pull out the wooden bench for her as if they'd arrived at the Ritz. By the time he was a teenager, it was an eye-rolling intrusion into his all-important social life.

Aunt Margaret, no nicknames for her, died when West was a senior in high school, and the strangest thing happened. He missed her, missed tea and time with her he would never get back. She'd helped him grow up, knocking every chip off his adolescent shoulder with a simple story or a pouty face. She'd been his friend when the comparisons to his brothers became too much. She'd kept his secrets and trusted him with hers. West didn't know how significant Aunt Margaret was until she was gone. Life seemed to work that way.

He'd thought about having tea a few times after she died to keep the tradition alive, but something far less important usually got in the way. He had never met anyone like her until a few days after he checked into the Fairmont.

He'd been surrounded by photographers while trying to make his way into the lobby. Towner burst through the crowd of cameras, her winter-white bob perfectly quaffed, exclaiming, "Mr. Drake needs to get inside. Please stand back. His dear sister is in labor." The piranhas had parted on an "aww" and allowed West to pass. He didn't have a sister.

As Towner escorted him to the service elevator and explained that he could use the side alley for his "comings and goings," West had thanked her and discreetly handed over a folded hundred-dollar bill. Her help was well worth the money, but she had instead pushed up the brim of her glasses, shaken her head, and showed West a picture of her newest granddaughter. That was it, a picture, some random conversation about when peaches were in season again, and a handshake.

It was the beginning of their relationship. Towner informed him less than a week later that she did not want to be called Ms., Miss, or Mrs. She was sixty-eight and none of those titles fit anymore, so she said. West, who was raised to respect his elders, couldn't bring himself to use her first name, so they settled on Towner. "Like Madonna," he had told her. He occasionally still tried to tip her, especially when he called on Towner to deal with his less-than-proud moments, but she never took the money.

He smirked at the thought of the hotel concierge being his only true friend and decided his Aunt Margaret would certainly approve.

The driver notified West they would arrive at the convention center with five minutes to spare, which was good news. He didn't want to listen to Hannah if some *National Geographic* rising star had to walk on stage alone. Like that would be a huge loss. The woman took pictures in freezing water, or with bears. She was obviously more than capable of walking on a stage. He had asked Hannah for more substance, but he'd secretly hoped she would stop sending him to publicity things altogether when he moved from LA. He should have known better; Hannah had selective hearing.

"These groups are happy to have you. And why wouldn't they? You're pure star power, hon," she had said last month when she set the event up and was far less pissed at him than she was on the phone.

Closing his eyes and resting his head back on the leather seat, West wondered how many more of his fifteen minutes of fame were left.

Acknowledgements

I would like to thank:

Katie McCoach and Nikki Busch for polishing my words and putting up with my last minute everything.

Teachers and coaches who inspire and find inspiration in a future that simply would not be possible without them.

My family for putting up with my moods, imaginary friends, and often absent mind.

Readers for inviting me into your lives. The honor is never lost on me.

Tracy Ewens is a recovered theatre major who writes smart contemporary romance from a beautiful piece of Arizona desert. When not working on her next book, she drinks copious amounts of tea, prefers an exit row seat, and reads well past her bedtime.

www.tracyewens.com